TAINTED NIGHT, TAINTED BLOOD

I hurried to the front of the house and pressed my back to the wall. The place wasn't large by vampire standards. It was bigger than where I lived, but not by much. Countess Telia still had a ways to go before she could move up to the mansions the other Counts and Countesses preferred.

I crept along the wall to the nearest window and peeked in. Furniture lay strewn across the room. A mirror had been smashed, leaving shards of bloody glass all over the floor. A coffee table had been shattered as well, adding to the destruction.

And there was blood everywhere.

My stomach rumbled as my inner demon made itself known. I hadn't fed for over a week and it was starting to get to me. I really should have hunted before coming. Then again, I hadn't expected to find bodies lying around with blood splattered all over the walls . . .

Books by E.S. Moore

TO WALK THE NIGHT

TAINTED NIGHT, TAINTED BLOOD

Published by Kensington Publishing Corporation

Tainted
Night, Tainted
Blood

E.S. MOORE

KENSINGTON PUBLISHING CORP.

http://www.kensingtonbooks.com

KENSINGTON BOOKS are published by

Kensington Publishing Corp.
119 West 40th Street
New York, NY 10018

All Kensington Titles, Imprints, and Distributed Lines are available at special quantity discounts for bulk purchases for sales promotions, premiums, fund-raising, and educational or institutional use.

Special book excerpts or customized printings can also be created to fit specific needs. For details, write or phone the office of the Kensington special sales manager: Kensington Publishing Corp., 119 West 40th Street, New York, NY 10018, attn: Special Sales Department, Phone: 1-800-221-2647.

Kensington and the K logo Reg. U.S. Pat & TM Off.

ISBN-13: 978-0-7582-6873-0
ISBN-10: 0-7582-6873-4

First Mass Market Printing: July 2012

10 9 8 7 6 5 4 3 2 1

Printed in the United States of America

For Lena

1

The body lay crumpled in the driveway—a heap of cloth that could have been anything if not for the distinctive smell that drifted on the light breeze. If I had simply been driving by, minding my own business, I might not have even noticed it. It was halfway up the paved drive, almost blended in with the darkness.

But I *had* been looking for it, and the corpse assured me I was in the right place.

Countess Telia was known for her cruelty. She hadn't been active very long, at least as a minor power of her own. She was the head of one of the newest Fledgling Houses and a vampire who tortured dozens of Purebloods to the point of insanity just for the fun of it. Once she was done with her playthings, she would release them, letting her victims return to their families to suffer their final days crippled and mindless.

It appeared this time she had gone too far.

I parked my modified Honda DN-01 just off the road and hid it behind some trees. The motorcycle was completely black, including the piping, so it would be hard for anyone who wasn't expressly looking for it to see it.

Even a vampire would have a hard time picking it out of the shadows.

A dog barking in the distance was the only sound as I slipped into the brush. I crouched down, listening and watching for any sign of pursuit. House Telia was deep within vampire-controlled territory, so the chances of someone spotting me were actually pretty good. I wanted to make sure none of the local vamps or wolves decided to follow the girl on the motorcycle in the hopes of having a little fun.

As far as I could tell, no one had followed me. I breathed a sigh of relief and drew my sword. The demon-crafted blade shone in the moonlight, but I was pretty sure it wouldn't matter now. By the time Telia saw me coming, it would be too late.

The gun came next. My modified Glock 17 fit comfortably in my hand. The bullets were made of silver, and thanks to Ethan's modifications, they wouldn't pass all the way through a supe's body. They moved too slowly for that.

I rose from my crouch, careful not to let my leather creak in the all-too-silent night. I was dressed in full-on black. It was my usual work attire. It just wouldn't do to run around fighting vampires wearing a white T-shirt and jeans. I had an image to keep up.

I slipped from the cover of the trees and started up the driveway. The body was just a hump on the paved surface, barely discernible as anything other than a pile of bloody rags. I could smell death on the air and knew this victim had been tortured to the point where there would probably be little left.

I approached, wary nonetheless. Even though I was pretty sure the victim was dead, I nudged her with my foot and touched the silver blade to her flesh to be sure.

Nothing happened.

The dead girl's shirt was shredded in the front and there was blood everywhere. She had been torn from groin to sternum by what looked to be werewolf claws. It wasn't exactly Telia's style, but I wouldn't put it past her to give a young girl like this to one of her wolves. She had to keep her minions loyal somehow.

Countess Telia was new, a recent break-off from one of the Major Houses. Mikael Engelbrecht, my snitch, hadn't been able to tell me which Major House she had come from, but he implied it was one of the biggies. He would have told me more, but he was in the pay of the House that Countess Telia once belonged to, so he refused to divulge any more than he had to. I didn't like it, but I had to respect his loyalty to his customers, especially since I was one of them.

Still, that didn't stop him from telling me about Telia's exploits, how she had cut the arms and legs off one of her victims and dumped him outside his home, his wounds sewn closed so he wouldn't bleed out. His tongue and eyelids had been removed, as were his nipples, ears, and any other dangly bits that she could get to with a knife. He survived in body, although his mind was long gone.

Why she hadn't been killed by the Major House she ditched was beyond me. Vampires didn't like it when their underlings defected. A vamp thinking she could leave a Major House to start her own usually turned up dead within an hour of making her claim.

But there Telia was, torturing victims and reveling in their blood just like any other baby vamp, albeit a more violent one. I was there to put a stop to it.

I left the body where I found it and started up the drive, keeping close to the trees so anyone who would happen to glance out a window wouldn't see my approach. I moved in near silence, my vampire-light feet barely making a sound on the pavement. I'd even learned to minimize the sound of leather with my walk. Being a vampire had its advantages at times.

It wasn't until I was halfway up the driveway that I

noticed the other bodies. All of the lights in the house were blazing, including the outside light. It spilled out over the corpses, illuminating them like actors on a stage. I could see the dark stain of blood against the black pavement.

I froze and gave the house a good long look. One body, I expected. Three was a bit much.

I hadn't noticed it before because I hadn't really looked, but the front door was torn nearly off its hinges. The window beside it was intact, but the curtains were hanging at an angle, as if someone had tried to tear them down.

And there were no sounds, no moving shadows that told me where Telia or her minions were. Had her little torture party turned into something much more deadly? I had no idea what she did in there most nights. It was entirely possible she had set three Purebloods loose, sicking her wolves on them for pure entertainment.

If so, then where was she? I should have seen a flicker of a shadow, heard the howl of a wolf. She would have wanted to watch the events as they took place.

I approached the two other bodies, keeping my gaze on the house as I went. They could be in there, watching me. The night was still young, so I was sure they hadn't bedded down for the day.

The first corpse turned out to be another Pureblood, this one male. He had been stripped naked and lay in a pool of his own blood. His ribs showed through flesh pulled tight, as if he had been starved before being released. His stomach had been ripped open and his throat slashed.

I nudged him like I had the other corpse to make sure he was really dead. Sometimes it was hard to tell between a Pureblood and a young werewolf or vampire. It was possible this was some sort of initiation rite that Telia cooked up for her newest recruits. Torture them, let them bleed a while, and then take them in.

But this guy was definitely dead. If she had tried to turn him, she had started the process far too late.

The last body was a few paces away, and at first I thought he was wearing a fur coat. As I got closer, I realized that wasn't the case and alarm bells started ringing in my head in earnest.

The werewolf was lying facedown, his head a few inches from his body. The cut was ragged, as if it had taken a few hacks to cut through the wolf's thick neck. There were marks on his arms and shoulder where he had tried to protect himself.

It hadn't helped. The wolf had been hamstrung, making him an easy target for whomever had done this. I wasn't sure if Telia had done it herself or if someone else was involved. Either way, I didn't like it.

I hurried to the front of the house and pressed my back to the wall. The place wasn't large by vampire standards. It was bigger than where I lived, but not by much. Countess Telia still had a ways to go before she could move up to the mansions the other Counts and Countesses preferred.

I crept along the wall to the nearest window and peeked in. Furniture lay strewn across the room. A mirror had been smashed, leaving shards of bloody glass all over the floor. A glass coffee table had been shattered as well, adding to the destruction.

And there was blood everywhere.

My stomach rumbled as my inner demon made itself known. I hadn't fed for over a week and it was starting to get to me. I really should have hunted before coming. Then again, I hadn't expected to find bodies lying around with blood splattered all over the walls.

I fought the urge to feed, pushed it as deep as I could. The blood was probably tainted anyway. To taste it would be to risk contaminating myself further.

I slipped past the window to the door. I still had yet to see any movement from within. It was entirely possible Countess Telia had been attacked by a rogue wolf or two and was out chasing down the last of them. She could return at any time.

Or she could be inside, bathing in the blood of her victims. It was hard to tell with vamps, especially ones like her.

I stepped around the corner and into the house, my gun leading the way.

There was blood on the floor just inside the door, but there were no bodies. One of the dead outside could have been wounded here before staggering out into the driveway to die.

Either that or whoever had been injured here was somewhere farther in the house, wounded and angry.

I worked my way deeper, checking each room as I passed. The living room I had seen from the window was to my left, and I paid it only a casual glance as I passed by. The dining room and kitchen were likewise empty, though I did find what looked to be an ear lying on the kitchen counter. Whomever it belonged to wasn't anywhere to be found.

There were two other rooms on the ground floor, but I had yet to come across any sign that anyone was alive inside. I still had the basement and the upstairs to canvas, yet something told me I wouldn't find anyone in the house. For whatever reason, Countess Telia wasn't home.

Still, I headed for the stairs. I would check over the place first, freeing any Purebloods I found, and then would wait for Telia to return. I couldn't let her continue her torturous ways. Not in my town.

From the bottom of the stairs, I could see what appeared to be a man's boot resting beside a bloody wall. I slowly made my way up the stairs sideways, keeping my gun trained just above the boot in case the guy sat up.

I needn't have bothered. The boot turned out not to be connected to anyone. The hallway behind it was empty of everything but blood. I stepped around the boot and just happened to glance back at it as I passed.

There was a foot inside.

The alarm bells in my head weren't just ringing now. They were clanging so loudly my ears rang with the phantom sound. Something was definitely wrong here.

The first room on my right turned out to be a bathroom. The owner of the foot was inside, lying on the floor, a bloody mess. His head lay in the tub, severed from his body much like the wolf's had been. The job had been sloppy, most likely performed with a dull blade. The dead man's mouth was wide, exposing two extended fangs. Vampires don't turn to dust when killed like they do in the movies.

I looked around the bathroom in the hopes of finding something that would identify the victim. I didn't know what Telia's lone vampire minion looked like. If this was him, then something truly bad had happened here, and by the smell, it hadn't happened too long ago.

I left the bathroom, my body thrumming with excitement. Had the Major House come down on Telia after all? Or was it someone else? Could another House have decided they'd had enough of the Fledgling vamp and her torturous ways? Or another Fledgling House could have come after her, looking to make themselves stronger.

A surge of anger coursed through my body. If Mikael held out on me because he knew Telia's old House was coming after her, I was going to be pissed. What if I had shown up while the killing was going on? I might have been caught in the middle of a fight between vamps and wolves from a Major House and Telia's own. I could have been killed.

I wasn't positive that was what happened. Most vampires didn't fight with swords, let alone dull ones. They would have sent werewolves to finish the job. A few well-placed bullets would have wounded Telia and her minions; then the wolves could have torn them apart at their leisure.

This was different somehow. I wasn't quite sure how,

but I knew something else was going on. Had Telia tired of her House? Had she killed everyone in an orgy of blood and torture?

I crept down the hall, checking each room as I passed. There was no one inside and I had yet to hear the slightest sound. I could taste blood where my fangs had started pushing through in my excitement.

The door to the last room of the house was hanging open. As I neared, I could smell the blood coming from inside. Someone was dead in there. More than one some-one by the smell of it.

I neared and as the massacre inside came into view, I knew Telia's killing days were over.

The Countess lay sprawled across her bed. At least most of her did. One of her arms was lying on the floor just inside the door, and her head was lying under the window. She was naked and was propped atop the dead Pureblood tied to the bed beneath her.

I stepped over the arm and another body, this one a werewolf, came into view. The wolf was fully shifted, but his body was nothing but a bloody pulp of entrails and muscle. It looked like something had fed on his intestines.

"What the fuck?" I said, scanning the room. Now that I was farther in, I could see what had killed the Pureblood under Telia. His face was gone, having been chewed away by something. I had a feeling he'd been alive when Telia had been riding him.

I slowly approached Telia's headless body. I was pretty sure she had been beheaded by the same weapon that had killed the others. Whoever had done this had somehow snuck up on her and the first blow had severed her spine. With all the dead lying around, I had no idea how that was even possible. She should have heard something, should have known things weren't right within her House.

A strange feeling crept up my gut. I didn't believe this was an inside job. I was almost positive it wasn't done by a Major House either. This looked a lot like something I would have done years ago, before I was changed, before I had silver weapons.

I hurried out of the room and headed for the basement. If anyone was still alive, it would be down there. Vampires usually kept cages there where they held their Pureblood prisoners. If someone was trying to copy my earlier work, then there was a chance they left the Purebloods down there.

I threw open the basement door and ran down the stairs. I almost stepped on another werewolf corpse as I hit the concrete floor. I staggered to the side, bringing my gun to bear, just in case the wolf wasn't dead.

It didn't take more than a glance to know he wasn't getting up again. He didn't have a head.

I took a deep breath and immediately regretted it. My fangs pushed the rest of the way through my gums and I started panting. There was so much blood down here, it was intoxicating.

My gaze roamed the room, and my shock was all that kept me from giving in to my demon.

The Pureblood prisoners were mostly still in their cages. Those who had gotten too close to the bars had been torn apart, pulled through the bars piece by piece. Arms and legs looked gnawed upon, and someone's jawbone lay against the wall.

Those Purebloods who had managed to huddle far back in their cages hadn't been able to escape the hungry jaws of the beast that had fed here. The bars of their cells had been ripped open and they had been killed where they cowered, easy prey to the wolf who had done this.

My hunger warred with my disgust. I couldn't figure out who would have done this. Why would a werewolf need a sword when he had his claws? None of this made any sense.

I turned and fled up the stairs, knowing I was wasting

my time here. House Telia was no more, but it hadn't been by my hand.

I slipped in a pool of blood at the top of the stairs and nearly fell. I growled deep in my throat and bolted for the front door. I could feel the urge to feed so strongly it nearly had a hold on me. I couldn't give in. Not now. Not like this.

I hurried out of the house, down the driveway, to my Honda. The fresh air did me some good, cleared my head, but it did nothing to stop the anger that came bubbling forth.

Mikael had to have known this was going to happen. It was the only thing that made sense. Why else wouldn't he have told me everything he knew?

I started up my motorcycle and sped away from the house. Everyone was dead inside, even the Purebloods. Whoever had done this was just as dangerous as Telia had been. They had to be stopped.

And I was going to be the one to stop them.

2

The Bloody Stake parking lot was full when I arrived, forcing me to park just off the road instead. Patrons were coming in and out of the door in streams, most of them supes, but a few Purebloods here and there. It was busier than usual, and I wondered what could possibly be going on tonight of all nights.

It wasn't until I was inside that I remembered.

Just because The Bloody Stake catered to vampires and werewolves, as well as Purebloods willing to risk their neck for a drink, didn't mean it wasn't any less a bar. Hell, the sign out front of a woman repeatedly staking an over-dressed vampire probably brought in more customers than it turned away.

But being a bar meant Bart, the owner and only bartender, had to make money. And tonight was one of those nights when The Bloody Stake became something different, something I would never have set foot into if the guy I wanted to see wasn't inside.

Tonight was singles' night.

Bart wasn't a big fan of turning his bar into a singles' hangout, but it's hard to say no to quadrupling your nightly take. He rarely held special events like this, preferring the normal dangers of serving monsters to the risks of bringing in the desperate. The last singles' night took place five months ago after a pretty bad fight left him with a hearty repair bill. I wondered what disaster prompted this one.

I frowned at the crowd, wishing they would all just go away. Quite a few of the people there would die that very night. There were still a lot of people who didn't quite realize how dangerous taking a vampire or werewolf home to bed with them really was. You were less likely to find your heart's desire than you would be to find your heart sitting atop your chest by night's end.

I pushed past a group of women leaving with a guy who looked too drunk to stand. I wasn't sure which were the supes and didn't care. It was their choice whom they left with, and if someone ended up dead, it wasn't on my hands. As long as they did their business away from the bar, Bart wouldn't interfere either.

Music blared over the speakers, drowning out the shouts and screams of the people dancing and fondling each other. The Bloody Stake was packed nearly wall to wall, and all the tables that usually adorned the middle of the room were pushed to the side, leaving a large, empty space for the singles to dance.

Bart stood at the bar, watching everything carefully. His shotgun was in front of him, just under the counter. If anyone got a little too frisky in his bar, they'd be leaving without their head. The scar on his face and his limp were clear evidence that The Bloody Stake had its fair share of violent outbreaks.

I gave him the briefest of nods as his eyes passed over me. He looked surprised to see me there but returned the nod anyway. He turned back to his patrons, a grimace on his face.

I worked my way around the edge of the room until I spotted Mikael in his usual booth. There were four girls intertwined around him, which wasn't much of a surprise.

He always had girls hanging all over him. I had no idea why. He wasn't much to look at.

Two of the girls were pressed so close to him they might as well have been part of his attire. His slicked-back hair shone in the dim lights of the bar and despite the girls plastered against him, it wasn't mussed. Only the backs of the other two girls were visible. Their heads were beneath the table somewhere, doing something I didn't even want to think about.

I turned away, disgusted. Mikael wasn't the most pleasant of people, but I counted him amongst my friends for some strange reason. His taste in women was pretty wide, though usually they were all young and pretty. How he managed to attract them was beyond me. Maybe there was more to him than appearances. Money probably had something to do with it.

But even though I was used to it by now, it didn't mean I wanted to watch. I scanned the bar instead, allowing the girls time to finish their business so I could have a little sit-down with him.

I didn't like it being so busy. I was pretty sure there was more than one person in the bar who would have loved to know who I was. There was a pretty big bounty on my head, although no one but those I trusted knew what I looked like or knew my real name. I made sure of that.

It was hard to make out much of anything in the mass of twisting bodies. There were just too many people gyrating against each other for me to get a good look at any one face. And thanks to the loose atmosphere, there were quite a few people who seemed to have lost a few articles of clothing. It was actually pretty distracting.

A girl just a few feet away was down to her bra and panties, and if she kept rubbing up against everyone like that, I was sure she wouldn't have even that before long. She looked high on something. Her eyes were glazed; her mouth hung open as if she couldn't figure out how to close it. She was prime pickings for anyone looking for an easy lay.

Or snack.

It was almost too much. Usually, The Bloody Stake was a place I went to in order to relax. I'd never been to singles' night before and I planned on never being there for one again. If I'd known it was this bad, I would have waited until tomorrow night to confront Mikael.

But I was here now and I wanted to get it over with. I glanced back over the table and found that the two girls were sitting back up. One was kissing him, and even from where I was standing, I could see his tongue probing her mouth.

Ew.

I started toward his table. I was so ready to get out of there.

I hadn't gone a handful of steps before someone pressed up against me from behind. Bone-thin arms wrapped across my chest and warm breath blew across my ear.

"Hey, beautiful," the girl said. She stank of alcohol and sweat. "How 'bout you slip out of that coat and we see what you have to offer."

She reached for the edge of my coat, fingers tiptoeing across the leather. My hand shot up and I grabbed her by the wrist a little too hard. She cried out as I twisted.

I could almost feel Bart's eyes on me, so I let her go before I got myself into trouble. The girl backed away, blue eyes wide. She wouldn't have been too bad to look at if she wasn't so damn skinny. The guy next to her didn't seem to mind, however. As soon as she was close, he grabbed her around the waist and licked the side of her neck.

I turned away and continued on to Mikael without glancing at Bart. There was a good chance he might ask me to leave if I acknowledged him. He didn't like violence in his bar even though he catered to the most violent of monsters. Most people respected his limits. I was usually one of them.

Dancers moved out of my way as I stalked across the room. They'd seen what I had done to the girl and didn't want to have any part of it. The look on my face probably kept those that liked it from making advances of their own.

Mikael saw me coming and pulled away from his company. He whispered something into each of their ears, which caused them all to giggle, and they slid out of his booth one by one. He made sure to give each a nice pat on the ass as they passed.

I was sure the disapproval was clear on my face, because his smile widened as I sat down across from him.

"I'm surprised you are here on this wonderful evening, my sweet," he said, his thick accent slurring his words. He sounded as slimy as he looked.

"You seem to be enjoying it."

"Of course." His grin widened. "How best to sample the quality America has to offer than to taste the youth? It is quite refreshing."

"I'm sure it is," I said, trying not to think about him tasting anything, especially after what I had seen. The music was so loud I was forced to lean across the table to hear him, and I could smell him. He smelled like sex.

"Why have you come to me tonight? Is there more I can do to be of service to you?" He winked. "Perhaps you are ready to sample a taste of Sweden." He waggled his eyebrows.

I knew he was joking, but the thought made my stomach flip anyway. I had to clench my fists and bite the inside of my lip to keep from saying something nasty. As much as I liked what Mikael did for me, he could be trying at times.

"Who else did you tell about House Telia?" I asked. I spoke just loud enough for him to hear, not wanting anyone else in the room to catch wind of our conversation. Who knew who might be lurking in the shadows, waiting for someone to say the wrong thing.

Of course, Mikael had chosen The Bloody Stake to do his business for a reason. Anyone who wanted to keep their life wouldn't even think about eavesdropping on anyone else's conversation. It was just too damn dangerous.

"What do you mean?" he asked, frowning. "I give only information that is asked and paid for."

"But House Telia? You couldn't tell me everything I wanted to know."

His smile returned. "But that would have no bearing on your business," he said. "Only you have asked about Countess Telia and her new House. I gave you all I could under the circumstances."

I stared at him long and hard, wondering what those circumstances might be. I knew he was telling the truth, that he had told me everything he was able, yet I felt that there should have been more. He should have warned me.

I hated the fact that Mikael had basically worked out who I was. He'd always suspected, and it wasn't until recently he was certain I was Lady Death. I never came out and actually admitted it, choosing instead to pretend I might know her, but he knew. He was smart that way.

Normally, I would have killed him for that knowledge. I didn't go around spouting it freely, and anyone I didn't want to know about it ended up dead pretty fast. It was the only way I could keep doing what I did without having people hunting me left and right.

"She's dead," I said, figuring it best not to belabor the point any longer. He knew who I was, why beat around the bush?

His brow crinkled. "I figured she would be soon enough, but why are you telling me this, my sweet?"

"Because it wasn't clean."

He looked at me like I was speaking some sort of foreign language. "I don't understand."

I took a deep breath. Even though I knew he knew, it was still hard to just come out and say it. It would be admitting something I didn't want anyone else to know. Doing that didn't come easy.

"I didn't kill her," I said, finally. It felt sort of good to say it. I really didn't talk to too many people about what I did for a living.

Still, my fingers flittered near my belt and I had to ball them even tighter to keep from drawing a knife and sticking it in Mikael's throat. Old habits die hard.

He simply nodded and leaned forward, all business. "How did it happen?"

"They were dead when I got there."

He blinked. "And?"

"And I was wondering if you knew who did it. I don't like walking into something like this without knowing the whole story. If you knew someone was coming after her, you should have told me."

His face didn't change, but I could tell he knew something.

"What?"

"How did they die?" he asked. He glanced around the room before his gaze resettled on me.

"It looked like a werewolf with a sword," I said. "Many of the bodies were torn up pretty bad and it looked like they were fed upon."

"The sword was not of silver?"

"I don't think so. If I were to guess, I would say the thing hadn't been sharpened in a few years. Whoever did it had to work at it."

Mikael nodded as if it made perfect sense. "I told no one of your plans," he said. "No one else asked about this House. The House I spoke of before is not involved in this in any way."

"Are you sure?"

"Yes."

"But you know who might be?"

"Perhaps," he said. He folded his hands and glanced down at the table in front of him.

I sighed. "I don't have any money on me. I'll have it the next time I see you."

He studied me a moment before nodding. "You are good for it. I can trust you."

I just stared at him.

"There have been some strange happenings as of late, much of it attributed to Lady Death."

"Like what?" I shifted in my seat, uneasy. I didn't like the sound of this at all. If people were blaming me for things I hadn't done, it would only draw even more unwanted attention my way.

"Mostly rogues," Mikael said. "They are found by others, torn up, heads separated. A few times families have died, killed in the same manner." He gave me a look. "I did not believe it was you, but not many fight with a blade and hunt those of their kind."

I ground my teeth together. "People are blaming me for this? You should know better."

He shrugged. "It is hard to say. I thought perhaps you were practicing for something. These kills had your mark, even if they were sloppier."

"But why haven't I heard anything? You could have said something."

"Perhaps you did not ask the right questions. I give only the information asked of me." He waved a hand. "Besides, these were just rogues. Who cares about them anyway, yes? And it was all so new, if it is someone coming after your title, you would take care of them eventually."

"Okay, but why kill Countess Telia? Could they have known I was coming for her and decided to show me up?"

"I do not know," Mikael said. "But I think it is more likely a coincidence. House Telia was new and small. They would make an easy target for anyone looking to test the waters."

I supposed that was true, but I didn't like it. How long before testing the waters turned into coming after the competition? If someone was trying to copy me or take over my work, then what was to stop them from hunting me next?

"I would be careful on this," he said. He glanced across

the room again and I followed his gaze. If there was anything to see other than the dancers, I wasn't seeing it. "If these killers are looking to replace you, you may be next on their list."

Even though I just had the same thought, a chill ran up and down my spine upon hearing it from someone else's lips. This was supposed to be a quick and easy run. Things were getting far too complicated.

"What can you tell me about who is doing this?" I asked. If the killer had me on their list, the best thing I could do would be to come after them first. The more I knew, the better prepared I would be.

"Very little," Mikael admitted. "I wish I could tell you more, but there is not much to tell. I, like many others, assumed Lady Death had a hand in the deaths. Maybe you were training an apprentice, someone who could help you in your mission to rid the city of the filth." He smiled a little at that, as if he thought the idea ridiculous.

"You assumed wrong," I said.

"It appears so," he said. "And I do not like it. I am rarely wrong." He sighed and scratched his eyebrow. "It makes for dangerous times. Who is to say they will not come for someone here tonight, that they aren't here themselves? I could be next. You could be."

I couldn't stop my gaze from traveling to the dancing crowd. What if the killers were here? Could they be watching me even now?

As far as I could tell, no one was looking our way. A few stray glances passed over us, but nothing that seemed to have any intent behind it.

"So you can't tell me anything else?" I asked.

Mikael shook his head. "I am sorry," he said. "Whoever is doing this is more dangerous than they appear. House Telia might have been a small House, but it *was* a vampire House. You don't become a House of your own, even a small one, without power."

I ran my fingers through my hair and was surprised to see the slightest tremble to them. Someone was out there killing werewolves and vampires, hunting them, and it wasn't me. Why did that bother me so much?

Of course I knew. Purebloods had died—people who might have been completely innocent of any crime. Someone who wanted to copy me would have known I never killed the innocent if I could help it. This had been nothing more than a slaughter. I couldn't abide by that.

And there was the fact I was a vampire myself. If they were killing all supes, no matter who, then how long before someone came after me?

Thoughts of the Luna Cult Den drifted to my mind, but I pushed them away. I didn't need to be thinking about them right then. They could take care of themselves.

I couldn't think of anything else to say, so I thanked Mikael for his time and rose. I had no idea how I was going to handle this. The best I could hope for was that the killer slipped up and got himself or herself killed.

I barely noticed the people bumping into me as I made for the door. I kept my hands close to my weapons out of habit, but would never draw them in The Bloody Stake. They were illegal here just as they were everywhere else. If someone were to catch wind that I was carrying silver in a bar full of vamps and wolves, I could be in for a long, bloody night.

I managed to get outside without incident. I breathed in the chill night air and made my way to my Honda. As much as I wanted to do something about the killer, I couldn't do anything now. I didn't have enough information to even think about starting a search.

It was still pretty early, but I'd already had enough of the night. The only thing I wanted to do now was go home and take a long, hot bath. Who knew? It might be the last one I'd ever get to take.

3

I hadn't gone far when I noticed the truck following me. At first, I tried to dismiss it as my imagination working overtime. I wasn't a stranger to paranoia. In my line of work, it's almost a necessity. You never stopped looking over your shoulder if you wanted to live.

I kept my eyes on the headlights behind me, certain I was overreacting. No one had followed me out of The Bloody Stake that I had seen. Just because a vehicle was behind me didn't mean it was after me. I wasn't the only person who ever drove these roads.

Still, I wasn't about to let my guard down. I couldn't discern the make of the truck or the driver in my mirrors. The lights were too bright and the night too dark. The driver wasn't on my ass exactly, but he stayed close enough that it bothered me.

I turned down a side street I knew led to a residential district that was on the decline. The street wasn't the worst I had driven, but it was starting to crumble around the edges. Scraggly bushes were creeping into the road and if someone didn't come along and clear them away, they would soon overtake it.

The truck turned down the street behind me and my paranoia leaped to new heights.

I sped up now that there was no traffic to worry about. The truck sped up behind me, its engine coughing with the increased speed.

There was no question about it now. The truck was following me.

Houses passed on either side as we zoomed down the road. Most of them were utterly dark. Shades were drawn, lights were off, but a few had glows around upstairs windows, just barely visible in the all-too-dark night. No one wanted to be a target, telling the prowlers that someone was home, but life did have to go on. Sometimes people couldn't help but leave a light on now and again.

The road curved ahead and I tore around it far faster than I should have. I started to tip but managed to drop my boot fast enough to rebalance myself and finish the turn. A move like that might have torn the leg right off of anyone else. As a vampire, it was almost too easy.

The truck skidded behind me as I took another turn and sped up on a straight stretch. There were no lights ahead hinting at any sort of civilization. The tightly locked houses soon became empty shells where the inhabitants had either moved to a safer location or had died. It wasn't a good idea to live this close to a place like The Bloody Stake. It was just asking for trouble.

I risked a glance over my shoulder and saw the truck slip off the road for an instant before popping back on. The driver swerved a few times before reorienting himself on me and speeding up.

I smiled, the thrill of the chase tingling throughout my body. I leaned into the wind as I shot forward, looking for a good place for a confrontation.

It took only a moment to find it.

Empty houses sat on either side of the street, just around a curve. My pursuer had been losing ground fast, even though he had to have had the gas pedal pressed to the floor. I had only a few moments before he would be on me, however, so I acted fast.

I turned hard and went a short distance through a yellowed yard, coming to a halt at the side of a house that stood just off the road. I leaped off my Honda, yanked my gun free, and waited. The guy driving the truck wouldn't be able to see me until it was too late.

A second ticked by. I could hear the truck rumbling closer. I tensed.

As soon as my pursuer came into view, I fired. His tire blew, and I could hear his curse over the tortured sound of metal as the rubber flew free. He slammed on the brakes, still in the process of trying to make that last turn, and the truck spun sideways.

For a second, it looked like he might make it, but just as he was about to coast to a stop, the back tire slid off the road and the truck tipped over. It turned over twice before slamming to a stop at the base of a tree in the yard across the street.

I rose from my crouch and drew my sword. Just because his truck was a mess didn't mean the driver was down for the count. I headed toward the wreck, gun trained on the bottom of the truck, eyes scanning every which way.

Something moved in a window across the street. It could have been just the flutter of a ratty curtain in the breeze through a broken window. Or it could have been something else, someone watching.

I didn't have time to worry about it. There was a grunt from within the truck and I stopped to wait for the driver to get out. Glass shattered as he kicked out the windshield. I couldn't see him from where I stood, but I could hear him slithering out. I was glad he survived. I wanted answers.

"Bloody fucking hell," he said as he emerged. "Fucking bitch broke my goddamn arm."

I stood there, aiming toward the sound of his voice. I

wasn't going to say a damn thing until I saw him. I didn't know if this was just some Pureblood out chasing down chicks for kicks, or if he was something more.

I didn't have to wait long to find out. My pursuer rose and walked around the truck, staggering slightly. He cradled his arm against his chest, hissing in a sharp breath with every step. I could smell the blood from where I stood. The bone had probably popped through the skin.

"You owe me some serious shit for this," he said, coming closer.

"I don't owe you a thing, asshole." I trained my gun on the middle of his face. He kept his head down as if his neck was hurting. "Why were you following me?"

The man took another step closer and raised his head, eyes falling on me where I stood. He had piercings all over his face and his spiked hair was purple. A knot of scar tissue glared out from his forehead, telling me all I needed to know about him.

He stopped walking and sneered at me as his gaze traveled to my gun. He spit a wad of blood and snot onto the ground and wiped his mouth with the back of his good hand.

"What does Adrian want?" I snarled the words, barely keeping myself from pulling the trigger. This guy had followed me before. He and his friend had dropped a goddamn werewolf on top of me in the middle of the road, scratching my bike all to hell. He still owed me for that.

"Fuck you," he said. His eyes darted from side to side as if he planned on running for it. Like a good boy, he stayed put.

"Why were you following me?" I really wanted to shoot him, but answers came first. I could shoot him later. "I don't like being followed."

He laughed. "Stupid bitch thinks she's all important." He glanced toward the truck. "She wrecks my goddamn ride and thinks I owe her an explanation." His grin turned sinister. "Maybe I was just looking for a fuck."

I had to restrain myself from shooting him right then and there. I knew I probably should have. Nothing good could come out of one of Adrian's wolves chasing after me.

Adrian Davis was a defector from the Luna Cult. He had sided with a vampire Count in order to secure his own power base. He wanted me to join him, become his mate or some shit. I had no intention of ever working with that asshole.

Purple Hair started hacking, blood splattering his lips. It dropped him to his knees and his head lowered. "Fuck," he cursed, spitting out more blood.

"You might need to get that looked at," I said, taking far too much satisfaction in his misery.

He started to rise again but suddenly shifted his weight at the last moment and went into a roll. I fired and my bullet took him in the broken arm. He screamed in pain, but the silver didn't slow him down. He was shifting before he hit his feet.

His face contorted, bones snapping and re-forming as his body remade itself. The piercings around his nose popped out, tearing gashes in his face. The ones in his ears and lips merely moved with the change, giving his wolfish grin a strange metallic look.

He screamed in agony as his broken arm shifted, the muscles tensing around the break. A jet of blood shot out of the wound, falling a few feet away from me. It distracted me enough that I didn't get another good shot at him.

He bound around the side of his truck just as I realigned my aim. My bullet ricocheted off the tail end, bouncing harmlessly into the night.

"Damn it," I said. I walked slowly sideways, keeping my aim where I last saw the wolf. He couldn't be far. The only place he could run was out in the open.

As soon as I stepped around the back of the truck, he leaped out at me. I was too far back for him to come anywhere close. I squeezed off two shots, both hitting, and he dropped to the ground. Before I could fire a final bullet into his brain, he was on his feet and charging.

I drew my sword and swung in a fluid movement that was all reflex. The silver blade took him in his good arm, nearly severing it at the elbow. He howled in pain and fell to the ground in a heap. Bloody froth fell from his lips and he rolled over onto his back to face me.

I stayed well back. Even an injured werewolf was dangerous. I considered shooting him in the head and finishing him off but stopped myself. I still needed answers.

I took a moment to glance around. I wasn't totally positive Purple Hair was the only one in the truck. He might have had a friend. I also was worried about that flutter in the window. Who knew who might be watching?

"Why did Adrian send you?" I asked, my gaze returning to the wolf. There wasn't much I could do about the house now. If someone was in there, they would be best served just to stay inside.

The wolf snarled at me and struggled to sit up.

I shot him in the leg.

He cried out and fell back, limp. He was bleeding all over, and I was pretty sure the crash had caused some serious internal injuries. Shifting as he had probably made them worse.

"I'd shift back if I were you," I said, poking him in the groin with the tip of my sword. "You aren't dead yet, and if you answer my questions, you won't have to be."

He shifted back, screaming all the while. The bullets lodged in his body ground against the bones, tearing bigger holes in his muscles. The pain had to be almost unbearable.

"Fuck you," he said the moment he could speak again. Blood dribbled from his lips.

I took a step toward him. He was nude now, his clothes having fallen off him when he shifted the first time. There was no place for him to hide a weapon, at least no place he could get to quickly with a broken arm and a nearly severed one. If he tried to shift again, I could easily kill him before he completed the change.

"I could get you help," I said. "You don't have to die. Just tell me what I want to know."

He tried to sneer again, but it turned into a grimace of pain. He was sweating profusely and was shaking. The slightest breath had to be pure agony.

"Why would Adrian send you after me? He had to know you stood no chance."

He groaned and his eyes rolled into the back of his head, showing only whites.

"No, you don't," I said, kicking him in the broken arm.

He screamed, eyes flashing open. They turned a wolf yellow for an instant before turning back into his normal browns.

"I asked you a question."

"I don't have to fucking answer a thing." He spoke through gritted teeth. Something was whistling and I wasn't so sure it was his nose. He might have punctured a lung.

"I could leave you here to die," I said. "I'm pretty sure your injuries are bad enough even a werewolf would struggle to recover." I made a point to look around at what I hoped to be empty houses. "Or I could finish you off now. It matters little to me."

"Then do it," he spat. He screamed as he tried to shift positions on the ground. He moved his broken arm as if to clutch at the nearly severed one and screamed again. "Fuck."

"I could take you to someone for help," I said. I wasn't so sure it would matter. He was losing a ton of blood. If he had been a Pureblood, he would have been dead by now. "All you have to do is tell me why Adrian sent you. He had to know it would end like this."

The wolf started panting, his chest rising and falling in

quick, hitching breaths. He licked at his lips and blood all but poured from his mouth. He wasn't going to live much longer.

And he knew it too. He forced a grin and started laughing. It had to have hurt like hell to laugh like that, but he kept on doing it. Blood bubbles rose and burst from his lips. His wounds were pumping at an alarming rate. Blood stained the ground, and despite the fact he was a werewolf and taking his blood would drive me insane, it awoke the hunger within me.

I stepped back quickly, my fangs bursting free. Blood ran down my chin and my breathing started coming fast. I fought it as hard as I could. If I so much as tasted his blood, I knew I wouldn't be able to stop. I had waited far too long to feed. I needed blood and I needed it soon.

"Kill me," the wolf gasped between breaths. His laughing slowed and turned into something that sounded more like a death rattle. "Please. Kill me."

I looked down at the man, wanting nothing more than to give him his dying wish, yet I was afraid to get any closer. My hunger needed sated. A bullet would kill him, but it wouldn't feel as good.

"Kill me!" he shouted. He followed it up with a scream that had to have been heard miles away. His eyes were blazing and he was shuddering uncontrollably. The blood coming from his arm was slowing.

I wasn't totally sure he would die on his own. He might suffer there, linger near death, but eventually recover.

I couldn't have that.

I raised the gun, intent on putting an end to him and getting the hell out of there before my control broke.

Flashing blue and red lights stopped me. I dropped my aim and spun around as a police cruiser pulled up. I hadn't even heard the car approaching. My eyes flashed to the window where I had seen movement and I wondered if whoever was inside had called the cops on us.

The cop got out, eyes wide, scanning the wreckage. My coat hid my sword, though if he looked hard enough, he would see my gun.

"Is everyone all right?" he asked. He looked from me, to the overturned truck, and then finally to the bleeding wolf on the ground. His eyes widened and he started to turn away.

I broke. Everything went blood red and I leaped at him, dropping my sword and gun. The officer managed to get an arm up in time so that I didn't immediately sink my fangs into his neck, but it did him little good.

I slammed him up against the cruiser, only wanting one thing. It was the only thing that mattered. The smell of blood was overpowering, my need overriding every last ounce of control I had. The cop screamed, but his pleas went unanswered.

I bared my fangs at him and he fell abruptly silent. His eyes widened just as I buried my face in his neck and started feeding.

Some part of me knew what I was doing was wrong, that this man was innocent. But I also knew he was most likely safe to feed upon without testing him against silver. The Pureblood police regularly underwent silver tests to make sure they weren't infected. An infected cop was relieved of duty and promptly forgotten about.

The officer fought beneath me, pushed at me with hands far too weak. He reached for his gun, but I intercepted him out of pure reflex, grabbing his arm and twisting it behind him. I felt it snap as I twisted too far. He screamed and kicked feebly at my legs.

His fighting weakened and my brain kicked back on. I wanted to keep feeding, wanted to drain him of every last drop. If I were to kill him, I would be able to go without feeding longer. There was something about that last pull that sucked the essence straight out of a victim. If I stopped now, I would have to feed again all too soon.

But as much as I wanted to keep going, I forced myself to stop. I jerked away from him and staggered back a few steps, appalled at what I had just done. The cop slumped down the front of his cruiser, blood dribbling from the wounds in his neck. He stared at me with mostly glazed eyes.

I didn't know what to do. He would die if I left him there. I glanced at the wolf, but he had stopped struggling. I wasn't sure if he was dead or unconscious, and it really didn't matter. I had bigger problems to worry about.

I opened the cruiser door and tore open the glove compartment. There were napkins there and I grabbed every one I could find. I slapped them against the wound in the cop's neck, and raised his hand and pressed it against the napkins.

"Hold these tight," I said, slapping him lightly on the face. He gave me a dazed look but held on to the napkins. His broken arm hung limply at his side.

Once I was sure he wasn't going to pass out on me, I reached into the car and grabbed his radio. "Officer down." I gave our location and let the mic drop to the floor as the person on the other end started asking rapid-fire questions.

I stepped back, wishing there was more I could do. If I took the cop to a hospital, I was sure they wouldn't let me leave. They would want to know what happened, and when they found out, they would try to detain me.

I couldn't hurt anyone else. Not tonight.

I hurried to my Honda, hating myself with every step. I should have done more. I shouldn't have attacked him. I never should have let myself get so far gone.

I grabbed my sword and gun on the way and started the motorcycle. It rumbled to life, sounding too loud in the suddenly quiet night. I pulled back onto the road, giving the cop one last apologetic look.

Then I left him there. To live or die? I didn't know.

I wasn't so sure it mattered.

4

"Holy crap," Ethan said, eyes following me as I walked through the side door and across the kitchen.

I hardly paid him a glance. I tore off my coat and tossed it on the dining room table, along with my shoulder holster and belt. I was in no mood to talk to anyone, and though he usually took the hint, Ethan was following me.

"What?" I said, turning on him. I could still feel the dried blood on my face and wanted nothing more than to get it off. It was a mark of my guilt.

"What happened?" he asked, paling.

"Nothing." I sounded far more sullen than I wanted. "Aren't you supposed to be working on something?"

He raised the coffee mug in his hand to eye level. "I needed fuel."

"Oh." I started to turn back toward the stairs.

"Kat." The concern in Ethan's voice stopped me. "What happened tonight? You look . . . bad."

I sighed. I really didn't want to get into what happened right then, maybe not ever. It was bad enough I was going to relive those moments with the cop for the rest of my life, especially if he died. Did I really need to talk about it so soon?

I turned to look at Ethan. He was wearing one of his cartoon T-shirts. It was smudged across the front as if he had spent quite a while in his lab below the basement doing something that involved dirt. His hair had grown over the last few months and it hung in his eyes, stringy, as if he had been sweating profusely.

I took Ethan in when he was just a kid. A vampire Count had killed his entire family, and we sort of bonded. I broke him out of his cell, mostly in my own rage at having my brother changed into a mindless beast and having my own life as a Pureblood ended.

Funny thing was, I've never asked him his last name. It wasn't until now that it even crossed my mind. He was always just Ethan to me, a comfort in a world where blood and death prevailed.

Of course, everything wasn't all lollipops and daisies with Ethan. He had problems of his own, namely, a demon he summoned in his lab nightly. The demon helped make my weapons, as well as other little gadgets like the fingerprint readers on all the doors, but that didn't mean I had to like it.

"I'm fine," I said. As much as I didn't want to talk about it, Ethan was my only true friend. Even with his demon summoning, I could trust him more than anyone else. "It was just a really bad night."

"The vampire give you troubles?"

I went to the dining room table and sat down. I so didn't want to do this. "None at all."

Ethan sat down across from me. He pulled my sword from its sheath and frowned. "You fought."

"A little."

He put the sword back and stared at me. I knew he was only concerned for my well-being, but for some reason, the look in his eye felt full of accusation. I had to look away.

"Kat, please," he said, sounding hurt that I wouldn't look at him. "Are you really okay?"

I started to nod but ended up shaking my head.

"Did you . . ." He trailed off and cleared his throat before continuing, "Did you have to hunt tonight?"

"Sort of."

He raised his eyebrows at me.

I sighed again. I knew talking around it wouldn't help anything. I licked my lips and grimaced. I could taste the cop's blood. I could still feel his skin between my teeth, the smell of his fear. God, I hoped someone got to him in time. I don't think I could live with myself otherwise.

"Countess Telia is dead," I said, figuring if I was going to tell him anything, I might as well start from the beginning. I still wasn't so sure I would tell him the whole story. The cop was my problem. I didn't need to burden him with that.

"That's good," he said, eyeing me carefully. "And?"

I took a deep breath before letting out the rest. "And I didn't do it."

He opened his mouth and closed it a few times. "Oh, uh," he finally managed.

"Yeah."

He took a sip of his coffee and set the mug down on the table. "Her own people, you think?"

"I don't know. I don't think so."

"Then what?"

I shrugged. "Mikael told me that other vampires and werewolves have been turning up dead recently. Telia wasn't the first."

Ethan digested that a moment before speaking. "What else did he say?"

"That everyone thinks I'm the one doing it."

Ethan started to chew on his lower lip. He picked up his coffee and started to take a sip but set it down instead. "That could be bad."

"No shit."

"What are you going to do?"

"I have no idea."

He nodded. We sat there silently for a few minutes more, each of us lost in our own thoughts. I really wanted to get upstairs and take a shower. I needed to wash the blood from me, the guilt. The longer I sat there, tasting the cop's blood, the worse I was going to be later. I tended to dwell on things like killing innocent people.

But I didn't move. I was afraid if I went upstairs now, I might break down. This was almost too much. A whole lot of shit just fell into my lap and I wasn't ready for it. I mean, how was I to handle this killer, Adrian and his goons, and my own guilt over feeding on someone who didn't deserve it. That's a lot to deal with for one night.

"What about . . . you know?" Ethan gestured toward me.

"What?"

"The blood."

"What about it?"

He gave me a sickly smile. "If Telia was already dead, then how did you get all icky?"

There was nothing I could do but tell him. I told him all about the purple-haired werewolf, about the cop who showed up at the worst possible time. I told him every-thing, even though it made my stomach clench to think about it. Ethan deserved to know the truth. He was the one who had to live with me.

He took it all pretty calmly. I think that's what I liked so much about him. He knew that any moment I could vamp out and kill him in a hunger-induced frenzy, yet he never flinched, never showed fear. He knew what I was and he accepted it. We both had our problems. It's what bound us.

Still, it was hard telling him. I hated reminding him what I was. Sure, he and his demon provided me with silver weapons, but did he really need to know the details of my life? I wanted to protect him, not get him involved any deeper than he already was.

"Someone will help him," he said once I was done. "You called it in. You have nothing to worry about."

"I fed on him, Ethan." I couldn't keep the disgust out of my voice. "I could have killed him. I never should have let myself get that far gone. I should have been able to control myself."

"It'll be okay."

"And what if it's not?" I countered. "What if he dies? What if it hadn't been a cop, but some kid instead?" I paused for a good ten seconds before continuing. "What if it had been you?"

"I would have poked you with your own knife and ran." He grinned, though it was a tad bit forced. "Look," he said, "I trust you. You've just gone through some crazy stuff, and the were attack had you all stressed out. It happens."

I gritted my teeth and sat back. I wanted to spit, but it wouldn't have been ladylike.

"It'll work out," Ethan said. "You'll see."

"Right." I stood. As much as Ethan's little pep talks usually helped, I wasn't in the mood to feel any better. I wanted to suffer a little while longer. I wanted the guilt to wash over me and make me remember why I did what I did. It would serve as a reminder as to what I was, of what I was capable of doing if I wasn't careful.

I made it all the way up three stairs this time before Ethan's voice stopped me again.

"Kat?" he said. This time he didn't sound as if he was curious. This time he sounded scared.

"What?" I asked, glancing down at him. He stood with his foot on the bottom step, his hands bracing him to the wall as if he was afraid that if he didn't hold on to something, he might collapse.

"I, uh, I have a question."

The way he said it made my eyes narrow. "What?"

He let out a little nervous laugh. "Well, um, I, uh."

"Spit it out."

He jerked at my harsh tone but did well in holding his ground. I could be scary when I wanted to be. "Well, you see, now that you know about what happens in my lab, and who I work with and all . . ."

I nodded. "Belifal."

"Beligral," he corrected, his nervous smile wavering.

"Whatever."

"Well, since you know about him and all, and I told him you know, he was interested to know who it was that knew."

I glared at him.

"Right," he said, licking his lips. "No babbling."

"Right."

Ethan took a deep breath. "I didn't tell him anything more about you than he needed to know. He doesn't even know your real name. I never told him and never plan to. I swear." He held his hand up like a boy scout.

"What *have* you told him?" I let the anger show in my voice. I so didn't need a demon on top of everything else right then. I never wanted to deal with it if I could help it. Demons were something I didn't fuck with. Ever.

"Well . . ."

I sucked in an angry breath and Ethan's eyes widened. How many sentences could he start with that one word without ever getting to the point?

"He knows you're a vampire," he said. "He knows you and I live together, but we aren't, you know, together." He reddened. "He knows you hunt vampires and werewolves, and that you are pretty good at what you do. He obviously knows about the silver weapons since he is the reason I can make them at all."

"Okay," I said, not liking this one bit. Who knew who else summoned the demon. If the right vampire Count just happened to be a summoner, it wasn't too farfetched to think Ethan's little play friend might give me up for the right price.

"It's all stuff he could have figured out on his own, really." Ethan's face was so red he looked like he was suffering from sunstroke. "I think he knows you're Lady Death, but I never said so specifically."

"What's the point?" I asked. I didn't like the idea of my name, even my nickname, being known by a demon. Nothing good could come of it. "I want to take a shower sometime tonight and would really like some time alone."

"Okay, yeah, well . . ." Ethan scratched at the back of his neck and fidgeted. "He wants to meet you."

I turned to fully face him. "What?"

"He thinks he can be of more use to you if he met you face-to-face."

My mind whirled. What in the hell could a demon want with me? He had to know that if I killed vampires and werewolves for a living, demons wouldn't be too much farther down my list. Hell, once I met him, the other monsters in my life might not seem so bad in comparison.

My gaze traveled toward the stairs leading down to the sitting room, as if I could see all the way down to the basement, to the next set of stairs leading into Ethan's lab. "Is he down there now?"

If possible, Ethan's face reddened even further. "Yeah."

My next words came out clipped. "You left a fucking demon alone down there? In *my* house?"

Ethan stepped backward and nearly fell off the step. He might have if he hadn't been clutching the wall so hard. "He's in a circle. He can't get out."

"And you know that for sure?"

He nodded. "He can't get out unless the circle is broken."

I wanted to scream and rant at him. There was no way it was ever a good idea to leave a demon alone anywhere, inside a circle or not. Sometimes, despite how smart he could be, Ethan could be frustratingly stupid.

But what could I say? I knew almost nothing about demons and how to summon them. As far as I knew, the demon wasn't even truly in this world. It could be a projection, some sort of glamour perhaps.

That brought someone else to mind. I quickly squashed the thought. I didn't need to be thinking about *him* on top of everything else.

"No," I said.

Ethan blinked. "No?"

"I'm not going to deal with this."

"He might be able to do something for you."

"I said no!" I screamed, taking a step down toward him.

Ethan scrambled back, eyes going so wide they were nearly all whites.

"I don't want to fucking deal with this shit," I said. "Tell your demon he can shove his help up his ass. I don't need him."

Ethan was nodding frantically and I realized how scary I must look to him. I had dried blood on my face, on my clothes. I could feel fresh blood coming from my gums, and my fangs were out and ready.

I turned away and hurried up the stairs, leaving Ethan shaking against the wall. I went straight to my room and slammed the door behind me.

I already hated myself for what I was, what I had so recently done. Now I had to add scaring the hell out of my only friend in the world to the list of shit I fucked up. This was definitely not turning out to be a good night.

I stripped out of my clothes, fighting back tears that threatened to break the surface. I would not cry. I was stronger than that.

As soon as my clothes were off and tossed in the basket reserved for bloody clothing, I went into the bathroom and turned on the shower, making it as hot as I could stand it. Stepping in, I let the water wash over me, hoping that by the time it was done, all the pain would be gone, stripped away like flesh in acid.

The water washed my skin clean. It could do nothing for my soul.

5

I didn't feel any better the following night. No matter how hard I tried to forget about what had happened, it kept replaying in my mind. It had been a long time since I'd attacked someone who hadn't deserved it in some way. Those kinds of things stick with you.

I rose from my bed and went to the window. Heavy drapes were sewn together and taped to the wall as not to allow in any light during the day. I peeled back a corner and looked outside, hoping the night would raise my spirits.

Moonlight shone over the trees, giving life to them. It was a crisp, clear night, and the sound of bugs and night birds reached my ears.

But it did nothing to ease my mind.

I slapped the tape back in place and got dressed. The jeans were tight, but the T-shirt I grabbed was loose-fitting. It hung to midthigh and was well worn. I threw on some running shoes and went to the mirror to pull back my hair to keep it out of my face.

I looked nothing like the girl who had come home the previous night. The blood was gone; the black leather was in the hamper to be cleaned. I was a bit pale, but these days, so were a lot of other people.

I looked normal. Without my fangs poking through, without the gun and knives and sword, I could almost pass for human. I forced a smile, exposing my teeth. There was no hint of the vampire I truly was. As long as I didn't touch silver or give in to my hunger, no one would be able to tell.

I never wore makeup, but I had some sitting on the counter. It always ran when I was fighting. Sweat and blood tended to do that. There wasn't much point in putting on makeup when the first splatter on your face would ruin all the work.

But I had no intention of fighting anyone tonight. I just wanted to be normal for an evening, even if it was a lie.

The lipstick touched my lips and I jerked back, scolding myself. What was I thinking? No matter how much makeup I put on, no matter what kind of clothes I wore, I was still Kat Redding, Lady Death, vampire and werewolf hunter. Nothing would change that.

Still, I needed this. After last night, I really needed to do something normal. I needed to get away from all the blood and death, even if it was only for a night.

It took me a while to apply the makeup correctly. I had to wipe it off more than once and start again. My hands shook slightly as I put on the eyeliner, but at least it went on reasonably well.

I stood back and looked at myself. With the makeup, it was even harder to tell my true nature. I smiled again, this time trying to make my eyes soften as I did. It didn't quite work, but at least it was a start.

Ethan was still in bed when I emerged from my bedroom. He had gone to bed late, so I didn't blame him for sleeping in. I imagine he hadn't had much of a good night, especially if he had to tell his demon what I'd said the night before.

I made my way quietly downstairs. My coat was hanging from the back of the chair and my weapons were gone. Ethan had probably spent most of the night working on them, fixing the nicks and scratches that would inevitably mar them after a night of fighting.

I grabbed my coat and considered heading out without my weapons but decided against it. If I went out unarmed, I would probably end up in a fight somewhere, wishing I had them. Just because I wanted to have a quiet night didn't mean the bad guys would let me.

My belt was on the table in the basement. I grabbed two new knives and slid them into the hidden sheaths at the buckle. A new sword came next. I buckled on the belt and slid on a shoulder holster. There were a handful of modified Glocks on the wall and I grabbed one, making sure to grab a few extra clips just in case.

I threw my coat on over it all. It settled on me comfortably, yet it made me feel dirty at the same time. Ethan had cleaned the blood off, bless him, but I could still smell it there, deep down within the leather. I fingered the spot where a werewolf's claw had torn a hole in it, touching the tight stitches that held it together. The coat, much like my own body, had endured quite a lot over the years.

I checked myself over to make sure I wasn't forgetting anything. There were a couple of silver dust packets in my coat pocket, but I wouldn't use them unless I really had to. They got in my eyes and on my skin and took forever to wash off. The sting always lasted for weeks.

I headed out into the garage and mounted my motorcycle. In minutes, I was on the road, driving without direction, just getting away.

I wanted to forget the past night even though I knew Adrian would need dealing with. Of everything else, he was the first on my list. Whoever was killing the vamps and wolves could wait. Adrian knew more about me, might even be able to trace me back from the Luna Cult. I couldn't have that.

I took turns without thinking about them, breathing in the night air. It felt so good just to be out and not looking to kill someone, I almost closed my eyes and just relaxed. The cool night air calmed my nerves where a day in bed hadn't.

I found myself drifting away from Columbus and moving out toward the suburbs. Vampires and werewolves were just as prevalent there as they were in the big city, but there was more open space, more chances to get lost. I knew the road I was taking, though it had been a while since I had traveled it.

Something tugged at me, some feeling that I couldn't quite pinpoint. I slowed down, letting cars pass by me. There were quite a few people out and I was given more than one appreciative look by passersby. I wasn't sure how many of them were supes and how many were Purebloods. And honestly, it didn't matter. I wasn't looking for trouble tonight.

I turned down a road that was less familiar, though I had come out this way once to put down a rogue wolf years ago. The traffic thinned here, the houses appeared farther and farther apart.

The strange feeling increased and I kept going, having no idea where I was headed. There was nothing out here as far as I knew—no town, no park, nothing that I would have the slightest interest in.

And then I saw it. A little sign beside a road I had never seen before. I stopped my Honda in front of the sign and had to lean forward to see it. Even with my enhanced vision it was hard to see.

"Welcome to Delai," I said, frowning. I'd never heard of the place.

I looked around. I vaguely remembered the area, but I didn't remember the sign or the road. It was entirely possible I had missed it before. I *had* been on a hunt all those years ago. It's easy to miss the little things when blood and death lie just ahead.

I started down the road, curious as to where it led. Fresh

pavement had been lain recently, so the ride was smooth and peaceful. My tires hummed on the road, a hypnotic lullaby that would have put nearly anyone to sleep.

I traveled for a good couple of minutes without seeing anything. There were just enough trees to obscure sightlines, so I was unable to see lights to the town anywhere ahead.

And when I did see them, I stopped my bike and just stared.

The entire town was lit up. From where I sat, it was hard to make much of anything out, but I could see the unbroken line of occupied houses, the distant lights that spoke of a shopping district farther ahead. It wasn't that it was big; it wasn't. It was just how peaceful it looked that had me sitting there, stunned.

I slowly moved down the road in awe. I wasn't used to seeing so many lit-up houses in one place.

I paused in front of a small house with blooming flowers lining its face. A large window faced the road and the curtains were parted, giving a good view of the people inside. There were three of them. They sat around a table eating dinner. They didn't talk, but they didn't seem afraid of the night either.

The next house wasn't much different. The window was smaller, but the scene had the same feel to it. A young couple sat on a couch. The soft glow of the television lit up their faces. As I watched, the girl rested her head on the guy's shoulder and he put an arm around her.

Something deep down rumbled at that. I'd never experienced a true social life, never even really considered it. My world had always revolved around killing and the night. My brother and family had been my world when I was a Pureblood. I'd known nothing else.

I looked away, angrier than I should have been. I never should have come here. Even though I had only passed two houses, seen a couple of families, I already knew I didn't belong.

And yet I kept going. I rode farther into town, looking from side to side. A car crossed an intersection ahead, but as far as I could tell, it was the only vehicle on the road aside from my own. It was strangely quiet, as if everyone had gone inside to relax at the same time.

Of course, that wasn't so odd. The night was a time when most Purebloods stayed inside.

But if all the people in their comfy houses were Purebloods, then where were the vamps and wolves?

My eyes settled on the glow ahead. I couldn't tell what it was like in the middle of the town from the outskirts, but I was sure it couldn't be as peaceful as it was out here. Nowhere was this quiet these days.

I made my way down the road, doing my best not to look into the windows of the houses I passed. Nearly all of them left their blinds parted, their curtains pulled back. I saw so many people simply enjoying life, it was disconcerting. People didn't do that anymore. When the night fell, the blinds came down and the lights went off.

A few more cars moved down the road ahead of me as I got deeper into Delai. The road into town was surprisingly long, the landscape dotted with houses bunched in small neighborhoods. It wasn't until I reached the heart of the town that I saw people outside.

The gas station came first. A few people stood outside their cars, pumping gas. They stared straight ahead, eyes blank like just the tedium of what they were doing was putting them to sleep.

A movie theater with subdued lighting appeared open for business. A small line waited outside for their tickets. The people didn't talk to each other. They just stood and waited, staring at the back of the person's head in front of them.

I knew it wasn't all that late, yet it *was* nighttime. The

place should have been shut down. This wasn't High Street. There were no streetwalkers here, selling their skin and blood and sex for a night of thrills.

So where the hell was I?

It was then I saw the diner. The sign out front proclaimed it to be DeeDee's. A few cars were in the parking lot and a couple of people stood next to them. They didn't seem to be doing anything.

I felt drawn to the place. I hadn't even realized how badly I needed this until I was there. I needed a night away from all the death, and why not here? It seemed safe enough.

I pulled into the parking lot, making sure to keep my weapons hidden. While I didn't think the people standing around were dangerous, I didn't want them getting the wrong idea about me. You didn't go walking into strange places with guns and swords waving about unless you were looking for trouble.

And tonight, trouble was the last thing I wanted.

I found a space in the corner of the lot and shut off the engine. A tingling sensation ran up my spine as I got off my Honda and headed for the door.

No one tried to stop me. No one tried to talk to me. A few watched my progress but didn't seem disconcerted by me.

I reached the front door to DeeDee's Diner. I hesitated a moment, took in the fresh night air, and then opened the door and stepped inside.

Only a few heads turned as I entered the diner. While I didn't get the feeling that I was unwelcome, I felt out of place anyway. No one smiled. They just watched me as I crossed the floor toward a table in the back corner.

DeeDee's looked bigger from the inside than it had on the outside. Booths lined the walls, each with its own window. There were at least a dozen, if not more, tables throughout the place, not counting the booths. A long counter was straight ahead, and another dozen stools gave customers a place to sit and sip their coffee.

Through an opening behind the counter, I could see cooks busily working on orders. A cashier stood behind the counter, and a pair of waitresses stood side by side, watching me. Another waitress was busy moving around between customers, refilling drinks.

Soft rock music from a few decades past played over the speakers hidden in the ceiling. In fact, the entire place had an old-style feel to it. It felt like I had been transported back in time, back when things were simpler, when people didn't have to constantly look over their shoulders to make sure the monsters weren't creeping up on them.

And I liked it. I took a seat, putting my back to the corner so I could look out over the entire diner. I could see the door from where I sat. I did it more out of habit than anything. I didn't feel threatened here, which was an all-new experience in itself.

One of the waitresses behind the counter walked my way. She wasn't smiling, but she didn't seem upset either. I wasn't used to that.

"What can I get ya?" the waitress asked as she came to a stop beside me. She sort of smiled at me, but it didn't look right on her face, like it was painted on.

There were menus on the table; I picked one up and flipped to the drinks. "A Coke," I said, glancing at the waitress's name tag: VALERIE.

"K." Valerie wandered back behind the counter to get my drink.

Everything on the menu sounded good. It was all deep-fried, and the smells coming from the kitchen had my stomach rumbling. Even though blood was the main source of nutrients for a vampire, regular food was just as important. I wouldn't die of starvation or thirst, but it would surely put me in a bad way if I didn't eat normal food every now and again.

Valerie returned a few minutes later with my Coke. She gave me another odd smile and readied her pencil over a pad of paper. "You ready to order?"

"Just a burger and fries," I said, setting the menu down. "Put whatever you think is best on them."

She jotted my order down and tucked the pad into her apron. "Let me know if I can get you anything else." She spun on her heel and went to fill my order.

I felt itchy sitting there waiting. I sipped my Coke, at a loss as to what to do. I didn't come to places like this to relax. Give me a beer at The Bloody Stake any day and I would be content.

Yet, sitting here felt somehow peaceful. I couldn't put my finger on it, but something about the place relaxed me, made me feel at home. Not even the blank faces on most of the people could unsettle me.

Which was somewhat worrying in itself.

A pair of men walked through the front door. Immediately, one of them turned my way and crossed the diner toward me. His companion followed behind.

I sat up, my hand going to the hilt of my sword.

"Hiya," the man said, sitting down across from me. "Name's Levi." He held out a hairy arm. I stared at the proffered hand, my face going hard.

The other man sat down in one of the free chairs. He didn't say anything, didn't even seem to notice me sitting there. He stared straight ahead, face slack.

"That's Ronnie," Levi said, withdrawing his hand. "He doesn't say much."

I glanced between the two men, trying to decide if they were a threat. Levi was a big man, as was the smile that seemed stuck to his face. At least he was smiling, which was more than I could say about the rest of the people here. Tufts of hair stuck up from Levi's shirt and his eyebrows were nearly crawling from his face. He was as hairy as they come.

Ronnie was his complete opposite. He was thin and might have been good looking if it wasn't for the scruffiness of his features. It looked as though he hadn't shaved in a few days. His clothes hung limp on him, almost like dead things. His shoulders were slumped, his eyes sagging.

"Welcome to Delai, our little slice of heaven," Levi said. "I wanted to make sure you felt welcome."

The two men didn't seem dangerous, so I moved my hand back to the table. A calmness flooded over me; it seemed to come straight from Levi's smile.

My plate of food arrived. Valerie set it down in front of me and gave Levi a quick glance before heading back to the counter. I didn't watch her go.

"Not the talkative type, eh?" Levi said. He leaned back. "That's okay. I just wanted to meet you and make sure everything is as you hoped."

"I'm fine," I said. I was having too many odd conflicting feelings and I didn't know why. One minute I was nervous, the next, as calm as if I was safely tucked away in my own bed. I didn't know if I should get up and leave or sit back to stay a while.

"Go ahead and eat," Levi said. "The food's great here. I'm sure you'll love it."

I frowned at him. He didn't know me, know my tastes. "We'll see."

"I know you will." He winked. "I know it's all kind of strange here," he said. "It's normal. Not everyone gets comfortable right away. It'll take time."

"I'm not staying."

Levi's smile slipped for an instant before returning. "I didn't think you were. I do hope you choose to come visit us again. You might like it here."

I shifted in my seat. Why was this guy bugging me? I should have told him to piss off the moment he sat down.

I picked up a fry and tasted it. Levi was right. It was pretty good.

"We don't abide by trouble here, mind you," Levi said. "I don't expect you are bringing any with you, but I just wanted to let you know. You have nothing to worry about here."

I took a bite of my hamburger and stared at him, giving him the coldest stare I could manage. He didn't seem fazed.

Levi leaned forward, crossing his arms on the table in front of him. He looked to either side and then spoke as if he was telling me a deep, dark secret. "Your sword is showing."

I glanced down and noticed my coat was hanging open. The sheath was too long to hide easily when sitting. I flipped my coat over the weapon and sat back. As good as the food was, I didn't want it anymore.

Levi smiled and sat back. "She'll fit right in, don't you think, Ronnie?"

Ronnie looked startled to be addressed. He looked up, eyes wide. He glanced at me, then at Levi, before he nodded and resumed staring at the top of the table.

"Well, I won't keep you," Levi said, rising. Ronnie stood almost immediately. "If you ever get some free time, come on back. I have a few things I'd love to show you. We could always use a new hand around here."

I didn't answer. I didn't know what to say.

Levi laughed. "Hope to see you around. Don't be a stranger." With that, both he and Ronnie headed for the door.

I watched them go, unsure what to make of them. There was definitely something odd about both of them, but I couldn't figure out what it was. I strangely felt too good to care.

Through the window, I could see Levi and Ronnie approach a pickup truck. Levi turned as if he could see me staring and waved before getting in. As he pulled away, my good feeling drained, leaving me feeling more paranoid than ever.

I took a few more bites of my food and then tossed some money on the table without waiting for the bill. I rose and headed for the door, wanting to be as far away from the place as I could as fast as I could. As comforting as Delai had been, it was really time I got home. This entire night out had been a bad idea.

No one paid me any mind as I left the diner. I half expected someone to chase after me to force me to pay at the counter, despite the money I had left on the table. Not even the people still standing around outside gave me much more than a cursory glance.

I took the time to check over my Honda, making sure no one messed with it while I was inside. Everything appeared as I had left it. I got on and started it up.

I pulled out of the parking lot, unsure what to think about the place. Part of me had enjoyed the quiet little diner, the town around it. Part of me knew that a place like that shouldn't exist, not with so many monsters prowling the night.

I sped down the road like I was running from something. The houses zipped by, their occupants still involved in their normal lives, enjoying time with each other.

A tinge of regret fluttered through me as I put Delai behind me. I knew I didn't belong there, yet I wanted to. I really did.

I turned toward home, putting distance between me and the quiet little town. My life might be a mess, but it was all I had. And right then, I just wanted to be home.

6

By the time I got home, Ethan was well at work in his lab and he didn't come up until after I had retired for the day. I wasn't sure if he was avoiding me or not. It sure felt like it.

Maybe it was my own guilt at how I treated him that made me think that way. I shouldn't have yelled at him. He was only doing what he thought was right. So what if his idea of right involved summoning and conversing with a demon? I've done worse things in my life.

I spent the day pretty much brooding. I didn't know what to think about Delai and its inhabitants, so I didn't worry about them at all. I never had to go back. They weren't my problem.

What I really needed was a quiet night at home. Ethan was what was important to me. I couldn't have him mad at me, even for a little bit.

I was out of my room and down the stairs as soon as the sun went down. Ethan was up only a few minutes later, taking a shower. I took the opportunity to do something for him I had never done before.

I tried to cook.

All four eggs burst into the pan when I tried to break

them. I flipped them a few times, hoping I didn't get too much of the shell in the mess. I put on his coffee while the eggs were cooking and considered finding some bacon, but decided against it. I was butchering breakfast enough as it was without making it worse.

By the time Ethan came downstairs, I had everything on the table. He paused on the bottom step and stared. "What's going on?" he asked, sounding as if I was offering him a last meal before execution.

"I thought you might be hungry," I said.

"Uh." Ethan came the rest of the way down the stairs, looking from me to the eggs and back again. "Thanks?"

I smiled and pulled out a chair for him. He took a seat, giving me a long, confused look before examining his food. "What is it?"

I smacked him gently on the back of the head and went to sit across from him. A plate just like his sat across from me, though he was the only one with a cup of coffee.

"No, seriously," he said, looking down at the yellow and white mess on his plate. "What is it?"

I frowned. "Did I do something wrong?" I had to admit, the eggs didn't quite look right, but I'd never cooked before. That sort of stuff was always done for me by people who knew what in the hell they were doing.

A smile lit the corners of his mouth, making my own lips curl. It was good to see him smile. Maybe I had jumped the gun when I thought my bad mood the night before had affected our relationship.

"It looks like you burnt half of them and undercooked the other half." He prodded the eggs with his fork and peered closer. "What is that green in there?"

I looked at my eggs and frowned. "There's nothing green."

He laughed and picked up his coffee mug. He took a sip and spit it right back out, making a face. "Ugh."

"What now?"

"How did you manage to screw up coffee?" He brushed at his tongue. There were little black specs on it.

I sighed. "I don't ever do this, you know. You're the one who always makes your own coffee."

"And now I know why." He pushed the mug away. "Did you use a filter?"

"Where are they?"

He laughed again. The sound filled the whole house, making me smile despite my embarrassment. This was what I got for trying to do something that wasn't in my nature. Give me a gun and a sword and I could do no wrong. Stick me in a kitchen and I'm likely to kill someone by accident.

"I'll make a new pot," Ethan said, rising. "And thanks for the eggs, but I had a late-night sandwich. I'm not hungry." He grimaced as he went to the kitchen.

I sat back in my chair and watched him make his coffee. It was nice just to do something normal, even if I had screwed it up. We didn't have those moments where we just sat without worrying about whom I did or didn't kill.

I looked down at my plate. Could the eggs really be that bad? He hadn't even tasted them.

I picked up my fork and scooped up a large helping. They looked pretty bad, but I'd seen worse. I held my breath as I shoveled them into my mouth. Ethan came back into the room just as I finished wiping my tongue off with a napkin.

He sat down across from me, crossing his arms over the big Superman "S" on his shirt. He rubbed at his arms like he was cold. "So what's this all about?" he asked. "You aren't exactly Little Miss Homemaker. It's kind of frightening."

"I was just trying to be nice," I said. "And I wanted to let you know I was sorry."

"For what?"

"For the other night. I shouldn't have snapped at you. It was a bad night and I took it out on you."

"I understand."

"Then why were you avoiding me?" The question slipped out without me really meaning to say it.

He cocked his head to the side and raised his eyebrows. "What gave you that idea?"

I felt stupid having asked the question, but there was nothing I could do but plow on. "I don't know," I said. "I didn't see you last night and just assumed you were avoiding me. I wasn't exactly being pleasant."

"It was a busy night," he said. "Since you left so early, I figured you had something important to do, so I didn't bother coming up to check for you. I got some other things done." He smiled nervously. I wondered what it was he worked on. Maybe I didn't want to know.

I tried to think of something to say to change the subject, but my brain was stuck. I was such a fool thinking he had been avoiding me. I'd put him through worse before. What made me think this time would be any different?

Ethan rose and got another cup of coffee, this one of his making. He took a sip and let out a contented sigh as he sat back down. "So, did you get into anything exciting last night?" he said. "Any super-secret killings that will require my weapon-repairing expertise?"

I shook my head. "I just needed some time alone. I didn't even draw my weapons."

"Wow," he said, grinning. "I'm impressed."

I gave him a dirty look. "I don't get into fights every night."

"Mmhmm."

"I don't."

Ethan's grin widened. He took another sip of his coffee and held the cup out to me. "You want a cup? I'll show you what real coffee is supposed to taste like."

"No thanks."

We sat in silence for a few minutes. Ethan stared out the glass back door, sipping his coffee. I sat there just looking at him, wondering what I was doing wrong.

I couldn't help it. My black mood was slowly returning even though I had done everything I could to push it away. Things were fine. My life was just the same as it always had been. I would eventually get up and leave, deal with some vampires or werewolves, kick some ass, then come home to wash it all away.

It might not be much of a life for most people, but it kept me going. I could easily have given in to my darker nature and tried to form a vampire House of my own. I could have joined with others, could have killed Pure-bloods for the sake of killing.

But I hadn't. I was better than that.

So why was I so fucking depressed?

Ethan glanced my way and must have seen the misery on my face. "What's wrong?" he asked, turning back to face me.

"Nothing." I pushed away from the table and stood. I didn't want him worrying about my mental state on top of everything else. "I was just thinking."

He studied me a moment. I don't think he quite believed me. "So, you going out tonight?"

I looked down at myself as if to say, "What do you think?" I was wearing a pair of shorts and a tank top, not exactly fighting gear.

"Right," he said, reddening a little. "I think I might take the night off too." He glanced toward the stairs and shivered. "It'd be nice just to get away from things a bit."

I agreed wholeheartedly. I really didn't want to think about my last few days. I'd have to deal with my problems sooner or later. It just didn't have to be tonight. There wasn't much I could do anyway. I didn't have any leads.

"Then what do you want to do?" he asked, looking

around the room. "It's not like we ever do much around here."

"Television," I said immediately. "Let's sit on the couch and watch the television."

He gave me a strange look, but agreed.

We hadn't watched the TV together for years. I hadn't even turned the thing on for so long, I wasn't even sure how. I knew Ethan watched a few shows here and there, mostly during the day when he couldn't sleep. We were always too busy during the night to watch anything then.

Ethan grabbed the remote from an end table and plopped down on the couch. He started flipping through the channels, taking small sips of his coffee every few moments. He looked content, like this was something he had wanted to do for a really long time.

I sat down on the other end of the couch, legs pulled up under me, and just watched. I divided my attention between Ethan and the television, not really seeing either.

Something was bothering me. It took me a good long while to figure out what it was. When I did, my face reddened and I felt like a fool. Unfortunately for me, Ethan chose that exact moment to glance my way.

"What's up?" he asked, brow furrowed.

"Nothing." I could feel my face heating up even further.

That only egged him on. His grin returned and he sat up straighter. "You thought of something," he said. "And it embarrassed you. I *have* to know what you just thought about."

I glared at him, which caused him to smile wider. I turned toward the television and stared at it like I could burn a hole straight through it. Ethan watched me a moment longer, chuckled wryly to himself, and resumed his channel surfing.

I hadn't realized what I had been doing until then. The getting up to make him breakfast, the sitting down and watching TV together. I wasn't just trying to make things up to him. There was far more to it than that.

Delai. The goddamn town and its happy little citizens going about their happy little lives had gotten into my head. Did I really think I could have that sort of life? I wasn't about to lean over and cuddle with Ethan. I mean, no way.

Ethan glanced at me and smiled again. And just like that, all my worries vanished. Why did I have to overanalyze everything? Couldn't I just sit back and relax with my one true friend? We didn't have to do anything more. We would both be happy just spending a nice quiet evening together without any attachments, any blood.

I started to tell him how much I was enjoying myself when there was a knock at the door. All my good feelings were wiped away just like that.

Ethan immediately turned off the television and rose. I was already standing and halfway to the door by the time he turned around. The door was closed and locked, so whoever was out there wouldn't be able just to walk in on us. The curtains over the windows were closed and when I glanced toward them, I couldn't make out our visitor.

"Downstairs," I said, veering away from the door and heading for the stairs. My weapons were still in my room where I had left them, but I didn't want to leave Ethan's side to get them. "Get to your lab."

He moved without hesitation. He dropped the remote on the couch and headed for the stairs in a crouch, his coffee mug clutched to his chest like it was the only safe thing he knew.

We hurried down the stairs into the sitting room. Ethan continued on into the basement while I checked the windows facing the front of the house. The knocking came again as I glanced out the window, but try as I might, I couldn't catch a glimpse of who was out there. Since it was night, there was no shadow to give them away.

I turned away from the window and headed downstairs. Ethan was standing in front of his lab door, waiting.

"Go into the lab and don't come out," I said, grabbing a gun and slamming home the cartridge. "I'll call you on the intercom when it's safe."

The knock came again, this time more insistent. While I was checking to make sure I was ready, Ethan unlocked the door and slipped inside his lab. He closed the door behind him. I caught a glimpse of his face as it closed and it was clear he didn't like being locked away while I faced all the danger.

Tough. We never had visitors, and I wasn't about to risk his life just because he didn't like being left out. I wasn't so sure why I thought whoever was out there wanted to hurt us, but I wasn't about to risk it. A careless mistake could get us both killed.

I took the stairs by threes and went back to the foyer. There were two vertical frosted windows by the door. I could see a vague shape moving outside but couldn't tell whether it was male or female, large or small.

The knock came again and I moved to the door, keeping myself out of the line of sight to the windows. I pressed my ear against the wood and listened, hoping to catch my guest mumbling something so I could identify who it was.

But there was nothing. Anyone could be out there. It could simply be a pizza guy who managed to get himself lost to one of Adrian's goons, sporting a submachine gun full of silver bullets.

There was nothing to do but check. I didn't want my guest to go away. I had to know who it was so I could stop them from ever coming again.

My hand moved toward the lock. I turned it slowly, hoping they wouldn't hear the click on the other side. For the first time since moving in, I wished the door had a peephole. We'd never needed it before. I guess it was time I had Ethan install one.

I counted slowly to three and then yanked the door open, bringing my gun up to around head level as I did.

Jonathan Alucard, Luna Cult Denmaster, stood on the stoop, a surprised look on his face. His eyes widened for a fraction of a second before he raised his hands in surrender.

"Sorry to drop in on you like this," he said, his glamour-perfect face breaking into a coy smile. "I had no other way to contact you and we really need to talk."

I stared at him, my gun wavering for a second before my aim firmed. No one came to my house and lived. It was a rule, damn it.

Jonathan's eyes traveled from the barrel of my gun, to my face, and then to the house behind me. He didn't seem all that concerned I was ready to blow his brains out. "May I come in?"

My muscles tensed and I really considered doing it. He was a werewolf. Not only that, but a sorcerer as well. I shouldn't trust someone who might be able to do bad things to me with a flick of his wrist.

But instead of blowing him into next week, I dropped my arm, cursing myself as I did. I stepped aside and let him pass.

"Thank you," he said, nodding slightly as he stepped past me and into the house. He looked around for a moment before heading to the dining room.

"Fuck," I said. I glanced out into the driveway to make sure no one else was lurking out there before closing the door and following him to the dining room table.

So much for the rules.

Damn it.

7

"I know you don't like visitors," Jonathan said. He looked uncomfortable sitting at the table. He kept lacing and unlacing his fingers as if he wasn't quite sure what to do with his hands.

"No shit." I placed the gun on the table, the barrel aimed right at him. I kept my hand on it to let him know how much I didn't like having people show up unannounced on my doorstep.

"I wouldn't have come if it wasn't important."

"Okay," I said. "Then speak."

He sighed and ran his fingers through the hair on the left side of his head. He looked much better than he did the last time I had seen him. It had been at The Bloody Stake, and he'd still been suffering the results of our semi-successful joint run against House Tremaine. The limp was gone and all his wounds appeared to be healed, though that could be deceiving.

Jonathan was a sorcerer, which allowed him to hide what he wanted to hide. He claimed he could only cast glamours, but I refused to believe it. Any sorcerer who wanted to live would claim they could do very little. Anyone stronger was sought out and killed.

Jonathan used his glamours to keep the Luna Cult Den hidden. He was able to hide the Den, making the old library on the Ohio State campus look run-down and abandoned from the outside. On the inside, it was anything but.

He'd used his glamour on me once as well, making me appear as a Luna Cult member so we could infiltrate House Tremaine together. It had worked, to a point. I hadn't been able to keep myself from killing a few wolves along the way, which, in turn, gave us away when Adrian Davis sniffed me out.

Before I met him, Jonathan had kept his face hidden with a dark hood aided by a glamour that made his face all shadows and darkness. Only recently had he started using his magic to hide the damage done to his face, reconstructing it so that anyone looking at him wouldn't cringe.

The slightest hint of guilt crept into me. I'd been the one who'd ruined his face. He was once a member of House Valentino, a House I had taken down after they had turned me into a vampire. My blade had cut a large chunk of his skull off, leaving him mutilated and near death. He survived and had a change of heart, choosing to turn against his vampire masters and fight for the liberation of the werewolf.

Yeah, I wasn't so sure why I was siding with him either.

Jonathan looked up at me and a sadness came into his eyes. "I was wondering if I would ever see you again," he said. "I thought we had gotten past our differences and could at least be friends."

I frowned. "Is that what this is about?"

"No," he admitted. "But I needed to get it out. I dislike the thought of you risking your life alone when you could have my help."

"I manage."

He rubbed at his forehead like a headache was coming on. "Things would be much easier if we could learn to work together. This animosity between us need not exist.

Maybe things wouldn't have gotten so far gone if you had come to me."

I frowned even harder. "What's happened?"

He licked his lips and brushed off his jacket, though there was nothing on it. He looked downright nervous, and it was making my trigger finger itch.

I moved my hand away from the gun just in case. I would probably feel bad if I killed him because he sneezed at the wrong moment.

He took a deep breath and leveled a stare at me. "Are you the one who has been killing all those vampires and werewolves?"

My blood ran cold. Could he really be talking about House Telia and the rogues Mikael had told me about? Or was this something else? I'd had a few kill runs since I had last seen Jonathan, so it could have been anything.

"Which ones?" I asked. I managed to keep the unease out of my voice.

He stared at me as if he was trying to discern the truth from my expression. I kept my face carefully blank as not to give anything away, though I wasn't sure why. It wasn't like I'd killed anyone he would care about. The vamps I had taken down were of Fledgling Houses with barely any wolves amongst them.

Jonathan seemed to reach a decision and eased back in his chair. "I don't think you're the one doing it," he said. "Even though the kills bear your mark, they aren't your style."

"House Telia?" I ventured, wanting to make sure we were on the same page before saying something I would regret.

"Among others," he said. "No one in the Luna Cult has been harmed, but I fear it is only a matter of time until something does happen. There is a lot of talk on the streets that Lady Death has gone mad and is slaughtering everyone as quickly and as messily as she can."

"I didn't do it," I said. "And I'm not crazy." I considered how much to tell him. I still wasn't positive he didn't blame me. "Countess Telia was dead before I got there. I saw the mess. It wasn't me."

He nodded as if he already knew. "While there are things that hint at you being involved in the kills, there is so much else that eliminates you as a suspect. To someone who knows you, it's clear you could have nothing to do with them. You of all people wouldn't use werewolves for your runs." He smiled at that.

"So if you didn't think I was the one doing it, then why are you here?"

"I need you again," he said. "We cannot let this continue. I don't like the idea of someone else running around killing weres and vamps uncontrolled. People are turning up dead in alleys at an alarming rate."

"How bad is it?" I shifted uncomfortably in my seat. I knew I would have to face this eventually, but to have the Luna Cult involved too . . . It just made things worse.

"Like I said, the Cult hasn't lost anyone, but others have. There have been weres we were looking to recruit who have turned up dead. All of them were beheaded, though it doesn't appear to be your work. There were claw marks on the bodies, and it looks as though they had been fed upon."

I nodded as he spoke. It sounded exactly like what I'd seen.

"And the more this happens, the more the vampire Houses will become interested in what is going on." Jonathan frowned down at his hands. "How long before they really start looking for Lady Death in the hopes of putting a stop to her before she comes after them?"

"They've searched for me before."

"But it's different this time. Wolves from Major Houses have died. You usually can only handle smaller Houses."

I bristled a bit at that. I knew I couldn't handle much

beyond a Fledgling House. I just didn't like being reminded of it. "What's your point?"

"Many of the larger Houses used to use you as a buffer. You take down the weaker, most dangerous of the small Houses, keeping them from rising through the ranks. The Major Houses like having you around so they can focus on keeping the stronger Houses in line."

"I seriously doubt that."

Jonathan shrugged. "Either way, weres and vampires are dying much faster than they had before. Whoever is doing this is working fast, and I have a feeling they aren't working alone."

I thought back to all the claw marks, the amount of carnage I had seen. Why would someone working alone claw someone to death if they had a sword?

"I agree," I said.

"With weres belonging to Major Houses dying, things are becoming more and more dangerous for you."

My frown returned. "And why should you care?"

Jonathan blinked at me as if I should already know. "We work well together whether you want to admit it or not. If someone manages to kill you, who would I go to when something like this arises?" He smirked.

I wanted to be angry at that, but couldn't. I didn't want the Luna Cult showing up at my doorstep every time they had a problem. I had problems enough of my own without taking on theirs.

"Why is it that every time I hear from you, you insist on telling me how much I'm in danger?" There was a little more heat in my words than I originally intended.

Jonathan's smirk turned into a warm, friendly smile. "Because I think you need reminding sometimes. You are so sure of yourself, so confident in your abilities, I sometimes think you forget to be afraid."

"You don't know me."

"I know you well enough to know that if something

threatens you, you will do something about it." He sat forward. "I only ask that you consider working with the Cult once more when you do. This affects us all."

Footsteps coming from the stairs jerked my head to the side. Ethan peered around the corner, eyes wide. He was holding one of my swords awkwardly out in front of him. If someone had been there, they could have easily disarmed him. He might fix my weapons, but he sure as hell didn't know how to use them.

"I said stay in the lab." I rose from where I was sitting, feeling strangely guilty. I picked up my gun and held it pointed to the ground.

"I didn't hear shooting, so I figured it was safe," he said shakily.

I eyed the sword and he gave me an abashed grin. There was no way he could have heard anything in his lab. The damn place was so soundproof a bomb could have gone off up here and he wouldn't have known.

"That doesn't mean you should have come up to investigate," I said.

Jonathan rose from his seat and was watching the exchange. Ethan's eyes traveled to our guest, but he quickly looked away. I couldn't read the look on his face.

"Sorry," he said. "I'll be downstairs."

With the way he said it, I felt horrible. It was clear I'd hurt his feelings. Somehow, I think he felt left out, what with me sitting around chatting with Jonathan while Ethan hid away in his lab, more than likely terrified I was dying upstairs.

Before I could say anything, he vanished back down the stairs. He moved so fast, I was afraid he might trip and skewer himself on the tip of the sword.

"I remember him," Jonathan said once Ethan was out of sight. "He was important to Count Valentino."

I turned to face him. "He's important to me."

"I understand." Jonathan looked at his feet like he was

ashamed. "I was never told why the boy was so important. Valentino had plans for him, but I was never privy to that sort of information."

It was then I realized how volatile the situation could have been. What if Ethan had recognized Jonathan? Was there an unspoken grudge? Jonathan had been there when Ethan had been imprisoned in Valentino's mansion. Just because Jonathan claimed to have had a change of heart didn't mean everyone would believe him.

Right then, I just wanted him out of my house.

"Is that all you came for?" I said. "I've been warned, but I think I can handle it on my own."

"I'm sure you can," Jonathan said. "But since this affects the both of us, I think it best we work together. I wouldn't want one of my wolves to get killed because they were in the wrong place at the wrong time."

"What do you want from me?" I held my back stiff. I had no intention of working with the Luna Cult ever again. The last time nearly got me killed. Not to mention the weirdness of it all, and I wasn't just talking about working with werewolves.

There was something about Jonathan that gave me a strange, queasy feeling deep in my gut. I hated that feeling, just as I hated the fact that I couldn't bring myself to hate him. No matter how rude or obnoxious I got, he was always calm and friendly to me. It irked me to no end.

"Come with me back to the Den," he said. "I drove myself here and left the car a few miles down the road. It was quite the walk, but I figured you wouldn't want me to drive all the way to your front door. I know how you value your privacy."

"And yet you came anyway."

He looked a little guilty at that. "Please," he said. "Just come to the Den with me."

"I don't see why I need to go to the Den. We've had a perfectly nice chat here."

He looked worried for a moment. "There are things we cannot discuss here." He glanced toward the glass back door as if looking for something. I didn't buy it. He was hiding something.

"Like?"

He looked away. "I cannot say."

A flash of anger shot through me. "So you expect me to drop everything and follow you to the Den without you telling me what this is all about?"

"I already did. We must take care of whoever is doing the killings. We can't let it go on."

"You know what I mean."

He lowered his head. "I cannot divulge that information at this time." He looked frightened. "If I were to tell you why I need you at the Den, you probably wouldn't come."

"And that's supposed to make me want to go?"

A small smile quirked the edges of his mouth. "I have hope your curiosity will urge you to do the right thing."

I ground my teeth in frustration. He was right. I was curious. Not only that, but he was right about the killings affecting the both of us. I couldn't stand by and let them continue unabated. Even though the killer was targeting vampires and werewolves, Purebloods were dying too. I couldn't stand for that.

"Fine," I said, nearly growling the word. "Give me a few minutes to get ready. I'm not going out like this."

Jonathan smiled. "You look nice, though it is strange to see you in something other than leather."

I really did growl that time as I spun for the stairs. "Stay here," I said. "Don't move or I'll have to reconsider my decision not to shoot you."

Jonathan bowed his head in acknowledgment and took a seat at the table. I glared at him for good measure and then stormed up the stairs.

What was I doing jumping in with the Luna Cult again? I had sworn to myself the last time would be the only time.

Now here I was, repeating past mistakes. What the fuck was wrong with me?

I tore off my clothes, leaving them crumpled on the floor. I quickly dressed in my leathers, donning the persona of Lady Death. There were werewolves involved in this. I wanted to be ready for a fight.

I grabbed my belt and shoulder holster and threw them on. The weapons from last night would be fine since I hadn't used them. I was as ready as I would ever be.

"One sec," I said, coming down the stairs. Jonathan had started to rise but sat down before he had fully straightened.

I went to the basement and pressed the intercom by the laboratory door. "Ethan?"

There was a moment of silence before he answered. "Yeah?"

"I'm leaving. I'll be back later." I started to walk away but stopped and pressed the button again. "Be careful and don't let anyone in until I'm home."

"K," came the faint response.

I went back up the stairs and turned toward the front door, opening it. "Let's go," I said without glancing at Jonathan. I stepped out into the night and started walking without waiting for him. I was ready to get this over with.

Somehow, I knew nothing good could come of working with the Luna Cult again. And yet I was doing it anyway.

Call me a glutton for punishment. I just couldn't help myself.

I sighed and let Jonathan take the lead. Nothing good might come of it, but at least I would be doing something other than sitting around.

I just hoped my decision to work with werewolves yet again wouldn't get me killed.

8

Jonathan kept silent as he led the way to his car. He kept a brisk pace, taking us through the woods surrounding my house instead of going down the driveway and following the road. I wasn't sure if he was doing it for my benefit or if he was just as paranoid as I was. Neither of us wanted to be spotted if at all possible.

I paused at the passenger door to his car. It was nice and all, but it had been a long time since I had ridden in a car with anyone. I preferred the open air of my Honda to being cooped up in someone else's vehicle.

And I was about to get into the thing with a werewolf. Even if he wasn't your normal wolf, Jonathan was still a monster. If he were to shift inside the car, I doubted I could fend him off in the confined space.

I opened the passenger door and got in anyway. Jonathan wouldn't hurt me. Somehow I knew that. He needed my help, sure, but I think it went much deeper than that.

Neither of us spoke during the first few minutes. We rode side by side, me feeling all kinds of uncomfortable. I glanced at him a few times, and it was clear he was warring with something himself. His face changed expressions constantly, as if he was having an internal argument and was somehow losing both sides.

Eventually, he sighed and seemed to relax. "You've been quiet as of late," he said. He never took his eyes off the road.

"I don't have anything to say."

"I meant over the last few months. You haven't come to the Den, haven't sent me word as to how things were going."

"You haven't done anything that required my sort of attention."

I meant it as a warning, but Jonathan smiled. "The invitation still stands. You are one of us as long as you don't come in with foul intent. No one will harm you while I am Denmaster."

I squirmed in my seat. I still couldn't get comfortable with the idea the Luna Cult accepted me as one of their own. Sure, there were a few who still didn't like me, but that didn't make it any easier. I probably would have liked it better if Jonathan was as uncomfortable sitting next to me as I was him.

The faint smile never left his lips as we continued on in silence. He looked so relaxed it made me want to smack him. My back was stiff, my hands hovered near my weapons. There was no way I was going to relax, not with where we were going.

Eventually, we entered the Ohio State campus. He stuck to the run-down portion of the old college. The Luna Cult controlled this area, though no one knew it. They kept a pretty low profile, hiding their Den in the mass of run-down, empty buildings. Lights from the occupied portion of the campus could still be seen from where we were, though they were far enough away that no one would see our approach.

He pulled into a small underground garage a few minutes later. It looked as though it was about to cave in from the outside. Part of one wall just inside had crumbled away, as if someone had smashed it a few times with a really large hammer. Pillars holding up the roof over our head were pockmarked and looked ready to collapse.

Once we were down a few levels, however, the place started to look a bit more respectable. Faint lights that couldn't be seen from the outside lit the way. I caught a glimpse of motion on one of the pillars and for the first time noticed the cameras that followed us as we rode down the ramp.

I knew the Luna Cult took their privacy seriously, but this seemed a bit much. I normally parked off in the middle of nowhere, hiding my motorcycle in an alley and walking the rest of the way to the Den. It appeared the Cult had a better method.

"We'll have to walk the rest of the way," Jonathan said as we got out of his car. "It isn't far."

I followed him out of the garage and through the campus. I couldn't help but gaze over at the lights where the Purebloods were staying. To think the Luna Cult was so close to where young men and women were living was unsettling. Sure, I had known it before, but to actually see it was something else.

"We don't hunt them," Jonathan said, glancing my way. He'd probably read some of my thoughts on my face.

"I find that hard to believe. How many wolves are in the Cult now?"

He smiled. "A few. The Columbus Cult currently is the only Cult with werewolves in their ranks as far as I am aware. We are special, and because of our removal of House Tremaine we have gained something of a reputation."

"Which draws others to you."

Jonathan shrugged noncommittally. "It is what it is."

I wasn't so sure how much I liked the idea of more werewolves within the Luna Cult. One or two was bad enough. If too many got together, how long before they became a problem?

"We make sure our newest were members follow our rules," he said. "We don't let them hunt like they would if they were rogues or under vampire influence. Those who have tasted blood, who have killed for pleasure and sport, are the hardest to break of the habit, but we do our best. We make sure their food is provided for without needless death."

I eyed him. He seemed genuine, but I found it hard to believe he could keep a group of werewolves from hunting if they wanted to. There were so many young people nearby, easy victims who might be too drunk or too stoned to fight back.

But in the end, I believed him. I hadn't heard about any excessive deaths at the campus. Sure, there were going to be a few. It was a way of life these days. Vampires and werewolves needed blood, and college campuses were usually easy targets, especially when a vampire House needed new recruits.

We reached the green leading up to the old library that served as the Luna Cult Den. Jonathan's glamour hid the true appearance of the building. It looked just as abandoned as every other structure on this end of the campus. Trash littered the green, and the Den itself looked dark and imposing.

He opened the door for me and the darkness seemed to ooze outward. I stepped through, shielding my eyes to the bright glare I knew was to come.

Light washed over me as I broke through the glamour. No one would be able to see it from the outside. Anyone who managed to approach the Den without getting hauled off by the Cult's guards wouldn't even know it was there unless they opened the door and stepped inside.

It felt strange to walk through the door again. It brought back all the memories of a time I sorely wanted to forget, of a time I nearly lost my life. I half expected Pablo, one of the more aggressive Pureblood Cultists, to be standing there, waiting to greet me with hostility, but when my vision cleared, the big Mexican was nowhere to be seen.

Instead, a small huddle of Cultists bowed their heads as my gaze fell on them. Jonathan came in behind me, smiling faintly as if he knew this was coming. A scrawny kid, whose tattoo of a crescent moon scored into his forehead looked worn and faded, stepped forward.

"Welcome," he said, bowing again. "We are honored by your presence."

I frowned and looked back at Jonathan. "What's going on?"

"They wanted to repay you for what you have done. They have waited a long time for this moment."

I looked back at the group and shook my head. "I don't need your thanks. I did it for me."

The kid faltered. He blinked at me like he couldn't quite understand what I was saying. "You helped us in our time of need," he said. "It is our honor to serve you."

I ground my teeth. While what I had done might have kept the Cult from being absorbed by House Tremaine, it had also resulted in the death of the original Denmaster, as well as quite a few Pureblood Cultists. I didn't deserve their thanks.

I wasn't sure what to say. I sure as hell didn't want the Luna Cult to serve me like they did their wolves. They could worship their werewolves if they wanted. I just wanted them to leave me out of it.

When I didn't say anything, the Cultist visibly slumped and returned to his companions. I felt bad, but I didn't want their thanks. It was a bitchy thing to do, I know. He would get over it.

"This way," Jonathan said, disapproval clear in his voice.

He led me up the stairs, marching as if he wanted

nothing to do with me now. I glanced back at the Pure-blood Cultists, feeling guiltier by the moment. They were watching me with sad, confused eyes. I had to look away, shame flooding me. Did I really need to treat them that way? They only wanted to be nice.

We reached the top of the stairs and Jonathan turned toward the gilded doors carved with werewolves in various stages of shifting. The small glass window above the scene was stained to look like the full moon. Two boys stood on either side of the door as if guarding it, which was new. There were no other Cultists on this floor.

One of the boys gasped as soon as he saw me and staggered along the wall as if he could melt through it. It took me a moment, but I recognized the kid. I never thought I would see him again.

"Jeremy." Jonathan's tone was hard. I wasn't sure if it was because of the kid's reaction or my treatment of his Cultists.

Jeremy straightened but didn't return to his place in front of the door. "It's her," he said, pointing at me. "She's the one."

Jonathan sighed. "I figured as much," he said. "Return to your post. She won't harm you here."

Jeremy took a faltering step back toward the door. His eyes never left mine as he slunk back into place. His companion snickered but didn't make a move.

Jonathan glanced at me. "We found him dying in the streets. We have you to thank for bringing him into our ranks, it appears."

I frowned. I remembered the kid. Jeremy Lincoln had followed me out of The Bloody Stake one night, intent on having me for dinner. In a misguided show of compassion, I let him go with a warning not to hunt within the city ever again. I thought he would flee town, find a new place to resume his hunt, yet there he stood, trembling in front of me like he expected me to kill him right then and there.

"He refused to eat for the longest time," Jonathan said. "He said a vampire threatened to kill him if he hunted. He wanted to live a good life, avoid killing or feeding at all."

"I didn't hunt anyone," Jeremy said, frantic. "I swear. I fought the hunger, but it nearly killed me. They forced me to eat." He lowered his eyes.

"We had a hard time getting him to eat anything, but after a while, the hunger was too much for him to bear."

I smiled at Jeremy and he flinched. "I'm glad I could help."

Jonathan's mood darkened for an instant, but he recovered quickly. "It nearly killed him," he said. "You shouldn't have done that. Not even you can turn away from what you are, yet you expected him to keep from feeding his beast."

I shrugged. "I could have killed him and saved him the suffering instead. Maybe I should have."

I didn't even move, yet Jeremy jerked back like I had leaped at him. His companion snickered again, drawing my eye. He paled and went silent. He was taller than Jeremy, but scrawnier. They looked to be about the same age. I wondered if they had known each other prior to the change. Neither had a Luna Cult tattoo, which indicated they were both werewolves.

"Enough of this," Jonathan said. "Make sure no one disturbs us. Paul, make sure the Cultists downstairs leave. I don't want any accidents. Return here once they are gone."

The kid beside Jeremy nodded and hurried away. I could hear him yelling at everyone to get out as he descended the stairs.

Jonathan's eyes turned toward the cowering Jeremy. "If you hear fighting inside, do not come in. Take Paul and leave. He won't want to go, but make him. I will not be responsible for your deaths should it come to a fight."

"What are you getting me into?" I asked, not liking what I was hearing at all.

"You will see why I take such precautions."

"How about you tell me now?" I took an aggressive stance, my hands going to my weapons. "I don't like surprises."

Jonathan glanced toward the door, nervous. "Please," he said. "Do not do anything to jeopardize our arrangement until you hear us out. It's important that we all work together."

"Who's on the other side of the door?"

Jonathan opened his mouth. I wasn't sure if he was going to answer the question or talk around it some more. I didn't give him a chance.

"Never mind," I said. I went straight for the door. "I'll find out for myself."

Jeremy scrambled out of the way. He didn't make a very good guard dog. I yanked open the doors and strode inside, my hands at the ready.

As soon as I entered the room and saw who was waiting for me, I cursed. "You," I said, drawing my sword without even thinking about it.

Across the room, staring at me with a face as blank as an empty page, stood Adrian Davis, Luna Cult defector.

9

"What the fuck is he doing here?" I asked, trying not to let my discomfort show. Adrian would enjoy it too much. My sword was held in my left hand and I could draw my gun with my right at a moment's notice. It was hard not to just shoot him where he stood.

"Calm down," Jonathan said, coming into the room and closing the door behind him. "We have a common problem and need to discuss this civilly."

"You killed him," Adrian said. His voice was controlled, almost casual, yet I could see the heat in his eyes. He stood across the room beside the couch. If he had been closer, I might have stabbed him simply for the pleasure of ending his miserable life.

"Your goon?" I said, putting as much disdain into the words as I could manage. "He was following me."

"He wasn't going to hurt you."

"He should have thought of that before getting too close. No one follows me and lives."

Adrian's eyelid twitched and he took a step toward me. "Eli was following my orders. He was not to engage you. He wouldn't have done so unless you forced his hand."

I shrugged. "Sucks to be him I guess."

His upper lip lifted into a sneer. "You owe me for his life."

I laughed. "I don't owe you shit, asshole. He shouldn't have been sniffing around where he didn't belong."

"Please," Jonathan said, stepping between us. "I didn't bring her here so you two could fight. There is much we need to discuss, and this verbal sparring will get us nowhere."

I ignored him. Adrian had one of his goons follow me. I didn't care why. If I hadn't noticed his wolf, he might have followed me all the way back home. I couldn't let that go.

"He deserved what he got," I said. The fingers to my free hand twitched. I so wanted to draw my gun. Only Jonathan's frantic face kept me from doing it.

Adrian took a deep breath, shuddering with it. He seemed about as willing to sit down and talk as I was. "And the others?" he said. "Why did you kill them? No one was to harm you. They had their orders."

Others? "Anyone I kill deserves it," I said. "If you send people to follow me, expect them to turn up dead. Their deaths are on your hands, not mine."

Adrian took another aggressive step forward. Even though he might appear calm from a casual glance, it was clear he was raging inside. This was the most excitement I had seen out of him since the night he had grabbed the silver bars to my cell in Tremaine's mansion.

"She didn't do it," Jonathan said.

"I don't need your help," I said.

"Can we calm down and talk about this?"

Adrian bared his teeth. They were sharp and pointed, hinting at his age. Only older wolves or ones who spent far too much time furry had teeth like that.

"Perhaps all the talking is done," Adrian replied.

I drew my gun and trained it right between his eyes. He didn't even flinch.

Jonathan reached toward my gun hand and I shifted my aim so he ended up face-to-face with the barrel of my gun.

"I wouldn't do that if I were you," I warned.

He took a step back and my aim returned to Adrian.

"I see this was not a good idea," Jonathan said.

"You think?"

Adrian stood stock-still, his eyes blazing. "She threatens me even here," he said. "She kills my wolves for no reason and then acts as though it is my fault she has lost control."

"It wasn't her," Jonathan said, slowly this time, as if talking to a dim-witted child. I wasn't so sure he wasn't. "Someone else is doing it."

"What the fuck are we talking about here?" I demanded.

"The same person who killed Countess Telia and the rogue weres and vampires has also killed some of Adrian's werewolves. He thinks you are responsible."

"I've only killed the one."

"She lies."

"No," Jonathan said. "You wanted to meet her here so you could see for yourself. She didn't do it. You have to see that."

Adrian studied me. His sharp features were drawn as he looked me up and down, as if he could read the truth in my posture. I wasn't so sure he couldn't.

"I trust her."

The voice came from behind me and to my left. I jumped, spinning my aim toward its source.

Nathan LaFoe stood there, hands folded over one another. He made the slightest flinch when I turned but otherwise didn't move.

I had been so distracted my Adrian, I never even noticed him standing there. I shifted so I could keep my eye on both Adrian and Nathan, trusting neither. Nathan might be a Cultist, might have broken me free of my cell at House

Tremaine, but he was never going to be a friend of mine. I'm pretty sure the feeling was mutual.

Adrian nodded once and seemed to relax. It was obvious he was still angry, but at least he didn't look as though he was going to attack me any time soon.

"Lower the gun," Jonathan said. "We are here to talk."

I hesitated but finally dropped my aim. I kept both my sword and my gun in hand, however, not wanting to relinquish their comfort. "Okay," I said. "Then talk."

Jonathan moved slowly across the room and took a seat on the couch. It looked soft as velvet and had silks thrown over the back, making it a bit too flashy for me. He gestured toward a couple of chairs that were new to the room. They looked to be just as comfortable, if not as garish.

"Please," he said. "Let's be seated and try to act civilly toward one another."

It seemed odd that I was being told to act civil by a werewolf, but there it was. I knew I was being hotheaded, but I had a reason. I trusted Adrian about as much as I trusted a vampire Count.

Nathan walked slowly past me, giving me the slightest of nods. His hair was still short, but he appeared to be growing it out from his crew cut. A scar ran down the right side of his face, following his jawline. It looked red and angry. He had gotten it sometime during the fight at Tremaine's mansion. Even though werewolves and vampires healed faster than a Pureblood would, they still got scars.

Nathan sat down on the couch next to Jonathan, though it appeared he wanted to stand. He sat on the very edge, muscles tense and ready to spring the moment something bad happened.

Adrian moved next. He walked nonchalantly, as if he cared nothing about me or my weapons. He might be resistant to silver, but that didn't mean a bullet to the brain wouldn't kill him.

He took the far chair, easing himself down like he wasn't used to sitting. His face went completely blank.

I really didn't want to sit. It was hard to stay defensive in such a vulnerable position. But if I wanted to get out of this without having to kill a few people, it might be the only thing I could do. I was sure Adrian wouldn't stand for me towering over him.

I crossed the room and took the chair as far from Adrian as I could get. I suppressed the urge to push it to a better angle. It would only amuse him.

"Let's clear the air," Jonathan said as soon as we were all seated. "We cannot have a worthwhile discussion while you are harboring misgivings about one another."

I doubted there was anything Jonathan could say to make me trust Adrian. It was hard enough being in the same room with him, let alone the same building. I kept my eyes on the ex-Cultist, waited for him to make a wrong move. I had no qualms about killing him.

"Lady Death did not kill your men," Jonathan said. "I believe her."

"Other than Eli," Adrian added, glancing my way.

I shrugged as Jonathan looked at me for confirmation. What else did he want from me?

"He followed me," I said. "Both of you would have done the same if someone was following you."

I had them there. Neither spoke, but I could almost see memories pass through their heads. Everyone sitting in that room had probably killed someone who knew too much or tried to tail them back to where they lived. It was in our nature.

"Adrian has told me why his man followed you," Jonathan said. "While I understand why you are upset, he had good reason."

"Oh really?"

"He thought you were killing his wolves one by one in

order to get to him. He sent someone to find you and watch you so he could confirm his belief."

Okay, I hated to admit it, but that made sense. I always followed wolves and vamps, checked out their homes, before I went in for the kill. I had to make sure they were what I thought they were. Could I really blame Adrian for doing the same?

"He told his wolves to stay away from you," Jonathan went on. "They weren't to get too close, only see what you were doing and report to him. None of them would disobey that order."

"Other than Eli," I said.

Adrian's eyebrow twitched, causing me to smile.

"Other than Eli," Jonathan agreed. "Have you had any other problems with Adrian or his wolves besides that one time?"

I shook my head. Adrian had stayed pretty clear of me since the last time we met. I'd hoped he had left town, even though I knew he had taken up living in Tremaine's mansion.

"And has Lady Death harmed you or yours in any way?" Jonathan turned toward Adrian.

I could tell he wanted to mention Eli again, but he kept that to himself. I would only mock him if he kept saying it. "No," he said. It came out terse.

"Then we are agree there should be little animosity between us?"

I couldn't help it. I burst into laughter.

All eyes turned toward me. None of them was amused. "What?" I said.

Nathan tensed in his seat and a glint of anger rose to his eyes. It was the old Nathan I knew coming back. As much as he was trying to be civil, I could tell he still hated me. This was the way things should be between us.

"Care to share?" Adrian said, his voice as dead as his expression.

"A little animosity?" I said. "I don't think that really describes how we feel about each other."

Jonathan frowned at me but didn't say anything, so I went on.

"Adrian defects from the Luna Cult, sides with Count Tremaine to gain power of his own, and he nearly gets us all killed in the process. And you say there is little animosity?" I laughed again. "Why in the hell is he here again? You should have killed him the moment he came crawling to you for help."

"We have a common problem," Jonathan said, clearly unmoved by my amusement. "Adrian wanted to know if you were committing the murders and he knew I was the only one who could easily reach you. Since we agree you aren't involved, I believe it is in our best interest to work together to solve our mutual problem."

My laugher died out. "I didn't do anything," I said. "I've taken down a few Fledgling Houses and took care of a problematic rogue, but I haven't done anything to Adrian or his people knowingly."

"I believe her," Adrian said. His voice was so calm it was jarring. His eyes glimmered, however, giving him away. He didn't believe what he was saying any more than I did.

Jonathan seemed to sink into the couch as if all his bones and muscles had given out at once. I didn't realize how tense he had become.

"Then how shall we go about dealing with this?"

All of us were silent. It might have been a good idea in theory to get us all together to discuss our mutual problem. In practice, it just wasn't feasible. I had no reason to trust either of them, and they had no reason to trust me.

"An alliance," Nathan said, suddenly breaking the silence. Everyone turned to face him. "We work together, comb the streets, and wait for whoever is doing this to make their move. If we all work together, we can have eyes everywhere."

"A truce," Adrian said, as if mulling the idea. He stared at me as he said it. "We will not move against each other until this problem is solved."

Jonathan nodded. "What do we know about this new threat?"

I sat there, stunned. Could I actually be thinking of allying myself with the Luna Cult again? Not only that, but with Adrian as well? Just the thought made me squirm in my seat. I should have already shot the lot of them and left with my dignity.

But no matter how uncomfortable I was, I sat there, listening as they went over the scant information I already knew. Adrian's wolves had been killed savagely by someone wielding what could only be a sword. It was the reason he thought I was involved, though he couldn't explain the claw marks without accusing Jonathan of being involved.

With every passing moment, I felt more and more uncomfortable. I couldn't believe Jonathan had allowed Adrian into the Den after everything he had done. If it wasn't for his wolves dying, I might have suspected Adrian of the murders myself.

I considered just getting up and leaving. The killers hadn't come for me. What reason did they really have other than I was a vampire? We were doing the same thing, had the same goals. I should be seeking them out in order to work with them, not turning against them so I could work with a bunch of werewolves. Again.

Of course I knew that was faulty logic. I knew Adrian and Jonathan. I had no idea who was doing the killings. And there were the Pureblood casualties. I couldn't forgive that.

"We should keep men on the streets, wait for our new little friend to make a mistake," Adrian said. He was still watching me and I forced myself to pay better attention.

"I can have the ancillary Cultists keep an eye out for

anyone suspicious," Jonathan said. "Nathan can lead our weres out on regular sweeps. We can watch the Houses near us, as well as the rogues living close to the Den. If anyone comes after them, we will know."

All eyes turned toward me and I knew I would have to say something. I was either going to have to back out of this or jump in headfirst. Neither choice sounded good. I didn't like working with werewolves, but I also didn't like backing away from a challenge, especially one that might save a few Pureblood lives.

"I can ride the streets and talk to some people," I said. "I know of a few places I could check."

Jonathan nodded, smiling. A small part of me hated him for that. He looked too content with what we were proposing to do, whom we were doing it with. I wondered if somewhere down the line, Jonathan and Adrian might work together to rid themselves of me.

I shook off the thought. I couldn't see Jonathan turning against me, not as long as I didn't come after the Cult. If I were ever to do that, I would make sure he didn't see it coming.

Jonathan and Nathan rose. I was quick to follow, not wanting to be seated when Adrian stood. He took his time, seemingly amused at my sudden movement.

"This is neutral ground," Jonathan said. "Report here if you learn anything. I will make sure everyone knows if something comes up."

Adrian nodded, though he didn't look happy about it.

"Fine," I said. "Are we done here?"

Jonathan looked around and no one seemed to have anything to add. "I'll drive you home," he said.

I could see the eagerness in Adrian's eyes. He would give anything to ride with us, to see where Lady Death called home. I was pretty sure he still had plans to make me his partner and mate. Someone like him wouldn't give up easily.

He blinked and the eagerness vanished, replaced by that dead look he was so good at. He started toward the door, brushing so close to Nathan they nearly bumped into one another.

A low growl emanated from deep within Nathan's chest. He stiffened and leaned forward. Adrian stopped, baring his teeth at the other man.

"Nathan," Jonathan warned.

Nathan backed down, taking a step back, hands clenched. I could see the animal in his eyes. He was just barely keeping himself from shifting.

A smile creased Adrian's face. He glared at Nathan a moment longer before turning toward the door. "I will show myself out," he said.

I watched him go. It was a struggle not to shoot him in the back, but I managed. How we were supposed to work together, I had no idea. This was definitely not going to be easy for any of us.

I glanced back at Nathan and my worry increased. His eyes were blazing as he stared at the place where Adrian had gone. He glanced at me and none of his hatred ebbed, just shifted.

Nope. This wasn't going to be easy at all.

10

Ethan was waiting for me when I returned home. One of my swords was resting on the table in front of him. He snatched it up as I came in but set it down as soon as he saw me.

"What did he want?" he asked. I was surprised to hear heat in his voice.

I didn't answer right away. It was obvious Ethan wasn't all that happy with me right then and I wanted to organize my thoughts. I sat down across from him and began removing my weapons and setting them on the table.

"We're going to try to find whoever has been killing the wolves and vamps lately," I said once everything was sitting in front of me.

"Are you sure you can trust him?"

Now that was a tricky question. I never really trusted anyone, aside from maybe Ethan, but nodded anyway. I couldn't let him think I was going into this unprepared. "This is something that needs to be taken care of, and the sooner the better."

Ethan took a deep breath and let it out slowly between his teeth. He ran his fingers through his hair twice,

messing it up even more than it usually was. His entire
body shook as he tapped his foot under the table.

"Is something wrong?"

He took another huffing breath and looked out the glass
back door. It was still deep night and only the outline of the
trees surrounding my property could be seen. The gloom
made it seem that much darker, as did Ethan's mood.

"That was that Jonathan guy, right? The one from the
Luna Cult?"

I nodded.

"And he came here, to our place, asking for your help
again?"

I didn't nod this time. I wasn't sure how to answer. I
could tell he wasn't happy about the arrangement at all. I
think he would have been much happier disposing of a
body than seeing me sitting around all buddy-buddy with
a werewolf.

I had to admit, I wasn't so sure I didn't agree.

"He knows where we live. Since you didn't do anything
to dissuade him from coming, he'll do it again."

"What's your point?"

"It isn't safe," Ethan said. "You know what they're like."

"They?"

"You know? Werewolves?" Ethan shifted in his seat, refusing to meet my eyes. "I can't believe you actually like
the guy after everything that's happened to you."

"I never said I liked him."

He gave me an incredulous look. "Right," he said.
"Who else could have come waltzing up to your front door
without you killing him? If you don't like him, then something else is going on."

I wanted to protest but kept quiet. I really didn't want to
think about my reasoning for not dropping Jonathan the
moment I opened the door. Ethan was right. If it had been
anyone else, I probably would have shot them.

"He and the Cult have their uses," I said, a bit too defensively for my liking.

"I know," Ethan said. "But he gives me the willies, you know? It's like living with a vampire and hanging around a demon isn't enough? I'm not sure I could handle you making kissing faces around a werewolf."

My mouth fell open. Kissing faces? "I think you're getting the wrong idea."

Ethan bit his lip. "He scares me," he said after a moment. "He gave me a look, one you didn't see. I swear he was thinking about hurting me, like he was afraid I was going to tell on him or something."

"That's stupid."

"Is it?" Ethan shook his head. "I'm not so sure."

I started to say something more, some other defense to why I hadn't turned Jonathan away the first moment I saw him, but stopped. Why was I defending myself? I knew what I was doing was stupid on so many levels. I mean, what would Ethan think if he knew it wasn't just Jonathan and the Cult I was working with, but Adrian Davis as well? He would probably bust a gasket.

Ethan started to reach across the table toward me but jerked back before coming anywhere close. "They had me for a long time." He spoke so low, it was a near whisper. "Valentino kept me locked up with barely enough to eat, forced me to watch my family die. I . . . I saw things, things I don't want to remember."

He struggled for more words but closed down instead. He looked away, tears glinting in his eyes.

I stared at him, shocked. In all the years we had lived together, he never truly told me what had happened to him those weeks he was held under Valentino's control. I knew his family had been killed, knew he had witnessed it, but other than that, I knew almost nothing else.

What had they done to him?

I probably should have said something, should have

comforted him. I should have put my arm around him, told him everything was going to be okay, even if I wasn't so sure I believed it myself. He needed that.

But I didn't. My life might be a fucked-up mess, but that didn't mean Ethan had suffered any less. Sure, he got to keep his humanity where I didn't, but was that really any better? He couldn't fight back as easily as I could. He needed someone there to watch out for him, and I was supposed to be that person.

But I had no idea how to comfort him. I wasn't sure he would even want me to try.

We sat there for a good long while, neither of us saying anything. It was one of those moments when nothing that could be said would ever make anything right, where not even a simple gesture of compassion could ever be enough.

"When do you start?" he asked, suddenly breaking the silence. His eyes were red, but the tears had stopped. He looked a lot more like the teenager I had taken in rather than the young man he had become.

"Tomorrow night."

He fidgeted a moment and then stood. "I've got some things to take care of." He gave me a weak smile. "Work, work."

Before I could say anything more, he took off toward the stairs and his lab, leaving all my weapons behind. I figured he would come back up and check them later. Probably when I was upstairs and he wouldn't have to face me.

I felt numb. After everything that had happened recently, this somehow seemed the worst. Ethan wasn't really all that mad at me, yet for some reason, I felt terrible for making him feel bad. Why couldn't I seem to do anything right lately?

I rose and went to the living room. It wasn't until the television clicked on that I realized what I was doing. I almost turned the damn thing off and walked away, but my timing had been perfect.

The news was on.

I stared at it, knowing what I was waiting for without really thinking about it. Part of me had to know, to see the results of what I had done.

I didn't have to wait long.

The report came on with a somber-looking reporter standing on a familiar street. I could see the spot where the truck had landed, though it was long gone by now. The stain of red was clearly evident just off to the reporter's right.

I scarcely dared to breathe. He talked of the injured officer, how he had been heading home when he called in a car accident. Their best guess was the werewolf lying dead nearby had been the driver and had attacked the cop. Before he could finish the job, someone else came along and killed the werewolf. It wasn't clear who, but the officer's family was thankful.

Thinking back to the flutter of the curtain in the house across the street, I expected the reporter to mention talking to witnesses, but if they had, he never mentioned it. Maybe the subtle movement *had* been my imagination after all.

The reporter babbled on a bit more, talking about the dangers of going out at night, how it is best to keep doors and windows firmly locked, before sending it back to the studio. The female anchor looked grim as she took up the story. What she had to say caused me to sag in my seat and a relieved sigh escaped my lips.

The cop had lived. He was in critical condition and had yet to wake up, but he was alive.

I turned off the television and went upstairs, shaking. I don't know why it bothered me so much. The guy had lived. There was still a chance he might die, but I was hoping he would make it. He would be able to tell everyone what had really happened, but I was pretty sure he never got a good look at me, so it shouldn't matter. It wasn't like the Pureblood police ever went after supes anyway.

It made me sick to think that such a thing could go unpunished. The cop hadn't done anything and I had nearly killed him. Something should be done. I didn't really care what.

I sat down on the edge of my bed, trying to come up with something that would make everything okay. Once again, my life was flooded with crap I didn't know how to handle: There was the whole cop thing, Adrian and his wolf I killed, the murderer, Ethan and his demon. What else could possibly happen?

I laid back and stared at the ceiling. I would get through this. Somehow, someway, I could do it. I managed to keep from going crazy when I was turned, I could do it again now. This was nothing compared to that. I just needed to weather this storm and wait for the next inevitable gale to wash over me. Things couldn't get any worse.

Could they?

11

The next night, I headed out in search of our killer. I
cruised the streets, watching for anyone who looked like
they might be a likely suspect. It wasn't easy. Every single
person walking the dark streets seemed just as likely as
the next.

I kept to the vampire districts, though I spent a major-
ity of my time on the back roads. I came across a werewolf
at one point, but he scampered away before I could get a
shot off. It was unlikely he was the killer, but I wasn't
going to take any chances.

I reported my meager findings to Jonathan and listened
to his reports, as well as what Adrian had brought him.
There wasn't much. No one else had died by claw and
sword over the last few days, making our search that much
harder.

I left as soon as I received the reports. After how Ethan
reacted to my hanging around Jonathan, I didn't want to
make it worse by lingering.

The next few nights were more of the same. I went out,
I looked, I came back empty-handed. Not even Mikael had
any news for me.

A few nights later, I rose from the long day, hunger

hitting me full force. I hadn't sucked the life out of the cop, so I was in a bad way by the time I had my things on and was out the door. I'd been so preoccupied with the shit-storm of my life, I hadn't thought to feed on someone more deserving until it was nearly too late.

I went straight to High Street, the one place I knew I could find likely victims in abundance. You could find anything you wanted here. If you were looking for danger-ous sex, drugs, or death, you could find it on High Street. Vampires and werewolves haunted the streets just as much as the Purebloods, and they weren't any less likely to die.

Neon lights lit the place up so much, it was impossible to see the stars, even on the clearest of nights. Strippers and hookers, both the male and female variety, walked the streets, selling their wares. Windows without curtains gave a clear view of the debauchery going on within many of the hotels. Nothing here was ever truly private.

I hated parking in the sole parking garage, but I had little choice unless I wanted to walk a good ways to get there. Every parking lot that had once existed on High Street had been turned into something else. Most people took taxis or walked simply because it was safer than leav-ing a vehicle somewhere where a monster could wait for you to return.

Of course, nothing was ever safe here. Coming to High Street was as much of a death sentence as walking down a dark alley at midnight.

A car pulled into the garage behind me and I watched it carefully as I pulled into a parking space. It went past, never slowing, and I breathed easier. The windows had been tinted so dark I hadn't been able to see the driver, but I was pretty sure whoever was inside hadn't been follow-ing me. I was just being paranoid, and paranoid here could save my life.

Stepping out onto the street was like walking out onto the sun. I had to shade my eyes until I was accustomed to the brightness after the deep gloom of the garage. Girls wearing nearly nothing walked past me, giggling and tottering against one another. They smelled heavily of vodka and other musky scents that left little to the imagination.

I grimaced and walked away from them, not wanting to be downwind of them for long. Just coming here made me feel dirty, but it was the best place to find a victim who wouldn't weigh on my conscience.

I walked up and down the street for a good hour, searching. Sometimes I could come here and find a likely target right away. Other times it was nearly impossible.

Tonight was one of the bad nights. Everyone stayed huddled together, walking in at least pairs, though most everyone was keeping to larger groups. It was the smart thing to do and I didn't like it.

A woman coming out of one of the hotels bumped into me. She was carrying a heavy metal case and I would have said she had probably been sampling everything High Street had to offer, but her hair was perfect, clothes unrumpled. I guess she hadn't found what she was looking for.

She looked at me with a strange glimmer in her eye as I passed. She didn't look quite right in the head, but that didn't mean she was someone I would feed on. Someone had to be more than crazy for me to feel comfortable killing them.

I turned away from her and continued on. I could feel her eyes on my back like she was sizing me up. I glanced back and she was indeed watching me. I had half a mind to go back and ask what her problem was, but she finally turned away. She was probably a new vamp looking for her first kill.

A few minutes later, I finally saw a likely target and I forgot all about the woman.

The guy was pretty tall, but I could handle a tall guy just as easily as a shorter one. His hair was long, unkempt, and his clothes hung from him as though they had been meant for someone much rounder. This guy was so thin he looked damn near skeletal.

He stood just inside an alley, a long brown trench coat hiding most of his figure. I watched as a small woman came up to him, handed him a few bills, and took a baggie of something white and powdery from him. She shambled off, heels clicking irregularly as she staggered away.

I watched him for a good ten minutes. He had a regular flow of customers and I didn't want anyone else to be standing there when I made my move. It was bad enough I needed to feed. I didn't need witnesses.

Finally, he slid back into the darkness of the alley and took out something to smoke. From the looks of it, it wasn't a cigarette.

Blood trickled down my gums as my fangs started to extend. The excitement of the hunt was taking over, even though this guy was as easy a target as I would ever have. I could almost taste his blood.

I approached him, glancing back and forth to make sure no one was watching. As I got near, the guy saw me and grinned, exposing gaps in his teeth. Up close, I could see what his hair had hidden. Most of his ears were missing, as if they had rotted away, rather than having been bitten off. His nose was in pretty much the same condition, leaving two large gaping holes in the middle of his face. His lips were chapped and bleeding, as were his gums where the teeth were missing.

"Heya sugartits," he slurred as I came close. The joint hung from his lower lip like it was stuck there. "I have whatever you need."

I forced a smile to my face. I hated feeding on drug dealers, especially ones who sampled their own product, and this guy looked as though he had more than sampled it. It was probably all he ever consumed.

Since I was only after his blood, the condition of his

body mattered little. While his blood might be riddled with disease and drugs, my vampire taint would keep it from affecting me. It was one of the benefits of being a vampire I was thankful for. Most diseases stood no chance against my immune system, and drugs were usually just as ineffective. I might get a little buzzed, but that was about it.

That didn't mean I wouldn't feel sick afterward. Feeding on a guy like this was like eating a rotten piece of fish. It might take care of your hunger, but it always came back to haunt you later.

I glanced down the alley as I approached. It was dark, dank, and lonely. It would be a perfect place to feed.

"What do you have to offer?" I asked, stepping close to him. He smelled as though he had never taken a bath in his life.

The guy's yellowed eyes widened. He licked his lips, exposing a tongue covered in sores. "Whatever you need, baby."

I managed not to show my disgust as I slunk past him and into the alley. I could feel his eyes on me, burning with fever, as well as with lust.

There was a nook deep in the alley and I stepped into it. It would hide us from too many onlookers. Someone coming down the alley might think we were just making out, though it was far more likely something more sinister was happening. No one ever truly wanted to believe what they saw.

The dealer followed, limping heavily. I could smell him approach and my stomach roiled. He smelled worse than the garbage littering the alley, which was saying something.

As soon as he was close, I grabbed him and threw him up against the wall. If I was going to do this, I wanted to get it done so I could do a little searching tonight. Just because I needed to feed didn't mean everything else could be ignored.

He grunted with the impact; his joint fell from his lips,

but his grin never faltered. He already had his pants unbuttoned and they slid down his bony hips.

He wasn't wearing anything underneath.

I had to fight a look of revulsion as I pressed up against him. From the little I had seen, everything on him was rotten. I jerked his head to the side, not bothering to test his blood for wolf or vamp taint. It was obvious by the decay of his body that he was neither.

Blood spurted from my gums, splashing his neck, as my fangs elongated. The dealer groaned and I noticed the other marks on his neck. This definitely wasn't his first time. Unfortunately for him, it would be his last.

I sank my fangs into his neck and he gasped. He pressed hard against my thigh and I shifted in case there was any sort of leakage from below. I so didn't want to have to get that sort of stain out of my leather pants, especially from this guy.

I fed on him, sucking down his blood in large gulps. He writhed against me in both pleasure and pain, doing everything he could to rub himself against me. He might have been getting off on it then, but after a few more moments, he wouldn't be. I had no intention of stopping like the other vamps had.

I pulled harder at his neck, biting down as if I planned on tearing out his throat with my teeth. He grunted and pushed against me all the harder, pumping his hips even though I was doing my best to avoid his lower half.

I growled, not wanting any accidents, and jerked his head back a little. A scream escaped his lips.

It was that scream that covered the sound of the approaching footsteps.

A sharp sting in my neck caused me to jerk back, stunned. I had a heartbeat to wonder, *What the fuck?* before collapsing to the ground.

Nothing worked. I tried to move my arms, but they were totally useless to me. My legs were dead weights; even my head felt too heavy for my neck. I could only move my eyes from left to right, searching for whatever had poked me.

She stepped into view an instant later. The woman set down the metal case and held a syringe up for me to see before tossing it away. She smiled at me, her face upside down from my perspective. There was insanity there.

I couldn't see the drug dealer, though I was sure he was dying. I had a chunk of his flesh in my mouth. I couldn't even move my tongue enough to spit it out.

"Such a pretty thing," the woman said. "Such a pity you chose this life." She smiled at me, eyes gleaming.

My head swam and it was all I could do to stay conscious. I knew she had to have used silver of some sort to paralyze me, but there was more to it than that. I had no strength, worse than anything silver could do. My head was woozy, the entire world swam. That didn't happen with just silver.

She vanished from view and I heard the case click open. She started humming as she moved things around inside. I could hear glass clinking and then something metallic being drawn through leather.

I immediately thought of my weapons, tucked away and useless to me.

Her face appeared again and she held up a serrated knife for me to see. "You chose the wrong night to hunt, my lovely little demon. It's unfortunate your victim won't see tomorrow. He might have liked to see the blood you took from him returned to the earth."

I fought my body. I tried to scream, tried to even whimper, but nothing came out.

The woman sighed. Her green eyes were nearly twinkling in the gloom. "You should thank me too," she said, leaning over me. "I will end your suffering, send you back to the hell you were spawned from. The Light will shine on you and perhaps you can still be saved. I will pray for you."

She turned the blade over in her hand a few times. She

seemed to be relishing the moment. It was almost like a ritual, something she had done over and over to the point it had become sacred.

"My hand is His hand," she said. "I strike in love." She lowered the blade to my throat.

Just as it touched my skin, it was suddenly yanked away. A blur of motion flew over me, striking the woman full on in the chest. I tried to turn my head to see who it was, but it was no use. My head swam even more and I started shuddering.

The scuffling was over quickly. The woman wasn't screaming or cursing or crying. I wasn't even sure if she was alive.

Footsteps approached, but I didn't see who had saved me. The world did a loop and I felt everything I had consumed from the dealer come back up, though I couldn't open my mouth to spew it out.

I couldn't even choke. I tried hard not to breathe, did everything I could to keep from drowning in my own vomit. I wouldn't die from suffocation, but I sure as hell could suffer for a very long time if I couldn't clear my airway.

It was too much. Blood and bile oozed from between my lips. My head fell to the side, my eyes glazed over. A hand touched my face, the skin rough and calloused.

The world went blissfully dark.

12

Everything came back into focus in a rush. I shot up and my head immediately went woozy. It felt like a dark fog was rolling through my brain. My eyes wouldn't focus and they burned as if someone had dumped salt in them. I lowered my head, closed my eyes, and then took a few deep breaths before things started to clear.

"Easy." Nathan's deep voice came from across the room.

I didn't look up at him. I wasn't so sure I'd be able to see much of anything just yet.

"What happened?" It felt like my skull was filled with cement. It hurt to think.

"Adrian brought you in," Nathan said. I could hear the disdain in his voice. "He said you were attacked and he saved your life."

I opened my eyes, wincing in the dim light. There was only a single lamp on to my right and yet it felt too bright. Of course, right then, even the glow of the moon would have been too bright.

I looked around the room, blinking rapidly to clear my vision. Everything was fuzzy around the edges, but at least I could see.

Nathan was sitting in the corner on a wooden chair that

looked far too small to support his weight. Curtains hung over the windows framing him. They were drawn closed, so I wasn't sure if it was night or day. I was so weak I couldn't even tell.

It took me a moment to realize I was sitting on a soft, comfortable bed. The sheets were pooled in my lap, and my coat was gone. At least I was still wearing my clothes.

I slid to the edge of the bed and put my hands to my head as another burst of dizziness came over me. I hadn't felt this bad since I was a Pureblood. Not even silver screwed me up like that.

"Where am I?"

"Where else?" Nathan said. "The Den."

I looked around again. There was a dresser across the room that looked to be an antique. Beside the bed was a nightstand holding a glass of water. I started to reach for it, stopped, and gave Nathan a sideways glance. He nodded and I grabbed the glass and downed the water in one gulp. It burned as it went down.

If I was in the Den, I was in a part of the old library I'd never seen before. I knew most of the Cultists, if not all of them, lived in the Den, but it really hadn't occurred to me they would have bedrooms like this. Of course, Nathan's bedroom might be special, since he was a werewolf. The Purebloods might only have cots in overly crowded rooms for all I knew.

I groaned and tried to stand. I staggered back and sat down heavily. My head was pounding and I was sick to my stomach.

"Where's Jonathan?"

"Downstairs with Adrian and our . . . guest." He didn't sound too thrilled with the last. "I'm to take you down as soon as you are able to walk."

I tried to rise again but fell back. My legs just wouldn't work. "What did she do to me?"

Nathan rose and crossed the room to stand over me, fingers flexing at his side. I wasn't sure if he was concerned about my health or if he was upset about something else. It wouldn't have surprised me if he'd considered killing me while I was unconscious. If I had been him, I might have considered the same.

"Thanks," I said. I licked my lips. Even after the water, both my tongue and lips were dry.

Nathan gave me a funny look, his ever-present frown deepening.

"For not killing me while I was out." I rubbed my temples. "And for letting me use your room to sleep it off." Whatever "it" was.

A bitter smile rose to his lips. "It's not my room. It's Jonathan's."

Looking around once more, I realized that made much more sense. The room was a little too flamboyant for Nathan. The sheets were silky smooth, the lamp subdued and artful. Nathan's room was probably militaristic and bland.

"Ready?"

I nodded and stood. My legs were wobbly, but I didn't fall down this time. Points for me.

Nathan led the way out of the room and into the sitting room where we had our meeting with Adrian a few nights before. The room was empty of people. I glanced back as the door closed behind us, hiding the entrance. I knew it had been there, but I'd never imagined a bedroom was tucked away behind the hidden door.

We crossed the sitting room as fast as my legs would allow. Nathan opened the gilded doors for me, staring at me with as much disdain as he could muster. Pablo was standing outside, guarding the entrance. He glowered at me as we stepped through but didn't say anything. I could tell he wanted to. The tattoo on his forehead nearly burned with his desire to say something nasty.

I did my best to smile at him, though I wasn't so sure it

reached my face. I felt numb all over. As far as I knew, I was glowering just as hard as he was.

Nathan headed for the stairs and I followed him. There were a few other Cultists milling about as we headed toward the office. None of them really paid me much mind. I had a feeling Jonathan had told them not to bother me when they saw me. He probably figured I wouldn't take well to sympathy of any kind.

We entered the office. I immediately leaned against the wall as Nathan shut the door and headed across the room to press the button behind the desk. The secret door opened and he headed for the yawning darkness.

"Come on," he said.

I hesitated. I really didn't want to go down there. I knew what was behind bars down in the Cult's basement. I didn't want to see the mixed-blood creature again. Once was enough.

Nathan stared at me, seemingly indifferent to my discomfort. He motioned toward the opening and I finally started forward. I hated feeling so weak. I shouldn't be afraid of anything, yet here I was tentative about going downstairs where everything dangerous was behind bars.

That thought straightened my back. I was fooling myself if I thought the only thing dangerous down there was locked away. I kept forgetting Jonathan and Nathan were wolves. I couldn't make that mistake too often or one of them would end up taking advantage of it.

Nathan led the way down into the basement. I used the wall for support, taking each step carefully. I still wasn't steady, but getting up and moving around had helped. A few more minutes and I might be able to walk without assistance.

I'd forgotten how big the basement was. It was as big as the entire building above us, making it seem almost cavernous. It might not have been so bad if there had been more than a bunch of cells, a table, and a few lights in the room.

Jonathan and Adrian were both waiting at the bottom of the stairs. They stood apart from each other, and I had a feeling they hadn't been talking much. I'd kind of hoped Adrian would have left by now, though I still wasn't quite sure how long I'd actually been out.

"I'm glad you are up and about," Jonathan said. He wasn't smiling.

My eyes immediately went past him to the cell where the poor mixed-blood creature had been. The beast had once been a werewolf, second in command behind the old Denmaster, Simon. Count Tremaine had mixed his blood with vampire blood, turning him into a mindless, raving beast.

His cell was now empty.

Jonathan followed my gaze and lowered his eyes. "We had to put him down," he said. "I couldn't let him suffer anymore."

I nodded, somewhat relieved. I didn't need that sort of reminder of my brother right then. I had enough on my plate than to be forced to think about Thomas, who had suffered the same fate as the Cult's creature. He was still out there somewhere, either dead or crazy. It amounted to the same thing in the end.

"Fill me in," I said, putting as much strength into my voice as I could. Nathan moved off to the side to stand close to Jonathan. "What the fuck happened?"

Adrian gave me a flat stare. "You were careless and she got the slip on you." He waved his hand toward a cell in the far corner. The woman who attacked me was standing behind the bars, glaring at us. "She injected you with something. I saved you."

I ground my teeth. "You were following me."

Adrian's shoulders did a little hop. I think it was supposed to be a shrug. "I was out looking for our killer. I happened to notice you and decided to see what you were up to. It was nothing more than simple curiosity."

"We haven't been able to get anything out of her," Jonathan said, moving to put himself between Adrian and me. I think he could tell I was getting pissed. "Not anything useful anyway."

The corner where the woman was kept was in gloom, much like the rest of the basement. Only a few lights were on and they barely gave enough light for a normal person to see by. Thankfully, I wasn't a normal person.

"Let me talk to her." I started walking toward her without waiting for an answer. Jonathan put his hand on my arm to stop me. I glared at him and he jerked his hand back.

"Are you sure you're okay?" he asked.

"I'm fine." I did my best not to wobble when I said it.

"You don't look fine."

I clenched my fists and nearly hit him. I so didn't need that pointed out to me. "I said I was fine."

He nodded and stepped aside. Adrian had moved to stand in the way. He refused to budge, forcing me to go around him. I think he got some sort of perverse satisfaction out of it.

The woman watched me approach with wary eyes. She was still wearing the same clothes I'd last seen her in, though now they were dirty and her hair was mussed. Her metal case wasn't with her, and I wondered if Adrian had brought it in with him or if he decided to keep it for himself. I would have to ask about that later.

"The Hand will fall upon those of darkness," the woman said as I stopped in front of her cell. "He will see to it."

"That's nice," I said. "Why did you attack me?"

She smiled. "Your blood is poisoned. It must be returned to the earth so that you may be free of your curse."

I frowned. I wasn't sure if she was as crazy as she sounded or if it was all an act. She kept smiling while she talked, seemingly unconcerned about her surroundings.

"You do know you'll die if you don't cooperate," I said.

The woman kept on smiling. "Death will set me free. I do not fear it. I will go to Him willingly if that is His wish."

I glanced back at Jonathan, who shrugged.

"What did you do to me?" I don't know why I kept trying. It was obvious the woman wasn't going to answer anything in a sane way.

Jonathan stepped forward. "It was a combination of silver, blood thinners, and something we cannot identify. I have someone looking into it."

The woman grinned at us. "It will set you free if you let His Hand guide you as it has me."

Adrian approached and held up the knife for me to see. Its edges were serrated and it looked dreadfully sharp. It wouldn't have taken much effort to saw my throat open with that. I managed not to cringe. More points for me.

"She was going to cut your throat with this," he said. "Until I stopped her."

"The blood thinner would have kept your blood flowing. You would have bled out pretty quickly." Jonathan looked uncomfortable at that.

I stared at the knife, my stomach doing a few tumbles. With the silver keeping me paralyzed, I wouldn't have been able to do a damn thing to stop her. My blood would have spilled freely, pumping in gushes, and I wouldn't have been able to cry out for help. It would have been a horrible way to die. To be so helpless . . . it was almost unimaginable.

"Who are you?" I asked, tearing my gaze away from the wicked-looking blade to stare at the woman.

She stepped back from the bars and crossed herself. She

looked up as if she could see the sky even though we were well belowground. "Deliver me from these demons. Take me into Your arms where I shall be protected from their taint."

I kept a tight rein on my emotions. This woman was seriously getting on my nerves, and if I were to lose control now and kill her, we wouldn't be able to get anything out of her. I could feel my teeth wanting to push through. This woman had nearly killed me. That was something I couldn't forgive.

"Did you kill the others? Why?"

The woman kept on praying or whatever it was she was doing. I don't think she was listening to me anymore.

"I don't think she is our murderer," Jonathan said.

"She attacked me."

"But she is not were. From what I can tell, she wouldn't have anything to do with a werewolf."

"And the blade is wrong," Adrian said. The knife was gone. He had probably tucked it away somewhere to keep. "I've seen the wounds on my men. They do not match."

I turned away from the cell. I couldn't stand to watch the woman anymore. I really wanted her to be responsible, but I knew they were right. My attack had been a coincidence. There was no way this one woman could be responsible for so many deaths.

I started to walk toward the stairs, but my legs gave out. I staggered a few steps and Jonathan grabbed me by the arm to support me. I glared at him and he let me go. I didn't need his help.

"We need to find out if she is alone," I said. "Maybe there are others who she works with. Perhaps they are who we are looking for."

Adrian walked past us and up the stairs. It appeared we were done.

Nathan glanced at Jonathan, who gave a quick nod. The

big wolf hurried after Adrian. I wondered if he was simply going to follow him out or if he was looking for a fight. Knowing Nathan, it was probably the latter.

"Are you really okay?" Jonathan asked once they were gone. I think he expected me to slump against him or something, because he stood so close I could almost smell his breath.

"Yeah," I said. I wouldn't show weakness, even to him. "I'm just pissed I let myself get caught up like that. I should have heard her coming."

Jonathan glanced back at the cell and I followed his gaze. The woman was watching us again, eyes gleaming in what I could only describe as complete and utter madness. The fervor there was so strong, it was a surprise we didn't burst into flames from the intensity of her stare.

"I will continue to question her," Jonathan said. "It's clear she has done this before. People like her could be dangerous."

"Do you think there are more of them?"

Jonathan met my eyes. He looked worried. "I don't know."

"I know."

I jerked at the gravelly voice. It came from the darkest corner of the room, farthest from the woman. It was hard to see even with my enhanced vision.

A shape stepped out of the shadows of the corner cell. He leaned against the bars and pressed his face against them. He was painfully thin and his throat was a mass of scar tissue. It looked hard and knotted, and was probably why he sounded the way he did.

"Davin," I said, recognizing the sorcerer vampire at once.

He laughed, a painful-looking grin spread across his face. "I can tell you what you want to know." His eyes gleamed with as much fervor as the woman's. "For a price, of course."

"Don't," Jonathan said as I started toward the cell.

I stopped and gave him a look. I didn't need to say anything. He got the idea. Dealing with a mad vampire couldn't be any worse than dealing with a crazed religious zealot. We needed to know who she was in case there were more like her.

Jonathan nodded and I turned back to question the vampire I had believed to be dead.

13

Davin didn't stop grinning as I crossed the room toward his cell. He was wearing little more than rags. Dried blood stained the fabric, and it took me a moment to realize he was wearing the same clothes he had been wearing the last time I saw him months ago. He smelled like death.

"I know," he said, his grin widening. There were two large gaps in his teeth where his incisors once were. He stuck his tongue through one of the holes and wiggled it at me.

I had to admit, I felt a tiny wince of pity for the fallen vampire. He'd once been a member of a Minor House, the second in command to Count Tremaine.

And now look at him. He could hardly hold himself erect. His legs trembled beneath him like his nearly insubstantial weight was too much for them. His cheekbones protruded from his face, the skin stretched so tightly over his skull he was little more than a skeleton. His eyes were deeply sunken, almost swimming in darkness where they had collapsed into their sockets.

Nathan had torn out his throat during the final fight with Tremaine. He hadn't had the chance to finish Davin off, so Jonathan had brought him here. I wondered if they had assisted him in his recovery.

"Davin," I said, stopping in front of his cell. I wasn't sure what else to say. The vampire would have killed me before. I wasn't so sure he wouldn't do it now.

"I've been down here a long time," he said. His voice was so degraded it was hard to understand his every word. While his throat might have healed, it hadn't healed all the way. The damage had probably been too extensive.

Jonathan came up to stand behind me. I glanced back at him and noted his unhappy expression. I don't think I was supposed to have seen the vampire.

"I've spent countless hours here, and yet this is the first time you've come to see me." Davin reached a bony hand through the bars, though it fell well short of touching me.

"I was busy."

He laughed, withdrawing his hand. "I see, I see. But now you are here and I have something you desire. This information I have, it could be useful to you down the road."

I shrugged. "It doesn't seem that important to me. We have her now. She'll break eventually."

Davin laughed again. "I doubt that," he said. "Her kind never breaks. I've seen it."

I wasn't sure what to think of that. The woman was a Pureblood. There was only so much she could do, so much she could withstand. I had a feeling that Nathan wouldn't have a problem with torturing her for information.

But if there was an easier way . . .

"Okay," I said, "tell me what you know."

He tsked. "Do you think I would give this information freely? I have endured so much here and I know I will never be set free."

"Then what could you possibly want?"

He smiled, exposing the gaps in his teeth. "I hunger," he said. "I have come near death many times, have felt my strength wane. It ebbs away like a retreating tide. But the tide always returns. I will never regain my full strength, not after what they have done to me, but I still hunger. I wish for blood."

I glanced back at Jonathan. He stared back at me, showing nothing.

"You haven't fed him?" I said, somewhat appalled. Why keep him down here if he was only going to starve him? The vampire meant nothing to me, but even though I would have killed him if given the chance, I wouldn't have tortured him like this.

"We have," Jonathan said. "But only enough to keep him alive. We do not want him so strong that he is able to use his abilities again."

"Look at what they did to me," Davin said. He jammed a finger into the hole where his left incisor used to be. "They have maimed me, ruined me, and yet they fear me." He laughed bitterly. "I must drink from a cup if I choose to drink at all. What harm could I possibly pose to anyone like this?"

I knew with enough blood, Davin could become a serious problem. He might never regain his incisors, though. Jonathan had probably torn them out clear to the root, if not deeper.

"Is that all?" I asked. "Blood?"

"What else is there?"

There was a gleam to his eye when he said the last. He wanted something else, and he was going to make me ask him.

"What do you want, Davin? I'm not going to stand down here all night." At least I hoped it was still night. I really didn't want to hang around the Den all day, waiting for the moon to rise, especially with Nathan and Pablo glowering at me every chance they got.

"I know I will not be released, even if my information might save you trouble later," he said. "I accept that. I know I'll be trapped down here until I am of no further use to my captors."

I shifted from foot to foot. This was too much like what a vampire House did to its prisoners for my liking. If the Cult was starting to veer toward keeping prisoners and torturing them, I might have to do something about it.

The thought made my stomach do a flip and I nearly staggered. I felt Jonathan move toward me as if he might support me and I waved him back. I was tired of people trying to help me.

"And?" I said.

"And I wish to see the moon," Davin said. "I don't mean I wish to be free. I wouldn't last an hour as I am now. I also know I will not be allowed a human to drain." He looked at Jonathan hopefully.

"No," Jonathan said, his voice firm.

Davin sighed and slumped against his cell. "Just the moon," he said. "I wish to be taken outside so I can look upon it again. I wish to bathe in its light, breathe the night air."

"I don't think they'll let you out long enough for that," I said. Jonathan grunted in agreement.

"They can leave me in chains," Davin said. "They can stab me with silver if they wish. I don't care. Just as long as I can see, it will suffice." He closed his eyes. He looked weary, like he was tired of living. "Please," he went on, "that is all I ask. One night under the moon."

I glanced back at Jonathan. He stared straight ahead, not looking at anything. I couldn't tell if he was considering it or not.

I turned back to Davin. I didn't like the idea of letting the crippled vampire out any more than Jonathan did, but what could it hurt? He had no fangs; he was unable to use his magic from what I could tell. All anyone would have to do is stick a silver knife into him and he would be helpless.

Yet, alarm bells were clanging so loudly in my head I

was surprised no one else heard them. Davin was up to something, I was sure of it.

"Please," he said again. "I promise my information will be valuable. It could save all of your lives." His gaze traveled down the length of cells to where the woman stood.

I glanced that way. I had to admit, I was more scared of people like the woman than I was of Davin somehow escaping. She had managed to sneak up on me. If there were more like her, then it could put a serious kink in my way of doing things. I couldn't have that.

"All right," I said without consulting Jonathan. This was my deal. If I had to be there when they took him out to see the moon, then I would be.

Jonathan made a sound deep in his throat but didn't protest.

"Is that all?" I gave Davin a hard look, daring him to ask for something else.

He looked relieved. "Yes," he said. "Thank you."

I didn't want his thanks. "So tell me what you know."

Davin used his fingers to push back his scraggly hair. He walked deeper into his cell and sat on a cot. I'm not so sure his legs would have supported him any longer if he had tried to remain standing.

"The Left Hand," he said. "That is the group she belongs to."

I frowned. "That means nothing to me."

Davin smiled and closed his eyes. "Not many alive know of them. They make sure of that." He opened his eyes and gave me a sinister smile. "In a way, they are a lot like you."

"That woman is nothing like me."

Davin's smile only widened. "They sneak through the night, hunt their victims, and then kill them as quickly and as quietly as they can. They leave no witnesses. Does that not sound familiar to you?"

He had me there. "How many of them are there?" I asked, doing my best to ignore the comparison.

Davin shrugged. "Dozens? Hundreds? No one knows. I'm not even sure they know themselves."

"But *who* are they?"

"The Left Hand. As in the left hand of God." Davin's eyes gleamed as he spoke. "They think of themselves as messengers. Their message is of a cleansing, to rid the world of taint so that the humans can live without fear of the night." He sneered.

"If they wanted to send a message, wouldn't they want everyone to know about them?" I glanced back at the woman. She was grinning as she listened.

"I don't know why they work as they do," Davin said. "That is something only they can tell you . . . if you can get anything useful out of them."

It all sounded unreal to me. Purebloods never fought back against the supes. They just resigned themselves to the day, leaving the night to the rest of us. It might not have created a perfect harmony, but at least it hadn't devolved into a war.

Davin was silent for a moment and I assumed he was done. I wasn't so sure the information he had given us was all that useful. I might have to run the name The Left Hand past Mikael sometime and see if he knew anything.

I started to turn away when the vampire spoke up again.

"You are Lady Death, are you not?"

I glanced back at him, surprised. It wasn't until then I realized he'd never truly known who I was. Not even Count Tremaine had figured it out until the end.

"I thought so," he said. "It makes sense. I should have seen it back then, back before I was left to this."

I didn't know what to say to that, so I kept silent.

"More will be coming," Davin said. He sounded completely resigned, as if he knew he had nothing to live for.

I don't think the prospect of blood and seeing the moon again was enough for him.

"More?"

"Of The Left Hand," he said. "She is but the first."

"How do you know?"

"I've seen it before," he said. "Before I lived here, I belonged to another House in another town. They came, slowly at first, and then all at once. They killed so many and we caught none of them. My House was destroyed and I fled here, barely escaping with my life."

"You seem to do that a lot."

He gave me a bitter smile. "I do," he said. "Though this is not so much of a life."

"When will they come?" I asked.

"Soon," he said. "It could be weeks, a month." He shrugged. "It's hard to say. They will sneak in one by one, kill as quietly as they can, and then vanish like smoke."

"They can't be that bad," I said.

Davin spread his hands. "I'm only telling you what I know. You would have to ask her if you wish to know more." He gave me a hard look. "I'm just glad I'm not going to be out there to deal with them."

I glanced across the room at the woman. She was still grinning. It made me want to break her neck.

I walked away from Davin, leaving him slumped on his cot. Jonathan followed me as I approached the woman again.

"How long until others arrive?" I asked.

She gave me a sweet smile full of venom. "You'll know when you feel the bite of our blade on your throat. His Hand will guide them to you."

I'd had enough. I turned and stalked toward the stairs, just wanting to get out of there. Jonathan gave me a worried look, his shoulders as tense as I'd ever seen them.

"You'll all die," the woman said to my retreating back.

"The Left Hand will strike you down. We will leave no survivors!"

I kept walking, ignoring her. As long as the others weren't here, she was nothing but talk. I would deal with them when I had to. There was already too much shit I had to worry about without having to watch for Pureblood assassins.

The last sound I heard as Jonathan closed the hidden passageway behind us was the sound of the woman's mad laughter.

14

"Do you believe him?"

We were sitting in Jonathan's office. Nathan stood by the door, arms crossed. Adrian thankfully had left, leaving the three of us to discuss what we learned from Davin.

Jonathan tapped his fingers on his desk. "I don't know. It's hard to believe anything he says."

"But why would he lie?"

"To get something for nothing," Nathan said. He sounded angry.

"I don't like it."

"Neither do I." Jonathan gave me a pointed look. "We should keep an eye out for others like her."

"Don't we already have enough to worry about?" I really didn't want to add another problem to my growing list. It was starting to get to be a bit too much, even for me.

"Do we have a choice?" Jonathan sighed. He rubbed at the right side of his face where his glamour hid his scarred features. It was odd to watch. His fingers didn't sink into the flesh or anything, but it didn't look right either. "If Davin is telling the truth and others like that woman show up, we could be in some serious trouble."

Nathan grunted. He'd been filled in by Jonathan and it was clear he didn't want to believe Davin. I wasn't so sure I wanted to either.

"They're Purebloods," he said. "What could they possibly do to us?"

I looked at him like he was a moron. He didn't deign to notice.

"We should just stay vigilant," Jonathan said. "If one of them can sneak up on you," he gave me a nervous look, "then we should all be watchful. None of us is safe."

"But what about our murderer?" I said. "Are we sure this woman isn't responsible? She seems crazy enough to walk right into a vampire House."

"She wouldn't have survived," Jonathan said. "You saw what it was like. I just don't think she could manage it on her own."

"Maybe she had help."

Both Jonathan and I glanced at Nathan. He shrugged and looked away.

"It's possible."

"But unlikely," Jonathan said. "Does she seem like someone who would work with werewolves? We know a wolf is involved if the claw marks on the bodies are any indication. We can't start assuming that one possible murderer is responsible for every murder that takes place."

I felt that one was aimed at me. "Then where do we stand?"

"The same place as before." Jonathan sat back in his chair. He was staring at the top of his desk and I wondered if there was something on one of his monitors that was interesting. "We keep looking, but now we watch for suspicious Purebloods walking around with poison."

I shuddered. "How long was I out?" I asked. I was feeling much stronger, but it felt good to sit down for a few minutes. I still had to get home at some point and wanted to leave soon. It was hard to find the willpower to rise.

"Not long," Jonathan said. "Adrian brought you straight to us and we took you upstairs. I had just enough time to question the woman before you came down."

That was a relief, though it didn't make much sense. "But the silver should have knocked me out longer. It never wears off that fast." Especially since it had been injected straight into my bloodstream like that. I should have been out for hours.

"The silver wasn't pure," Jonathan said. "There was just enough to keep you down for a few minutes, an hour at most. Whatever was in the injection that knocked you out was the most potent."

"She wouldn't need you paralyzed that long to finish you off," Nathan said.

He was right. If the plan was to incapacitate me long enough to cut my throat, they could use the slightest traces of silver in the mixture and it would do the job.

Of course, that did beg the question as to where she had managed to obtain the silver. It wasn't like it was easy to get hold of these days. The silver I used came from a demon, and I was pretty sure she would have nothing to do with something like that.

I stood, feeling uncomfortable sitting in the presence of the two men. I wasn't sure why. Maybe it was because both the werewolves had seen me vulnerable. Maybe it was because I was angry at myself for getting jumped like that.

Whatever it was, I just wanted out of there.

"Where's my coat?" I asked, checking myself over. I still had on my shoulder holster and belt. All my weapons had been left untouched, which was a good thing. I wouldn't have put it past Adrian to take something with him when he left.

Jonathan glanced at Nathan, who turned and walked out of the room. I started to follow.

"Wait," Jonathan said, standing.

I turned to face him. Nathan closed the door behind him, leaving the two of us alone.

"Are you sure you're okay?"

"How many times are you going to ask me that?" I responded.

"It's just . . ." He struggled for something to say. "I was worried there was more to it than what we were told."

"I'm fine." I was getting aggravated at having to repeat myself. If one more person asked me if I was okay tonight, I was going to gut them. "She got lucky. I was feeding and my victim was a bit too into it. He distracted me."

"That isn't like you."

I clenched my teeth to keep from yelling at him. "It won't happen again," I said, my voice low and controlled. "I made a mistake."

"Okay." Jonathan still looked worried, and it bothered me to no end. "I just don't want anything to happen to you because of this."

"It's my choice," I said. "I'm doing this because it needs to be done. This is what I do. I'll live."

"I hope so."

Nathan returned before I could say anything and he handed me my coat. I checked the pockets to make sure my spare clip, as well as my silver packets, was still inside, then slipped it on. It felt comforting to have its weight on my shoulders again.

I didn't say anything as I made for the door.

"Kat," Jonathan said from behind me. I nearly growled as I stopped. I was so ready to get the hell out of there.

"What?" I said.

"How are you going to get home?"

Fuck! My Honda was sitting in the parking garage on

High Street. Unless I was willing to go for a nice long walk, I was going to have to bum a ride.

"I'll drive you," he said. I noted a hint of satisfaction in his voice.

We went to the Den's garage and got into Jonathan's black car. I sat as close to the door as I could, as if sitting close to him was going to somehow infect me with his taint. It was stupid, I know, but I just wasn't looking for company right then.

He tried more than once to start up a conversation, but I ignored him. I had too much on my mind. I just wanted to get out on the open road and get home before the sun decided to make an appearance. The night was quickly fading and I still felt like I had so much more to do.

He dropped me off right beside my motorcycle. I thanked him grudgingly and got out to inspect it. I didn't trust it not to have been messed with. Not here.

As far as I could tell, everything was fine. I got on and started it up. The vibrations of the motorcycle beneath me felt comforting. It was something familiar, something I longed for.

It felt like home.

Jonathan sat in his car watching. I drove off without giving him another look, though I did make sure he wasn't following me as I started down the road.

The night had grown cold since I had last been out. That didn't mean there were any less people on High Street. It was just as crowded as every other night. I doubted there was much of anything that would keep the usual patrons away.

I put the vileness behind me and tried to outrun my own thoughts. It didn't work. I couldn't stop thinking about my close call, about what Davin had said. Could this really be happening? My life hadn't exactly been easy before, but it was starting to get a little out of hand.

Without realizing what I was doing, I turned away from

home. I didn't want to face reality. If I did, then I would have to face my own mortality. Never before had I come so close to death. Even trapped in a vampire Count's cell had been better than lying there, staring up at the woman as she prepared to cut my throat.

If Adrian hadn't shown up, I'd be dead right now.

That thought only angered me more. Adrian had been following me, I was sure of it. As much as he might want to call it a coincidence, I knew better. He wanted something out of me. And I was pretty sure I knew what that something was.

The air started misting, which only added to my shitty night. It speckled my coat, moistened my cheeks, as I raced down the highway, weaving in and out of traffic. I was going too fast, driving too recklessly, but honestly, I didn't care. So what if I crashed? I'd live.

I took a hard turn and nearly lost control. Even with my reflexes, I was going too fast for the wet conditions. I righted myself at the last instant and kept going, trying to outrun my life.

It was stupid. I could never run from what I was. I might not have chosen what I'd become, but I did choose the life I'd been living. It was the only thing that kept me sane.

Or did it? I was really starting to wonder.

I didn't see the sign as I turned down the well-paved road, but I knew where I was going. I felt drawn to the place. The closer I got, the more relaxed I felt.

The lights ahead sparkled in the light rain. They called to me, told me of comforts waiting, of a friendly face willing to accept me for what I was.

15

DeeDee's was packed despite the late hour. I parked in the same place I had the last time I was there. It seemed to be the only place left open. No one really paid any attention to me, though I did notice a few heads turned my way.

I made my way slowly toward the front door, trying not to notice the blank stares. The first hint of doubt crept into my mind. I should have gone home, should have spent time with Ethan. I was a stranger here. I didn't belong.

And that was exactly why this was the perfect place. I needed to get away, to forget about Adrian, the murders, the crazy woman, everything, for a few hours. Where else could I get that sort of peace of mind?

Still, I felt like a fool for coming. Could I really relax after what I'd been through?

I started to turn around, but a large, hairy hand reached past me and opened the door for me.

"After you," Levi said, grinning.

I stiffened for an instant but relaxed. Just seeing a friendly face made me realize my doubts were groundless. This was where I needed to be.

I led the way into the diner. The smell of deep-fried

grease met me the moment I was through the door. It was somewhat comforting. It felt like the way things should be, the way the world was before vampires and werewolves made themselves known.

"Saved you a seat," Levi said, taking the lead.

I hesitated but ended up following him over to a corner booth where Ronnie was sitting. He had a plate of loaded cheese fries in front of him, but as far as I could tell, he hadn't touched them. He stared at them blankly, like he had fallen asleep with his eyes open.

"How did you know I was coming?" I asked, taking a seat across from Ronnie. He didn't seem to notice our arrival.

"It came down the pipeline that a girl on a motorcycle had entered town," Levi said, sitting down beside his friend. "I figured there weren't too many leather-coat–wearing, motorcycle-riding young women who would travel through here, so I decided to wait outside to see if you'd show."

I squirmed a little at that. Levi seemed far too comfortable with me. Even if he thought I was a Pureblood, he still should be hesitant about accepting me. I didn't exactly have the nice and friendly look down.

I flipped my coat closed over my sword. The last time I was here I hadn't been dressed in my Lady Death guise. Full-on kill mode didn't mesh well with the dressed-down, easy atmosphere of Delai.

"So what you here for this time?" Levi asked, stretching his arm across the back of the booth. Ronnie gave the slightest flinch as Levi's arm passed behind his head, but he quickly settled back to his usual blankness.

I shrugged, eyeing the fries. They looked damn good. "I just needed to get away for a little bit. This seemed as good a place as any."

"Help yourself." Levi gestured toward the fries. "It's what they're there for."

I grabbed a few fries and slowly chewed. Just the act of eating eased my mind. I felt more at ease than I had in a long time. I sort of sank into my booth and a low groan of pleasure escaped my lips at the greasy, fattening taste of the fries.

"Good, aren't they?" Levi said, smiling.

I smiled at him but caught myself. The smile slid from my face and I sat back up, dropping the last fry in my hand back onto the plate.

What the hell was I doing? I should have gone out looking for the murderer, and yet I came here. There was too much to do back home to be sitting around, eating fries, and chatting with strangers.

But every time I considered getting up and leaving, my mind would ease and all my troubles would slip away. It was as if the air of the diner calmed me, made me see that I didn't have to go rushing back to my troubled life so fast.

Unfortunately, the good feeling never lasted. I couldn't get comfortable with people dying needlessly.

Levi must have seen the thought pass over my face because he leaned forward, hairy arms crossed on the table. "What's bothering you?" he asked. "You look as though the entire world is resting on your shoulders. You should stop and let someone else hold the load for a while."

"It's nothing," I said. I looked out the window, feeling oddly ashamed. What was wrong with me? "It's been a rough week."

"Care to talk about it?"

"No."

I could feel his eyes on me. I refused to look at him, knowing if I saw him staring at me, I might break down and tell him everything. I really didn't want to scare him off now. He seemed to be the only person in this place who was willing to get to know me.

Suddenly, he burst into laughter and I couldn't help but look at him. He was smiling ear to ear.

"What's so funny?" I asked. I felt my old rage start to climb. I didn't like being laughed at.

"Nothing," he said, waving his big hands in front of his face. "It's just that you are trying to be so tough, so impenetrable, you're missing out on what makes life fun."

Ronnie glanced up. He looked at me, and for an instant I thought I saw something deep down behind his eyes. I wasn't sure what it was, but I swear it was there. He looked back down and continued his silent vigil.

"I manage just fine," I said. "Maybe coming here was a bad idea." I started to rise.

"Hogwash," Levi said. "It was the best idea you've ever had."

I hesitated, stuck between standing and sitting. I knew I should just get up and leave and never come back. I had too much to do.

Once again the need to leave vanished, replaced by a contentment that fell over me like a comforting arm. How could something feel so wrong yet feel so right at the same time. Was it something in the air? The food? Or was it just Levi and his jovial nature that drew me?

"Come on," Levi said, standing. "Let's go for a walk."

I stood the rest of the way. I checked to make sure my weapons weren't showing. I didn't want to scare anyone.

"I should probably just go," I said, feeling foolish. I'd never felt so out of place before.

"We should really walk," Levi said. Something in his voice told me he would brook no argument.

Normally, I would have argued. The old me might have. Something about Delai was changing me, and I had no idea what it was. Instead of arguing and making a scene, I found myself following after Levi as he led the way out of the diner.

Eyes followed us as we left. Levi waved to a few men in the parking lot. They watched us go without showing any sort of reaction. I think one of them might have blinked, I wasn't sure.

The entire town seemed sedate outside of DeeDee's. It made my worries seem like so much useless garbage. It was like a breath of fresh air after years locked in a too-small room without windows or doors.

"You feel like you don't belong," Levi said once we were out of the parking lot. We were walking down a well-cared-for sidewalk. There were no cracks, no weeds growing up between the slabs of concrete.

"That isn't so strange," I said. Streetlights lit our path. We were walking away from the small commercial district and heading toward the far end of the town to a place I hadn't seen yet.

"But you feel out of place even more than usual," he said. "You don't feel like you could ever belong in a place like this, around people like these." He made a circle with his arms, encompassing the entire town.

I gave him a sideways glance. "Don't try to read me."

"It isn't hard. I can tell by the way you hold yourself you aren't comfortable here. You look like the rabbit in the wolves' den. There is nothing to be scared of here."

"I don't like being watched."

"It's more than that," Levi said, seemingly oblivious to the implied warning. "There's more to you than you like to show. You are deeper than the tough girl you let everyone see. Put away your weapons and that god-awful coat, and maybe more people would see it."

I remained silent. I hadn't come here for a psych evaluation. All I had to do was turn around, get back on my Honda, and go home where I belonged. I never had to see this place again.

But I kept walking. Neither of us spoke for a few minutes. I think he was letting his last comment sink in. I tried not to think about it.

The streetlights gave way to porch lights and soon we

were walking in near dark. I could see the silhouettes of people through curtains, going about their lives as if nothing could bother them. I wanted to stop and just watch, to see what a normal person did with his or her time. It was a struggle not to.

"You could be among friends here," Levi said, eventually. "We aren't so different from you."

"You'd be surprised."

"No," he said, "I wouldn't."

I glanced at him and I could see the seriousness in his face. "You don't know anything about me."

"I know you live a violent life," he said. "That's clear by your constant need to keep yourself armed."

I pulled my coat a little tighter around me. "Anyone who wants to live at night should," I said a little too defensively.

"Look around," he said, stopping. We were in a small neighborhood. A couple of kids were methodically throwing hoops in the light coming from above the garage door. Across the street, an old woman walked her dog, never once glancing around in search of something that might leap out at her.

I looked at the sky. It was far too late for anyone to be out, at least anyone who wanted to live. The sun was just an hour away, if not less. It seemed odd that these people weren't tucked away in the comforts of their own homes.

I opened my mouth to say something, but I had no idea what I *could* say. I didn't know how to handle this after a life of watching every shadow, knowing it most likely contained something with fangs.

"It's peaceful here," he said. "We don't fear the night like so many others."

"How?" I asked, looking around. "I don't understand."

"We have our ways." He smiled and something glimmered behind his eyes. Suddenly, I wasn't so sure Levi was just another Pureblood. There was more to him, something hidden behind that smile and those kind words.

"I wouldn't fit in," I said, turning away from him. I started back the way we had come. "No matter how much you might think I could, I would never be able to live a normal life here."

"Your kind always says that."

I stopped walking and turned to face him. Levi was smiling at me.

"What did you say?" I said. My throat constricted. If he knew what I was, then he knew I brought danger. I took a step toward him, my hand touching the hilt of my sword.

"Oh, don't do that," he said, rolling his eyes. "I'm not saying I want you out of here. Don't you remember what I said? You could find a place here. You just have to let me help you."

"I don't need your help."

"Are you so sure of that?" he countered. "I see someone who is afraid to admit when she's scared, someone who is running from something. No one ever comes here if they aren't looking for a way out."

I stared at him, wanting to hate him, but I couldn't. I turned away and started walking back toward DeeDee's. Levi hurried to catch up. He put a hand on my arm and I jerked away, spinning on him.

"Don't fucking touch me!"

He raised both hands in surrender. "Okay, okay," he said. "I just want to let you know I understand. Your life sucks. You came here for a reason. You shouldn't leave until you are sure there is nothing here for you."

"There's not."

"And how do you know?" he said. "You've haven't stuck around long enough to find out."

"I have too much to do," I said, walking again. Levi walked beside me but didn't try to touch me this time. "I can't turn my back on that."

"I don't expect you to," he said. "But don't you think you deserve a break sometimes?"

I didn't say anything. I could use a break, sure. Everyone could. But did I really have time to relax when people were dying back home? I didn't think so.

"Stay the day," he said, stopping me again.

I stared at him. Was this guy nuts?

"I mean it," he said. "It's going to be morning soon. I'm pretty sure you don't want to be out when the sun rises."

"I'll be fine," I said. "I'll drive fast."

"But why do that when you could stay here, see what our little town has to offer?"

I looked around. Every house was lit up. "Doesn't anyone sleep around here?"

Levi laughed. "Only when they have to." He sounded full of pride, like it was of his doing. I wasn't so sure it wasn't. "The night had been taken away from so many people for so long, they no longer wish to waste it. Here, they don't have to."

I frowned. I still didn't like it.

"Stay, please," Levi said. "What can it hurt?"

There were quite a lot of people here I could end up hurting if I lost it at the wrong time.

"I can't."

"You can," he said. "You don't have to save the world tonight. It'll still be here tomorrow."

I wanted to keep arguing with him, but something deep down stopped me. Did I really want to turn my back on this? Was this a chance for me to step away for a little bit, to clear my head? If I went home, all I would do is go to my room and wait out the day. Was I ready to deal with all the thoughts that would arise from loneliness?

"Fine," I said. My stomach did a strange little flip when I said it. "I'll stay."

"Good," Levi said, clapping his hands together. He

acted like I had just made his day. "I have a spare room made up especially for you."

That made me hesitate, but I didn't back down. I'd made my decision, no matter how misguided it was. I'd have to live with it.

We walked back to DeeDee's, our pace hurried. I still wasn't sure this was the right thing to do, but I was committed now.

Levi ran inside the diner to let Ronnie know what was up. He came back out a moment later and told me to follow him. He jumped into a red pickup truck and waited as I started my Honda and fell in behind him.

It wasn't raining now. I wasn't so sure when it had stopped.

Levi honked as he pulled out onto the road, waving into the rearview mirror. I waved back, surprising myself.

Something was going on here.

And right then, I really didn't care what it was.

16

Levi lived in a quiet little neighborhood in the middle of town. Trees surrounded many of the yards, obscuring the lights from downtown that would otherwise ruin the blissful atmosphere.

He pulled into his driveway and parked in front of the garage. The house wasn't large, but it wasn't small either. It looked inviting, nearly as much as Levi was himself. The curtains fluttered closed and a face I didn't catch vanished within the house.

I pulled in behind him and shut off my motorcycle. Levi was waiting by the front door for me.

"Someone's inside," I said as I stepped up next to him.

"It's probably Eilene, my wife. She often waits for me by the window."

He unlocked the front door and held it open for me. I hesitated, unsure this was really what I wanted, but I went in anyway. I wouldn't make it home before the sun was up. I really had no choice unless I wanted to look for some hole in the ground I could hide in.

"Eilene," Levi called. "Sienna. We have a guest."

A timid face peered around the corner as Levi led me into the living room. The girl was probably eighteen or nineteen, but the innocence in her eyes made her look younger. Her hair was blond, which was a stark contrast to Levi's darker brown. Her eyes were such a bright green they nearly lit up the room.

"Sienna," Levi said. The girl came the rest of the way into the room. She kept her eyes down, only glancing up every few moments. "Where's your mother?"

"Upstairs," Sienna said. "She isn't feeling well."

Levi sighed. "Let her know we have a guest," he said. Sienna nodded and scurried out of the room.

"Daughter?" I said, skeptical. The girl looked nothing like her father.

"Adopted," Levi said. "She can be shy at times but once she gets to know you, she'll warm up."

He led me to the couch and gestured for me to sit. I glanced toward the window. The sky was getting lighter by the minute. I had maybe thirty minutes before the sun would rise.

"It'll be okay," he said. "I just want you to meet the family before I show you to your room. Eilene will be thrilled to meet you."

A moment later, Sienna came back into the room. She sort of slunk against the wall, out of the way, as if she was afraid to come any closer. She glanced at me through her lashes, trying to hide the movement with her hair. I pretended not to notice.

I pulled my coat tight around me, hiding my weapons. I probably looked dangerous dressed as I was. Showing off my sword or gun would probably make Levi regret ever bringing me. His daughter looked scared enough as it was. I didn't need to be making it worse.

The sound of footsteps approached and Levi hurried out of the room. He returned a moment later with a frail-looking woman on his arm. She was painfully thin, almost to the point of emaciation. Her hair was pulled back into a ponytail, exposing taut features. She reminded me of Davin in a not-so-pleasant way.

"Eilene," Levi said, guiding the woman to a chair across from me. She sat with his help, staring at me all the while. She looked terrified. "This is . . ." He glanced back at me. I had never given him my name. "A friend."

"Hello," Eilene said. Her voice sounded as pained as she looked. It hurt just to hear it.

"Eilene's been sick of late," Levi said. "She normally is a lot peppier and would have fixed you some tea or coffee."

"It's okay," I said. "I'm not thirsty."

"Are you going to take him away from us?" Sienna asked from her spot against the wall.

Levi's head jerked up and a frown marred his usually pleasant features. "Sienna," he warned.

She looked down at her feet and didn't say anything more.

"No," I said, feeling oddly guilty. Did these two women think I was trying to replace them? I didn't plan on staying here ever again. "I'm just visiting. I can always go somewhere else if would be easier for everyone. I don't want to cause any trouble."

"I'll have none of that," Levi said. "She just doesn't understand."

Sienna flinched as Levi gave her a look. She seemed to cower in on herself. If she could have pressed herself into the wall, I think she would have done it.

"It's a pleasure to meet you," Eilene said, bringing everyone's attention to her. "It's been a while since we had anyone new in town."

"It's an interesting place." It was the only thing I could think of to say.

Eilene smiled, but it didn't look natural. "Levi mentioned you before. He wasn't sure if you'd come back."

"I didn't think I would."

"You shouldn't have."

My brow furrowed at that. Levi cleared his throat like he was going to say something, but Eilene made a sound I took for a laugh.

"I'm just saying that it's hard to leave," she said. "Delai is one of those places, you know?"

I did. The place strangely felt like home. Even though I was a stranger in his house, Levi and his family somehow made me feel comfortable despite my trepidation. Maybe there *was* something in the air.

Eilene turned her head toward Levi. Something sparked in her eye, but I couldn't quite make out what it was. "Where's Ron?"

"DeeDee's," Levi said. "Garrett will drop him off later."

"Ronnie your son?" I asked.

"Just a friend," Levi said. "His family died and he had nowhere else to go, so we take care of him. He won't bother you."

The way he said the last made me squirm in my seat. There was something in his tone that made it sound like Ronnie *could* be dangerous. I'd only seen the other man twice now and as far as I could tell, he did nothing but sit and stare at nothing, much like most everyone else in Delai.

Aside from Levi and his family. They seemed different somehow.

"Shall I show you to your room?" Levi said, holding out an arm to me.

I stared at the proffered arm and suddenly wanted out of there. The dark hair covering it seemed somehow obscene, as if I was seeing more of him than was decent. I almost told him to forget it, that I would find somewhere else to stay, when Eilene spoke up.

"Let me."

Levi looked at his wife. She stared at him defiantly, as

if she was daring him to object. They locked eyes and something passed between them.

Finally, he nodded. "Take her to her room and then come back up," he said. "I have some things I wish to discuss."

Eilene rose. She took her time as if every movement hurt. "Come on," she said. "You too, Sienna."

The younger girl look surprised. Her eyes darted to Levi before going to me. They were round, full of fear.

"I don't bite," I said. Oh, if she knew the truth.

Levi laughed. "It's okay," he said. "I'll get cleaned up."

Eilene led me through the house toward a set of stairs leading down into the depths of the house. They led into a sitting room not much unlike my own. The fireplace was cold, but it looked inviting nonetheless. I could see myself spending quite a lot of time here.

A door off the sitting room opened up into a window-less room. Eilene flipped on the light. The room was pretty spacious. There was a bed big enough for three, as well as a pair of reclining chairs. A writing desk sat against the wall, and a swivel-back chair was pushed into the leg space.

And it looked lived in.

"Whose room is this?" I asked, stepping inside. There were no posters on the wall, nothing on the desk that would indicate someone held claim to the room, yet I was certain I wasn't the first to spend time here.

"Yours," Eilene said. She gestured toward a door just inside the room. "The closet is empty if you wish to hang up anything. We have some spare clothing you can use if you wish to change."

I looked down at myself. The leather might not be the most comfortable clothing to sleep in, but I wasn't about to change into something else. Not here anyway.

I started to thank her when I noticed the fear in her eyes. Eilene stared at me as if she expected me to attack her at any moment. Either that or take Levi from her. I wasn't sure which, and quite frankly, I wasn't so sure it mattered.

My guilty feeling returned. I didn't want to come in here and screw up this woman's life. She looked as though she had suffered enough without me coming along and ruining her relationship with her husband.

"Look," I said, turning to face the two women. They stood huddled close together as if for protection. "I'm just staying the day. I'm not going to stick around."

Eilene closed her eyes and sighed. "A vampire," she said, opening them. She looked sad.

I didn't want to answer, but I didn't want to lie either. "Yeah."

"I thought so. Why else would you need this room?"

"I won't hurt you or your family."

She glanced at Sienna. The younger girl looked so scared I was sure she would bolt and never stop running if I as much as bared my fangs. I felt bad for her.

They just stood there, looking at me, then at each other, like there was something they expected to happen. I didn't know what to do, so I walked the rest of the way into the room and sat on the bed. I'd take my coat off when they left.

"It can be nice here," Eilene said after a moment. "Levi tries to provide for everyone in town."

"That's nice of him."

Eilene sighed. "If you say so."

I cocked my head to the side at that. "What's wrong?"

"I . . ."

"Mom, please." Sienna looked pleadingly at her mother.

"She should know," Eilene said. The fear in her eyes ramped up to eleven.

"Know what?" I said. My skin was starting to crawl. I wasn't sure if it was the coming sun that did it, the way the two were acting, or if it was something more.

Eilene started to speak, but the front door opened upstairs. She snapped her mouth closed, her eyes going wide. "It's nothing," she said. "I'm just feeling ill is all. I wouldn't want you to worry you might catch what I have."

I didn't quite buy it but didn't say anything.

"I should go see if that was Ron," Eilene said, spinning around and hurrying away.

Sienna hesitated in the doorway. She refused to look at me for the longest time. I was about to ask her if there was something she wanted, when she finally looked at me.

"I think I might like you," she said.

Before I could respond, she hurried away.

I sat on the bed, dumbfounded. Something wasn't right here. As much as Levi might appear to have everything in control outside his home, it was obvious he had some serious issues to deal with within his household.

But that was none of my business. It was his wife, his life. If they were unhappy together, then they could deal with it. I wouldn't get involved.

I rose and closed the bedroom door. I took off my coat, as well as my shoulder holster and belt. I dumped the bundle on the desk, not wanting to hang them in the closet where I couldn't get to them quickly.

I went to the bed and laid back, hands behind my head. It would be hard to relax and let the day pass. At home, I could take a bath, go through my things, and find something to do. As a vampire, I didn't need sleep, but I did need to rest my body. Even a vampire could feel weary.

But there was a difference between rest and boredom. I wished Eilene or Sienna would come down to visit. I was curious as to what the older woman had really been about to say. I didn't buy the bit about her sickness. Something about it didn't ring true.

Of course, it really wasn't my business. Once the moon rose again, I was going to leave, get back to my mess of a life, and put all of this behind me. It was a mistake to ever have come. I had too damn much to do.

A little while later, a knock came at the door and Levi's voice came from the other side. "You there?"

"Where else would I be?" I said.

"Can I come in?"

"Suit yourself."

He opened the door and slipped inside. He looked indecisive for a moment before choosing one of the chairs closest to the door. He sat down, though he stayed sitting at the edge like he didn't plan on staying long.

"Are you leaving when night falls?"

"Yeah," I said. "Don't you ever sleep?"

He smiled. "Not if I can help it," he said. "Why are you leaving?"

I gave him a strange look. "Because I don't belong here."

He rolled his eyes. "We went over this."

"I can't abandon my life," I said. "It's nice of you to let me stay for the day, but I'm not planning on making it a habit."

Levi lowered his head. "Something is holding you back."

I scowled at him. "Yeah, my life."

"It's more than that. Something is keeping you from getting away from all the pain and death. Something is refusing to let go."

"I'll deal with it on my own," I said. I really wanted to change the subject. "Why is your family so scared?"

Levi looked up at that. "What do you mean?"

"They seem scared of something."

He sighed. "They don't understand why I do what I do. I try to help people. They're afraid it might get me killed."

"It might."

He shrugged. "Like your life is your own, so is mine. I'll manage it the best way I see fit. I can't be afraid." He stood and crossed the room to stand in front of me. "I want you to come back."

"I'll think about it."

"Come back and stay."

"Unlikely."

He smiled. "It might seem that way now, but once you overcome whatever is holding you back, you might see things differently."

"Doubt it."

He laughed. "Always so negative. I like that. It gives me something to work on." He reached out and touched me on the arm. "You'll find exactly what you are looking for. You'll deal with it and then you'll be free to return, your burden lifted."

A jolt of electricity ran up my arm from where he touched me. I jerked back, my hand going to my waist where my sword would have been if I hadn't taken it off.

"What did you do to me?"

Levi backed away. "I didn't do anything," he said. "It must have been static electricity. It happens a lot around here. I'll leave you to rest." He turned and walked out of the room, closing the door behind him.

I sat on the bed, rubbing my arm. I'd felt something, but what? I couldn't say, but it *had* been there, and it sure as hell hadn't been a static charge.

I stood and grabbed my weapons from the desk and tossed them on the bed before lying back down. I felt better having them close beside me.

No one came down for the rest of the day. As soon as my body told me the sun had gone down, I rose and made straight for the door. No one was upstairs when I came out. They must have still been in bed. That was fine by me.

I left the house without saying good-bye. I never wanted to see any of them again.

I mounted my Honda and tore out of the driveway as if I couldn't run away fast enough. I swept past the houses, through the downtown, ignoring the calm peace that seemed to permeate the place.

The farther I got from Delai, the more I realized the peace was a lie. Something was going on there, something that didn't quite fit with the way I saw the world. I didn't know if it was a good thing or a bad thing.

I only knew I didn't plan on coming back to find out.

17

I had every intention of going straight home, but I found myself riding back roads, avoiding the main part of Columbus. The night was clear, a bit on the chilly side, and that chill helped clear my head of all the swirling thoughts threatening to invade. I didn't want to have to think about Delai or Levi or anything else for that matter.

So much for time away. Going to the town hadn't helped. It only made me even more confused.

A howl lit up the night, so loud I could hear it over the wind whipping around me and the muffled sound of my Honda. Ethan had worked on the bike, making it quieter than a normal motorcycle, but it was still loud when you were sitting on top of it.

I coasted to a stop and listened, almost certain the sound had been a figment of my imagination. It had sounded like a werewolf's howl, not a dog's or a regular wolf. Real wolves didn't run around Columbus much, if at all.

A minute passed, then two.

Then the screaming started.

I leaped off my bike and pulled it just off the road where someone wouldn't hit it. As soon as I was satisfied it was far enough out of the way that no one would see it, I started toward the sounds of screaming and howling.

The road I'd been traveling was mostly deserted. It was one of those run-down places where rogue wolves tended to haunt. Very few Purebloods could survive out in a place like this. My best guess was that the fight ahead was some sort of territorial dispute.

It was just what I needed to bring back my edge.

While there weren't a ton of trees, they were still heavy enough I couldn't make out where the screams were coming from. I could see a house back behind me through the branches, but there were no lights shining inside. By the time I could see another house, the one behind me was hidden by the brush.

I drew my gun and sword, and my fangs started to extend. The blood oozing from my gums energized me. I was ready for this. It had been a while since I'd been in a real fight.

Another scream tore through the night. I couldn't tell how many wolves I was dealing with. It could be anywhere from a couple to a half dozen.

I patted my pocket, making sure the silver packets were still inside. I didn't really want to use them outdoors because a freak breeze could blow the dust back into my face. Small amounts would sting for hours. More than that, I would be helpless and paralyzed. I never wanted to feel that way again.

Another howl started but was cut off suddenly from somewhere up ahead. A roar followed in the brief silence.

My step faltered. I wasn't so sure I was ready for this. The fight sounded as though it was moving away, though the screams and howls kept coming. This wasn't a fight where the wolves would all walk away. There were going to be casualties.

I regained my rapid pace after only a slight hesitation. I couldn't be worried about a few rogue wolves. Even if a vampire Count had decided to kill off some rogues hiding out, I could take them. I almost hoped there would be more to it than that.

Something crashed in the trees ahead and I trained my gun on the sound. I waited for it to come for me, but whatever had snapped the branches wasn't moving anymore. I wondered if it was my howler.

I approached warily, ready to fire. I didn't have all the information here. I could be walking in on just about anything, including a torture house, something I never wanted to see again. Once long ago was enough for me to never want to repeat the experience.

An arm came into view, covered in blood. The fingers were twitching and I leveled my gun where his head would be. It was hidden by the base of a tree. I stepped around, ready to fire, but lowered my aim as soon as I saw what was lying there.

The wolf had started to shift but hadn't made it very far. His plaid shirt was torn in the front, as were his throat and chest. It looked like his heart had been ripped from his body, a sure way to kill both a vampire and a werewolf.

The fingers stopped twitching. Dead eyes fell on me, the life already drained from them. It had taken him a few moments to die, but die he did.

I stepped around the dead wolf and crouched down to look through the few remaining trees, into a clearing where a double-wide trailer sat. There was no sign of the killer or the dead wolf's heart. The house was the only thing visible. The windows were still intact and lights were on inside. The back door was hanging open but showed little of what might be hiding inside.

There was blood in the yard. As my eyes scanned the grounds a second time, I noticed another body pressed up against the base of the house. I'd overlooked it before because there wasn't much left of it. His head and arms lay scattered around the tattered torso like so much debris.

My throat constricted as I considered that. I glanced back at the wolf behind me, really looking him over. His chest hadn't been cut open with a knife. I could see scrapes on his face and arms that could only be made by were-wolf claws.

And his friend out there? I'd have to get a closer look, but it would be a shock if his head hadn't been severed by a blade.

This was exactly what I had been looking for.

A surge of excitement shot through me. I scanned the rest of the yard, but there was nothing within sight that would give the attackers away. I could still hear scuffling somewhere outside. It didn't sound like it was coming from within the house. It sounded too far away for that.

Someone screamed and I stepped out of the trees, making for the side of the house in a low crouch. I could see the driveway from where I was. A pickup truck was parked just off it. The doors were closed and weeds had started to grow up around the wheels. It had been there for a while.

I pressed my back up against the side of the trailer, straightening. I peeked through a window and, seeing nothing, moved on. The fighting was definitely going on outside. I just had to find the combatants and put an end to it.

I moved silently and quickly, keeping myself low. My eyes never stopped moving. If something so much as twitched, I was going to put a bullet into it. I wasn't positive we were dealing with our murderers, but it was a good bet I'd stumbled onto them. I was taking no chances.

I glanced around the corner of the house and when I saw no one, I slid around the side to work my way to the front.

An agonized wail was silenced almost as soon as it started. It sounded close, closer than I expected, and I froze. Something growled from about a dozen feet away, though I couldn't see it from where I stood.

The sound of tearing flesh came soon after.

I crept the rest of the way around the side of the house, gun trained ahead. As I reached the corner, two men came into view. The first was clearly dead, his head barely hanging on by a thread. Blood was splattered across the grass, turning it black in the dim light coming from within the house.

On top of him was something I never expected to see.

The beast's head was down, face buried in the man's sternum. Long claws came from his nearly human fingers. Shaggy hair covered a large portion of his nude body, though not all of it. His legs looked normal, his arms a little hairier than they should be, but they looked human.

My aim went straight for the beast on top of the dead wolf. My hand was trembling and I had to take a few deep breaths to steady it.

I'd seen this before. It was becoming an all too common sight these days.

Before I could pull the trigger, there was a barking command from somewhere out of sight. The creature's head snapped up at the sound and his eyes immediately fell on me.

"Shit," I said as the thing leaped for me. His face was a strange mix of wolf and human, one eye blue, the other a feral yellow. He opened a partly shifted maw to expose teeth that were all too human.

He came at me fast and hard, almost too fast to believe. I pulled the trigger and the thing fell face-first into the grass as my bullet took him in the chest. He shuddered, whimpering, and I quickly made my way to where he lay. I raised my sword and without giving it a second thought, severed his head from his body.

My mouth was dry as I wiped the blood off onto the grass. The sound of fighting had stopped, though I wasn't sure if it was because everything else was dead or if the sound of my gun silenced them.

I raised my gun and started scanning my surroundings. The road was to my left, but no one was over there. To my right and straight ahead were more trees, obscuring my view. It was likely anyone watching me would be there.

"Come on out," I said. My hands had stopped shaking, though I couldn't say the same about my insides. No wonder House Telia had been destroyed. While these part-vampire, part-werewolf creatures were still susceptible to silver, they were pretty much impervious to pain. Telia and the rogues they had been killing weren't like me. They didn't use silver.

A rustle in the brush brought my gun around. I tried to spot some hint of movement, but whatever had moved had fallen still. I kept my back to the house, not wanting to give anything the chance to sneak up on me.

I waited, trying to keep my mind focused on the task at hand, but it was hard. These creatures didn't hunt in packs. Either the one I had killed had been set loose on these poor rogues or someone was controlling the beast somehow. Whatever vampire was in charge was in serious need of taking down. Controlling werewolves was bad enough. Something like this was unheard of.

Savage. That was the word that came to mind. Any vampire who could control such savage beasts was extremely dangerous. Most vampires wouldn't even consider the mixing of blood because of the consequences. Not only would the other Houses look down on you, but the result was impossible to control.

Or so I thought.

More rustling from within the trees brought my head around. I couldn't worry about the who or why right then. I needed to stay alive first; then I could worry about tracking down whoever started this mess.

I took a deep breath and let it out slowly, centering myself. The world came into sharp focus. Every leaf sprang to new life. My vampire-enhanced vision showed me every root, every twitch of a branch from the breeze.

A shadow shifted next to a tree and I fired.

A startled yelp came next, followed by the sound of something heavy hitting the ground.

"Come on out!" I shouted. "Or I'll kill you one by one." I had no idea how many were out there. If they were all mindless beasts like the first, then they probably didn't understand me anyway.

A growl and a sort of bark that sounded almost like speech answered me. Five figures stepped out of the trees. Before I could get a good look at any of them, there was another bark and two of the things charged me.

I turned my gun on the first and fired. It took the wolf-thing in the chest. He went down hard, writhing as the silver coursed through his blood. I swung my gun around to fire on the next, but he had moved too damn fast. He was on me before I could take aim.

Claws raked at my face and I just managed to jerk back in time. I rolled away as another bark sent two other mixed-blood beasts after me. The last was obviously the leader.

I rolled to my feet and fired at the closest beast before he could fall on me. The bullet took him in the stomach and he dropped. Like all the others, it wouldn't be a killing blow, but it would incapacitate him long enough for me to subdue the rest before I went about beheading them all.

I didn't have time to raise my gun on the other two. I was forced to backpedal, and I moved to put the house against my back again. The two creatures attacked me from either side. Neither looked sane, yet they worked together like they knew what they were doing.

What the fuck?

I dropped into a forward roll as the two charged. I swung my sword in an admittedly wild swing. I got lucky and my blade caught one of the beasts in the leg. He cried out and dropped as the silver did its work.

I was just about to finish the roll and swing toward the

other beast, but I was yanked to a stop when he caught hold of my coat and yanked me backward.

Claws tore through my coat like it wasn't even there. They ripped into my back, tore the flesh, and buried themselves into my muscles. I screamed and tried to pull away, but I was trapped. Hot breath blew against my neck as the beast tried to bite me. I jerked away just enough so that its teeth sank into the leather of my coat instead of my neck. The claws in my back dug deeper, dropping me to my knees. Both my hands spasmed as if the creature had hit a nerve, and both my weapons fell harmlessly to the ground.

More blood poured from my gums as my teeth pushed fully through. The pain had brought my monster to the fore and with it, even more strength. I jerked forward and the claws tore out of my back. The pain ripped another scream from me, but I was free.

I spun, reaching down to the hidden sheaths at my waist, and pulled both my knives free. The creature leaped at me, snarling, bloodshot eyes boring into me, with an utter disregard for his own safety.

He hit me hard and we went down together. He vibrated on my chest, saliva dripping from his maw. His eyes rolled into the back of his head, and warm blood spilled out onto my hands and over my torn clothes.

I twisted both knives in his gut as I pushed him away. I didn't want to get too much blood on me, not with the wound in my back. Though it normally took a lot, it still would be all too easy for the blood to mingle, turning me into a mindless creature like him, especially if the wound was as bad as I thought it was.

I pulled my knives from the creature as I stood. I turned to face the last of the beasts, ready to finish the fight and all my troubles at once.

My eyes fell on the face and my entire world fell out from under me. All the pain I had ever felt, all the misery I had suffered for all these years, came crashing into me.

My grip on my weapons eased and they fell harmlessly to the ground. A strange, choking sob came from somewhere, and it took me a moment to realize it had come from my own throat.

"Thomas," I said, his name slipping from my lips like a gasp of pain. My eyes watered. My knees trembled and nearly gave out.

My brother bared his fangs at me, no hint of recognition in his mad gaze. The coarse hair on his face bristled with the movement. He raised a rusty sword in front of him, adopting an aggressive stance.

He snarled, growling like the animal he had become.

And then he charged.

18

I couldn't move at first. I was so shocked at seeing my brother alive, I could hardly think straight, let alone think about my own safety. For an instant, I was frozen to the spot, my entire world spinning at my feet.

And then instinct kicked in.

I dove to the side as Thomas reached me. His sword arched down to where I had been. His intent had been clear. If I hadn't moved, he would have embedded his sword in my skull. Instead, it caught the end of my coat, just barely tearing the thick leather.

"Thomas!" I shouted, coming to my feet. "Stop!"

He spun, snarled at me, and came again.

I waited until the last possible moment before moving. He came at me, his motions surprisingly fluid for someone who was supposed to be a mindless beast, and as I reached out to catch him by the bicep, his sword nicked me in the shoulder. An inch more and he might have cut me.

I yanked on his arm hard, jerking him off balance. I used his momentum to throw him to the ground, hoping to jar the weapon from his hand.

The sudden movement brought agonizing pain as something in my back ripped. I dropped to one knee as Thomas hit the ground. He kept hold of his sword as he went down. He blinked once as if the impact had stunned him, but before I could recover from my own pain, he growled low in his throat and was in motion again.

He rolled to his feet, swinging his blade in a low, wide arc as he came for me. I leaped over the swing and crashed to the ground as my knees buckled upon landing. Tears stung my eyes and my breath was coming in ragged gasps.

I couldn't fight him. Not like this. The pain in my back where the creature had torn into me was a screaming agony unlike anything I had ever felt. He had to have hit more than a nerve. The muscle was damaged, and if he had hit one of my internal organs, the bleeding could end up paralyzing me just as easily as silver. Just because I was a vampire didn't mean I could go on indefinitely with wounds like that.

At least Thomas's sword wasn't silver. It looked a lot like the blade he had used when we hunted together as Purebloods. As far as I knew, it very well might be.

I glanced at my weapons laying a few yards away but doubted I could bring myself to use them even if I got to them. This was Thomas. I couldn't hurt my brother like that, and I sure as hell couldn't kill him. It would be like killing myself.

Thomas came at me again, eyes wild. I avoided his swing, but he anticipated me this time and swung at me with his clawed hand. I managed to twist out of the way just as his claws tore into the leather of my coat and into my flesh. Stabbing pain shot through my arm and blood splattered the ground at our feet.

I spun to face him, grimacing at the pain coursing through my body. He was already swinging again, a blow meant to behead me and end the fight all at once. I ducked under the swing and swept my leg around, catching him in the calves. He crashed to the ground as I regained my feet and staggered back.

I winced at the pain, trying to think through both it and my confusion. Thomas shouldn't be here, especially not with others like him. It was impossible.

But as impossible as it was, he was back on his feet again, moving much faster than I could manage in my wounded state. While he looked as wild and mindless as every other mixed-blood creature I had ever seen, there was something more to him. He wasn't acting like the crazed beast he was supposed to be.

I dodged his attack but lost my footing when I tried to spin to keep him in front of me. I hit the ground hard and instinctively rolled out of the way. Thomas's sword missed me by inches. He snarled in rage and kept coming, swinging at me, keeping me from regaining my feet again.

With every jerk, my wounds seemed to get worse. I was wearing out fast, and I wasn't so sure I wouldn't bleed out if I didn't do something about my current predicament and do it fast.

Thomas howled as he swung at my head, missing me by scant millimeters.

"Thomas," I gasped, pushing away from him. My finger bumped into one of my knives and I grasped it like it was the last thing on earth that could save me. It probably was. "Please," I begged. "It's me, Kat."

He didn't seem to hear. He feigned to the left and I fell for it, jerking to the right. His clawed fingers caught me just under the chin, tearing the flesh. I jerked back fast enough so he didn't tear my jaw clean off.

Pain jolted me. My vision went black for a heart-stopping second and I was sure I was done for. After all these years, fighting and killing vampires and werewolves, I was to be undone by my own brother. It had a sort of poetic feel to it.

I managed to push back, flopping my body backward before he could finish me off. My head hit the ground hard enough to jar some sense back into me. I managed to roll out of the way as Thomas thrust his sword down where my heart would have been. His blade struck the ground and stuck there, nearly all the way to the hilt.

He was strong, but the hard earth was stubborn. He fought with the blade, snarling in such rage he was probably making it harder on himself than he had to.

I used the seconds it afforded me to work my way to my gun. I grabbed the modified Glock and aimed, a mere twitch of the finger away from ending the fight.

I couldn't pull the trigger. My hand tensed and I tried to will myself to alter my aim and at least shoot him in the leg. The silver would incapacitate him and I could figure out what to do from there.

But I couldn't do it. He was my brother. I couldn't cause him any more pain. He had suffered enough.

Thomas yanked his sword free and turned on me. His eyes were still his own, having not been affected by the partial change. I could see the brother I had lost in them. His features might be contorted from the mixed blood, but it was still Thomas. I might not be able to see it through his actions, but he was in there somewhere. He had to be.

I jerked my aim away and fought my way to my feet. My knees tried to buckle, but I managed to stand without falling. My head swam, my hand trembled. I was covered in blood, and most of it was my own.

"Thomas," I said, backing slowly away. He advanced on me, one foot in front of the other, sword held at the ready. He eyed my gun. I think it was the only thing keeping him from coming at me wildly again. "Think," I said. "It's me."

His upper lip raised in a sneer. He growled, tightening his grip on his sword. There was no hint of the man I once knew in his gaze.

He approached, stalking toward me like I had seen him stalk toward a vampire or wolf back when we hunted together. I didn't know if it was muscle memory causing him to act like this or if it was something else. I hoped there was something of the real Thomas in there. If there was, then I had a chance.

Of course, it was the fear that he was still in there somewhere that kept me from shooting him. If he had been acting any other way, had acted like the animal he was supposed to be, then maybe I could have done it. It was my fear of hurting my brother that kept me from ending both our suffering.

My sword was a few feet away and I considered rushing for it. I could try to fend him off while I tried to reach him. If I could just make him understand who I was, I was almost positive he would stop. It had worked with Nathan back at House Tremaine. I'd managed to talk to him, to get him to work through the Madness and leave me be. It would work with Thomas too. It had to.

I started to move toward the sword and Thomas shifted his advance to intercept me. I halted immediately, not wanting to provoke him.

The arm holding the gun fell to my side. I was too weak to hold it up any longer. I doubted I could even use my sword if it came to that. If he were to take me down again, I wasn't so sure I could get back up.

My legs trembled; the world wasn't just swimming now, it was in a full-tilt swing. I could feel the blood running down my back, my shoulder, my neck and chest. My right arm was throbbing, and it was getting harder and harder to keep my fingers curled around the gun. I wasn't even sure where my knife was. I must have dropped it somewhere.

There was only one thing I could think to do to survive this.

I feigned to the left just as Thomas had done to me. As soon as he shifted his weight, I took off to the right. I spun around, nearly fell flat on my face, and bolted for the backyard, putting every last ounce of strength I had left into it.

Thomas howled and I could hear him pound after me.

My left shoulder hit the corner of the house as I went past. I staggered a few steps before regaining my balance.

A pile of wood was stacked against the side of the trailer, chopped and ready for winter. I had just enough time to reach down and yank a long log out from the bottom and kick the stack. The wood tumbled down behind me.

Thomas cried out, an inhuman sound that chilled me straight to the bone. He fell hard but was on his feet just as fast. I glanced over my shoulder and saw he still had his sword in hand. He ran slightly hunched over, like he wanted to drop to all fours.

I pushed myself harder. My motorcycle wasn't too far away. I just needed to get to the trees and use them as a shield against him.

I felt something brush the back of my coat and risked another glance over my shoulder. Thomas was stumbling, lips peeled back in a snarl. He had swung his sword at me and had just barely missed. An inch more and he might have severed my spine.

I ran all the faster, pushing my weary legs well past what they wanted to do. My left knee nearly buckled as I burst into the trees, jumping over the dead wolf corpse. I bounced off a sapling and staggered around a large oak just as Thomas came in behind me. The quiver of his sword where it had struck the tree told me how close I had come to losing my head.

Black dots sprang into my vision as I ran. I was running on pure adrenaline. I had nothing left in the tank, and I wasn't even sure I would survive if I did manage to escape. I was losing a lot of blood.

It was starting to feel like I was running through waist-high water. My legs were screaming and my right arm was hanging useless at my side. I could taste blood in my mouth and I knew it wasn't from my fangs pushing through.

My Honda came into view and I nearly cried out in relief. I started for it, my body rejuvenated at the sight.

Thomas crashed into me just before I reached the edge of the road. We went down hard together. His teeth tore into my already useless shoulder and I screamed.

We rolled on the ground, with him latched on to me like a human-sized leech. Sucking sounds came from where his teeth had sunk into my flesh.

"No," I said through clenched teeth. I knew he was already tainted, but the thought of him consuming more vampire blood scared me. I didn't know if he could get any worse than he already was. I didn't want to find out.

I slammed us both up against a tree, using him to buffer me from the blow. His teeth came from my shoulder with a rip and I screamed again, nearly blacking out from the pain. As strong and resilient as I was as a vampire, I had never taken this much of a beating.

Thomas tried to bury his claws in me to hold me still. He caught a handful of my coat instead. He roared in my ear and tried to bite me again. I slammed my head back and the back of my skull connected solidly with his mouth. I felt a tooth break on my scalp and blood started pouring out of my head, matting my hair.

His grip on me loosened and I fought my way away from him. My coat came away, caught on his claws. I had lost my gun somewhere in the woods and was thankful he seemed to have lost his sword as well. It was probably still stuck in the tree back where he had tried to behead me. If he had still had his weapon, I'd probably be dead.

I bolted for my Honda, hoping I could reach it before he could work himself free of the tangle of my coat. I leaped onto the seat, started the engine, and gave it so much gas I nearly lost control.

I shot down the road, breath coming out in pained gasps. I didn't look behind me, fearing what I might see. I drove as fast as I could, putting distance between me and the bloody scene.

A rage-filled howl lit up the night, causing me to bear down harder on the gas. I sped up, woozy and bleeding from multiple wounds.

I was alive, but I wasn't sure how much longer I would last.

19

I staggered my way to the Luna Cult Den, not really paying attention to where I was going. I knew I couldn't go home and let Ethan see me like this. He would freak out, and right then, I couldn't handle that.

The sidewalk seemed to sway back and forth, and I had to consciously make sure each foot fell in front of the other. It was a miracle I'd managed to drive all the way there and not crash into something. I could hardly stand without falling.

I had no idea where the cameras were placed around the Den. I just hoped someone would see me and help me inside when I got there. My coat was gone, I was covered in blood, and I was so weak I wouldn't be able to fend off an attacker if someone decided to take advantage of my weakened state. There were some in the Cult I was sure would love to have the pleasure.

But where else was I going to go? If home was out, this was it. I had to take my chances that someone wouldn't take advantage of my condition and would get me help instead.

Nobody came out to help me inside, so I trudged up the stairs and fell against the door, breath ragged. I was still losing a lot of blood. While the lesser wounds had already stopped bleeding and had begun to heal, the one in my back was still bleeding badly. I might not die from the wounds, especially if I found someone to feed on to replenish what was lost, but it could be a near thing.

I somehow managed to get the door open despite the fact my right arm was totally useless. I dragged myself through the glamour-made darkness and fell face-first into the light, unable to support myself any longer.

My world swam in darkness, though I could still hear what was going on around me. Someone said something harsh in Spanish and a moment later, I was lifted roughly from the floor. I gibbered something close to "Sorry," though I wasn't quite sure what I was sorry about. I think it had something to do with getting blood on their floor.

Wind hit me in the face as I was taken back outside. I wanted to protest, to tell them who I was and that I'd come there for help. But instead of dropping me into the grass, I was carried farther, held by strong, supportive arms.

I could smell cinnamon on whoever was carrying me. I tried to focus on the face, but no matter how hard I tried, I couldn't make my eyes cooperate. Others moved around me, but like the guy carrying me, they were indistinct shapes, just barely glimpsed at the edge of my fuzzy vision.

Deep down, my sense of self-preservation, as well as my stubborn independent streak, tried to fight to the surface. This wasn't me. I didn't go crawling to others for help. I'd been hurt before and had managed to take care of it myself. If I had gone home, Ethan would have made sure I got blood.

But then he would know how fucked up things had become. I couldn't do that to him. If Ethan saw me so screwed up, he would certainly insist on helping me in some way that would put him in danger. I couldn't do that to him.

We passed from the chilly night into an underground

area I soon recognized as the Luna Cult garage. A few minutes later, I was put into the back of a car. The engine started and two shapes took their places in the front, leaving me alone stretched across the back seat. I tried to ask where we were going, but my mouth refused to work.

The drive wasn't long. I felt totally helpless and it pissed me off to no end. I tried to fight away the darkness that was creeping up on my vision, tried to make my body obey my mental commands, but it was no use.

The car came to a stop after ten minutes that felt like an eternity. Both people up front got out. A moment later, the back door opened and the cinnamon smell returned. I was scooped up and gently pulled through the opening.

They took me inside and set me down on a bed. The lights were dim, just enough to illuminate the room, but not so bright as to make it uncomfortable. It was soothing, actually. The place smelled clean, almost hospital clean.

My heart seized and I tried to sit up. I wanted nothing to do with a hospital. Supes died under the care of Pureblood doctors. It didn't happen all the time, but there were quite a few Purebloods who took matters in their own hands in a futile attempt to take back the night.

A hand pressed me back down and I could do nothing to resist. Agony flared in my back, along my shoulder and chin, and it was all I could do to keep from screaming. A needle was pressed into my right arm and my left hand shot around my body instinctively. I grabbed a wrist that felt strong, but was so thin it had to belong to a woman.

Sudden images of the crazy woman's face in the alleyway flashed through my head and I nearly panicked.

"It's okay." The voice came from my left and I turned my head to look. I could just make out the face as the adrenaline kicked back in, clearing my vision. Jonathan laid a hand on my good shoulder. "Let her do her job."

I laid back, though I was raging inside. I hated to admit it, but I was terrified. I'd never been beaten this badly.

What if something was hurt worse than what my body could fix? What if I didn't heal all the way and couldn't fight like I used to? I had seen it before. One look at Jonathan could tell me everything I needed to know about the limitations of our supernatural healing.

The needle went the rest of the way into my arm and the pain subsided almost instantly. I breathed a sigh of relief and settled back in, no longer caring what happened to me. Whatever I had been injected with had to have been pretty strong stuff. Most drugs didn't work on vampires. The taint in our blood killed it before it could affect us.

Someone tugged at my boots, pulling them from my feet. I was okay with that. It wasn't until the cold press of scissors against my flesh brought me sitting up again.

"No," I said, pushing away at the hand at my waist.

"She needs to remove the clothing to check your wounds. You are seriously injured."

I turned to glare at Jonathan, though I think all I managed was a delirious, blank look. He still got the message.

"We'll leave," he said, rising from a chair next to my bed. He motioned for someone else and I noticed Nathan was standing against the wall. He was covered in blood. It was probably mine.

The two men left the room and I turned to face the woman standing over me. She was small, petite, and would have been pretty if it wasn't for a missing eye and ear. Her hair was done in a way so that it fell over her face, concealing most of the damage, but there were just some things you couldn't hide.

"I'll be gentle," she said, her accent thick, though I had no idea where she had come from. "But I need to remove the clothing or I cannot do my job."

"Where am I?" I asked, taking in the room. There was a vase with flowers beside the bed. The walls were painted a light blue, and the floor was hardwood. The wood was darkened in a few spots as if someone had spilled something on it, most likely blood.

"You're in my home," the woman said. "I am Doctor Isa Lei. I will take care of you, make you better."

I leaned back, my strength waning. At least it wasn't a hospital. "Never heard of you," I said, laying my head back and closing my eyes.

"Not many have. I like it that way." The scissors went to work.

My clothes fell away and I was conscious that someone else had come into the room to help the doc roll me over, though I didn't look to see who it was. The movement brought some of the pain back, but it was distant. I just wanted to sleep.

Lei started poking and prodding me, pressing her fingers against the wound in my back. I hissed at the agony that brought but didn't move. I was hoping she knew what I was, knew what my blood could do to her. I wasn't sure if she was a wolf, a vamp, or a Pureblood, and right then, I wasn't so sure it mattered. I just wanted the pain to end.

Eventually, the prodding stopped and the needlework began. My wounds were scrubbed out, igniting the pain to new heights. My teeth were out and I was bleeding from the gums, making an even bigger mess on the bed than I was sure I had already made. The mattress felt squishy.

I was too weak to bite anyone, however. Once the scrubbing stopped, Doctor Lei started sewing me up. She seemed to take forever on my back and I wondered how bad it really was. It felt like she was sticking the needle all the way into the muscle.

The shoulder and chin didn't take nearly as long and didn't hurt nearly as much. She probably could have left them alone and I would have healed okay, though the scars would have been pretty bad.

After a few hours, she was done, and I was lying alone on the bed, sheet pulled up to my chin. I was still naked.

I felt weak as hell, but at least I didn't think I was going to die.

I expected Jonathan to come in right away to check on me, but after the first hour passed, no one had come into the room. Doctor Lei came in sometime during the second hour and sat down next to me.

"Are you feeling better?"

I nodded. My stitches pulled with the motion, but it didn't hurt as bad as it had before.

"I sewed you up with a special kind of stitching," she said. "They will help the healing process, though you will be out of commission for a good month. There will be scars, but the one on your face will be mostly invisible."

"My blood," I said, propping myself up. My back protested, but I wasn't about to take all of this lying down. I was too damn stubborn for that. The sheet started to slide down and I caught it, pressing it up against my chest. "And my clothes."

"The blood has been taken care of," Lei said. "None has gone where it shouldn't. You will need more blood to fully start the healing process, however. Master Nathan is obtaining some for you now."

Master Nathan? "Okay," I said. My head still felt as though someone had filled it with helium and it was going to float away. I think a lot of it was the blood loss, but some had to have been whatever she had given me for the pain.

"As for your clothing, I have some spare I keep for situations like this. They aren't much, just cheap rags really. You can keep them when you are done."

I was going to ask more questions, but just then, Nathan and Jonathan returned. I slid down in the bed so the sheet wouldn't have a chance to slide down again. I wasn't sure why I cared. Normally, I didn't care who saw me naked. It wasn't like they were going to risk touching me. I just didn't like the thought of those two men seeing me without my clothes.

"Drink this," Jonathan said, handing me a cup with a straw in it. I didn't have to smell it to know it was blood.

"Where did you get it?" I asked, taking the cup. I drank before he could answer, my hunger forcing my hand. I needed the blood to heal. I was nearly starving.

Nathan shifted uncomfortably behind Jonathan and looked away. He had changed his clothes at some point. All traces of my blood were gone.

"It was donated," Jonathan said. "There is more when you finish this."

I wanted to ask him who had donated the blood but decided against it. I probably didn't want to know.

"She needs rest," Doctor Lei said. "We should go."

"I'll get more blood first." Jonathan walked out of the room, leaving me with Nathan and the doc.

I turned my gaze to Nathan and he looked away again. "Thanks," I said, grudgingly. He had carried me when he could have killed me instead. It seemed like he was doing that a lot lately.

Nathan frowned and looked as though he was about to say something. Instead, he turned and walked out of the room, his back stiff.

"He is concerned," Lei said. "He doesn't know how to feel about you. I must admit, neither do I. You seem to have a strange hold on them."

I looked at her, but her face gave nothing away.

Jonathan returned with another tall cup of blood. He set it down by the bedside and took a step back. "Drink it before it gets cold," he said. Both he and Lei turned to leave.

I wanted to stop them. I needed to tell Jonathan about what I had seen. I knew who was killing the wolves and vamps, and he needed to know before he went out hunting for him.

But no matter how much I wanted to speak up, I kept

silent. I couldn't bring myself to talk about it. Not yet. Not so soon after finding out my brother was still alive.

I removed the straw from the cup and downed the rest of the blood. It was already getting cold and was so thick it made me want to gag, but it felt good going down nonetheless. I could already feel it starting to work.

Once the last cup of blood was gone, I settled in and closed my eyes. I knew I couldn't sleep, but I wanted to relax, if only for a little while. I would have to rise soon and tell Jonathan everything I knew. We couldn't let Thomas go on like this.

I did my best to let everything go so my body could heal. It was hard, but I managed not to go crazy thinking about all the shit that was piling up on me. I let the world fade and focused solely on getting better.

20

"What happened?"

Jonathan and Nathan were in the bedroom with me. I was wearing sweatpants and a sweatshirt Doctor Lei had provided for me. They were too big and too baggy, but I had nothing else. My clothes were in ruins and my coat was long gone. I felt naked.

The bedsheets had been changed while I got dressed. I could hear the crinkle of plastic beneath the sheets and vaguely wondered if it had been there before, or if I had been so far gone I hadn't noticed. It was probably the latter.

Jonathan was sitting beside the bed. Nathan had a chair in the corner, almost as if he was trying to stay as far away from me as he could while also sticking close. He kept his eyes averted from mine, which struck me as odd. Just because he had helped me didn't mean things had to change between us. He could still hate me all he wanted and I would understand.

I took a drink of water to compose my thoughts. I needed to tell Jonathan what had happened, but I was afraid of what might happen once I did. I was scared of what he would do.

And I was afraid I might break down and cry like a baby.

I scratched at my shoulder stitches. I itched everywhere. "I stumbled onto our killer," I said. I didn't look at anyone as I said it.

Out of the corner of my eye, I saw Nathan's head jerk around. At least he was looking at me now. Jonathan remained calm, although his breathing did speed up a little bit.

"Where? How?"

I took another sip of water. I wasn't exactly sure how to explain. I don't know why I went the way I did, how I just happened to end up where the next attack was taking place. It seemed too much a coincidence, but it *had* happened. I couldn't deny that.

"It was an accident," I said. "I wasn't out looking for them and the next thing I knew, I was in the middle of the fight."

"And they did this to you? How many of them were there?" Jonathan seemed almost stunned by how bad I looked. Did he really think I was that invulnerable?

"Five or six. I sort of lost count. I didn't have a problem with the first few, but the last two got to me."

Jonathan sat back, hand at his chin. "Did you get a good look at them?" he asked. "If this was some sort of Minor House play, it might be a good idea to stop them now before things get too far out of hand."

"Yeah," I said. I struggled for something to say, but I just couldn't bring myself to tell him what I knew. What if he went after Thomas without me? I was in no condition to go on the hunt with him. I couldn't let him kill my brother.

"I'm not sure how this does us any good," Nathan said from his corner. "If she was defeated by these people, then what chance do we have? We don't even know where they went. She would have to have recognized someone for us to even have a clue."

I looked away at that.

"Do you know something?" Jonathan asked. He sat forward and gave me a look so intense I could almost feel it.

I closed my eyes and took a deep breath. Why was this happening to me? "They weren't normal vampires or werewolves." I hesitated in going on, feeling all sorts of uncomfortable. "They had mixed blood."

"What?" Jonathan said. He stared at me like I had just told him they had been wearing togas and doing a line dance before they kicked my ass.

"None of them was normal. They fought together, worked as a team, but their blood was clearly mixed."

"Impossible," Nathan said. "The Tainted wouldn't work together. They wouldn't know how."

I gave Jonathan a questioning look. "The Tainted?"

His smile never reached his eyes. "When Tremaine tainted Byron, we figured it best to come up with a name for his condition. We feared it was going to become a common occurrence if we didn't do something to stop him."

"But the Tainted?" It seemed silly considering both vampires and werewolves had tainted blood.

"It fit," he said. "What else could we call them?"

He had me there. I wasn't about to go around making up names for things. I was surprised someone hadn't named them before then.

I took a moment to gather my thoughts, sipping the water as if it would somehow save me from having to talk about what came next. I drained the glass and set it aside.

"There's more," I said. "It doesn't make sense, but I saw it with my own two eyes."

I looked from Jonathan to Nathan and then let my gaze settle on my legs. I still hurt and couldn't stand up for long without help. I really wanted to be pacing, gun in hand, sword hanging at my side. Dressed as I was, I could find none of my usual comforts.

"They had a leader." My voice came out sounding dead.

"A vampire?" Jonathan asked, coming to the same conclusion I had at first. Nothing else really made sense.

"No." I took too deep a breath and my back muscles cried out in agony. I let out the breath, letting my pained voice carry with it. "It was my brother."

Dead silence filled the room. Jonathan and Nathan stared at me like I had gone mad. I wasn't so sure I hadn't. I stared right back at the two men, defying them to call me a liar. It clearly crossed Nathan's mind, because he frowned and looked away.

"I don't understand," Jonathan said.

"Join the club."

"How is it possible?" he asked. "Mixing the blood destroys the mind. There is nothing that anyone could do to fix that. Vampires have tried to control the Tainted before, but none of them has ever succeeded. It's just not possible."

"I would have said the same. It appears we were wrong."

Nathan was shaking his head like he didn't want to hear what was being said. I could have produced bodies and he probably would have denied their existence. He truly didn't want to believe me.

I didn't blame him. I didn't want to believe me either.

"Are you sure there was no one else there, someone hiding just out of sight?" Jonathan asked.

"As sure as I can be," I said. "Thomas appeared to be leading them, keeping them organized somehow. He made . . . sounds." I didn't know what else to call that strange barking. "He acted like he knew what he was doing. He had a sword and hunted me down like he used to do to other vampires."

"But he attacked you. That doesn't sound like something a brother would do."

Jonathan had me there. I hated even thinking about Thomas and what he had become. This wasn't the time to have those old memories dredged back up, though the situation sort of dictated it. It was like a fresh wound that was repeatedly being prodded, torn open again and again. I wasn't sure how much longer I could go before it drove me crazy.

"It makes no sense," Jonathan said.

"Keep saying it and maybe things will change," I said, unable to keep the bitterness out of my voice.

"I'm sorry," Jonathan said. He sounded it. "It's so hard to believe. The Tainted cannot work together. They can't even think. I'm trying to make sense of it and it's just not happening."

"Well, it happened," I said. "And I'll have the scars to prove it."

Jonathan nodded, eyes far away. "There has to be a reason to why they have banded together."

"And why it has taken this long for Thomas to get them together." There was no doubt in my mind he was the reason they had started working together. He had always been that kind of guy, wanting to take the lead. When we had run together, he had been the leader, though we never truly named him as such. It was just natural for him to take charge.

Both Jonathan and Nathan gave me a quizzical look.

I sighed. "It's been years," I said. "I've heard nothing about him, so I assumed he was dead."

"As would anyone."

"And yet, here he is. Why now? Why in this way?" I licked my dry lips, wishing I had more water. I started to say something else, but a thought came to me. It sounded crazy, but it was the only answer I could think of. "Maybe he is regaining his senses."

Jonathan frowned and Nathan gave a disgusted sound.

"Hear me out," I said. "He vanished for years, went underground. He probably survived by killing in the dark, sneaking around. Maybe in doing so it brought back some of his mind, his memories. He's basically doing what he's done before, hunting and stalking his prey. Only his victims and methods are any different."

"Or it could be by pure reflex," Jonathan said. "Nothing says he is getting better. Did he happen to know who you were while he beat you into a bloody pulp?"

"No," I admitted. "But I'm sure if given enough time, he might remember."

Nathan snorted again and I shot him a dirty look. He didn't seem to mind. It was obvious he thought I had gone just as crazy as my brother.

"It's impossible," Jonathan said yet again, making me want to slap him. "No matter how much we might wish it, once a mind goes like that, there's nothing anyone can do to fix it."

"How would you know?" I started to shout, but the pain in my back kept me from getting too loud. "You have no idea what is and isn't possible. You're just guessing."

"We had a member of our own tainted, remember. We tried everything we could think of and he only got worse. There was no saving him."

"But you didn't give him years," I said. "What if it takes that long for things to settle in their heads? Maybe the two bloods fight and eventually one side wins out. What happens then? Maybe Thomas can become normal, even if it means he will still be stuck physically between worlds. It doesn't matter, not if I have him back."

Jonathan gave me a level stare. I knew what was coming before he said it. "You can't have him back. I wish it were possible, but it's not. You have to understand that."

I clenched my fists, happy I could actually do it. My right arm was sore, but I could move it now. Doctor Lei had done a pretty damn good job.

"I understand what I saw," I said. "You weren't there. He came at me like the Thomas of old." That wasn't entirely true, but it was close enough. "We need to bring him in and I'm sure we'll find a way to save him."

"And how do you propose we do that?" Jonathan asked. I could tell he was starting to get angry. He hid it well, but the heat was in his voice. "Adrian won't like it. He wants those responsible for the deaths of his weres to suffer the same. He won't be willing to catch one just so we can reform him."

"Don't tell him," I said. He was right. Adrian wouldn't stand for capturing Thomas and trying to heal him. He might torture him for a little while, but that was about as far as Adrian would be willing to go. "Please, don't tell Adrian."

Jonathan studied me long and hard. I had a feeling he really wanted to side with me but was torn. He had a strange loyalty to Adrian I couldn't quite understand. The guy had betrayed him, yet he told me not to hunt him. It made no sense.

Finally, he slumped in his seat. "Okay," he said. "I won't tell him."

Nathan sat up and looked as though he wanted to protest. Then it seemed to occur to him that we were cutting Adrian out and he sat back with a smirk on his face.

"This isn't going to be easy," Jonathan said.

"No one said it was going to be."

"And you aren't helping."

I stared at him. He stared right back.

"I'm not sitting back on this one," I said. "You need me."

"How are you going to help in your condition? You can hardly get out of bed."

"Give me a day, I'll be fine."

Jonathan didn't look like he believed me but didn't argue. He probably realized it would do no good.

"But how are we to find him?" he asked. "It isn't like you stumbled on to wherever they are hiding. Your brother could be anywhere now."

I thought about it. It would be easy to assume Thomas was living in the sewers somewhere, or perhaps in the

middle of nowhere. He almost had to be. If he had taken
over some big mansion or was terrorizing a specific section
of the city, I would have heard of it by now.

But that wouldn't be like him. He had to have found the
sword somewhere. It looked almost exactly like the swords
we had used when we had worked together.

I paled. "I think I know," I said, my voice trembling as
I spoke.

Thomas was acting like he remembered his training. He
was coming after werewolves and vampires like he had
done when we had hunted together. The use of the Tainted
was new, but then again, he was using them as he used me.
They were fighting at his side, following his lead. That
wasn't so different than what he had done when we had
fought together.

And the sword. I kept coming back to the sword.

"Home," I said, fighting the tears that were trying to
force their way down my cheeks. I refused to cry in front
of the two werewolves. "He's gone home."

21

I wanted to leave that night, but it was far too close to dawn. Doctor Lei led me down into the basement where the windows were completely black. A few mattresses that smelled of stale sweat and blood lay around the room. I chose one that smelled the least foul and settled in for the long day.

Jonathan wanted to continue talks about what should be done about Thomas, but I was in no mood. He came down more than once to try to get me to discuss it with him. I steadfastly refused, knowing if I were to start plotting my brother's downfall now, I'd lose it.

Eventually, he left me alone to my thoughts. We planned on waiting another night before acting, which gave me time to figure out what the fuck I was going to do. I needed to go home, obviously. My gear was there, and Ethan would be having a fit by now.

Doctor Lei checked on me off and on. She never really said much outside a few grunts and mumbles about me moving around too much. As hard as I tried, I just couldn't sit still. My back ached something fierce, and she was forced to rebandage my wound more than once.

Finally, the day faded and I was allowed to leave.

Jonathan drove me back to my Honda and waited there as I checked the bike over.

"You could use our garage," he said as I started up the motorcycle. "You don't have to park all the way out here."

I didn't answer. I walked my bike out of the alley and took off down the road the moment I was clear. I wanted nothing more than to go home and take a long, warm bath. Lei's clothes, combined with the stitches and healing flesh, were making me itch.

The drive was nearly unbearable. Every bump in the road made me wince. I cried out almost continually when the road got especially rough. While I might be healing, it was clear I wasn't going to be nearly strong enough for a good fight for quite a while. Thomas and his Tainted had done a pretty good number on me. It felt like someone had taken my insides and stirred them around with a baseball bat covered in barbed wire.

I took my driveway slowly in a vain attempt to mitigate the jarring. I parked in the garage, closed the door, and entered the house through the side door. I fully expected Ethan to be in the basement working. I was wrong.

"Where have you been?" he asked, nearly stumbling over himself as he rose from the table. His face was puffy and red. His SpongeBob T-shirt looked as though he had been wearing it for days. His hair was a mess, and it was obvious he hadn't slept since the last time I had seen him.

"Out," I said, easing my way across the kitchen. I just wanted to go upstairs to my bath. Doctor Lei hadn't told me if my stitches would dissolve in the water or if it would be bad for me. Quite frankly, I didn't give a fuck. I was going to do it whether she approved or not.

"Out?" Ethan said, his voice rising in pitch. "Just out? I was worried. You've been gone for days and all you can say is out?" He laughed. It had a slightly maniacal sound to it.

I stopped and leaned on the table. "I'm sorry," I said. "Things came up."

Ethan started to say more but froze. "What happened to you?" he asked. "Jesus." He walked toward me, wincing as if he could feel every bruise and cut. "And where did you get those horrible clothes?"

I sighed. I really didn't want to get into it until I felt better. While I wanted to let Ethan know I was still alive, I had hoped to do it after my bath. I figured a good wash and a new set of clothes would have hid most of the damage. He never would have known how bad it really was.

But it was too late now. He was circling me, looking me up and down. He reached out every few seconds as if he wanted to touch me, but held off as if he was afraid to. I didn't blame him. I probably looked like hell.

"I found Thomas."

"Jesus," he said again. He stared at me wide-eyed. "He did this to you?"

"No," I said. "Not entirely." I suppressed a groan as I shifted my weight. "He had some friends."

"And all of that." He motioned toward the stitches under my chin.

"Doctor Lei sewed me up."

"Who?"

I didn't feel like explaining. "Thomas is alive, Ethan," I said. "He's alive and I think he is starting to remember who he once was."

Ethan sat down heavily. "But he did this to you?"

I started to shrug. Pain lanced through my shoulder and I settled for a nod. "He isn't there yet. I think if we can catch him, we'll be able to restrain him. It'll take time, but I think we can reach him."

"Who's we?"

"Jonathan and I." No sense in hiding it. "I'm leaving later to discuss it with him."

"Tonight?"

"No better time."

"Jesus, Kat." Ethan shook his head. "You've been gone for days, you look like someone dropped you into a meat grinder and then tried to sew you back together, and you want to go running off again? Take a break. I don't think I can handle another night wondering if you're dead or alive."

"I can't leave him out there," I said. I sagged into a chair, unable to stand any longer. "The longer I wait, the more likely it is that Adrian or someone else will find him. I can't take that chance."

"Adrian?" Ethan paled. "I think I'm going to be sick."

I frowned at him. "I'm not the only one who's been looking for Thomas. My brother's been the one who's been killing all the vamps and wolves lately. He's in a lot of trouble, and I plan on getting to him before someone else does, someone who won't be as understanding."

"And one more night will really matter?"

"You don't understand. . . ."

"No, *you* don't understand."

I looked up at Ethan, stunned. I couldn't believe he had actually raised his voice at me. I don't think in all the time I've known him he'd ever yelled at me.

He reddened and looked away. "I'm sorry," he said. "But I just can't accept this. You look like you can barely stand and you plan on running off after your brother. A brother who kicked your butt once already, I might add. Do you really think it's a good idea to go running off now before you've had a chance to recover?"

"I never said I was going after him tonight."

"You didn't have to," Ethan said. "I know you. You'll go talk about it for a few minutes, and the next thing you know, you'll be off chasing after him."

I looked down at my hands. Ethan was right. While I might prefer to have everything all planned out, this was Thomas we were talking about. I couldn't sit back and wait when I knew I could be out there looking for him. I was pretty sure I knew where to find him. Why wait?

"Kat," Ethan said. "I know you mean well. I know you want to do what is best for Thomas and everyone else around you, but you have to stop for a few minutes and breathe sometimes. If you don't, you're going to get yourself killed rushing into something you aren't prepared for."

A hint of anger started to rise, but I suppressed it. Ethan wasn't being selfish here. He was trying to look out for me. I was being stupid. I could hardly breathe without whimpering and I expected to go running off to subdue the very man who had hurt me so badly? What was I thinking?

"All right," I said, hating myself. I knew it was the right thing to do, but that didn't mean I had to like it. "I'll stay home tonight."

"Good."

"But I'm leaving tomorrow night at first dark. I'll want all my gear ready, plus a few extras just in case."

Ethan frowned. "Where's your stuff?" he asked, eyeing me critically.

"Gone." I left it at that.

He nodded as if it made perfect sense and started for the basement stairs. "I'm going to make sure you have everything you need. Don't you dare leave or I'll have to come after you."

I smiled at that. He could hardly leave the house without panicking, yet I believed him. "I won't."

Ethan hurried down the stairs. As soon as he was gone, I forced myself to my feet and dragged my way up to my room. I instantly shed Doctor Lei's baggy clothes and went to the bathroom.

I peeled off my bandages and dropped them into the trash. I started for the tub but stopped at the mirror to really look at myself. My eyes were sunken in, my face bruised, though the bruises would fade by morning. The stitches in my shoulder and under my chin were dark against my pale skin. I wondered what she had used to sew me up. They definitely didn't look like normal stitches.

I turned so I could see my back and nearly sagged to my knees when I saw the extent of the damage. The skin was so dark it was nearly black. It looked as though someone had run me through with a forklift. It was a wonder I could even move.

Feeling worse than I had before, I went to the tub to start the water. I applied a liberal amount of bubble bath, and as soon as the tub was full, I sank down into the hot water.

It was like slipping into acid. My back screamed as the hot water washed over me. I gritted my teeth and forced myself all the way in so that only my nose and eyes were above the water. I trembled there, in so much pain it made me sick.

But it eventually passed. The pain ebbed away and I was left floating in a state of utter numbness. It almost felt good.

I stayed in the bath for so long my entire body had started to wrinkle, which did little to help my wounds. All the bubbles had popped and the water had turned cold. It was now a faint pink.

I dragged myself out of the bloody water and dried off, careful not to press too hard against my wounds. Just the thought of touching them hurt. How I was ever going to fight and subdue Thomas, I would never know.

Leaving the bathroom, I picked up Doctor Lei's clothes. There was bloody pus all down the back of the shirt where I had seeped. It made my stomach churn. I tossed the bundle into the hamper. I would return them to her and thank her later, even though she had said I could keep them. It was the least I could do.

Still naked, I went to the closet and pulled out my old leather coat, the one that was too long. I tossed it on the bed, along with a pair of jeans and a loose-fitting T-shirt. As much as I would want to go out in full leather, I was pretty sure it would be impossible to get anything too tight on my body for weeks.

I sat down cross-legged on my bed and grabbed a pair of scissors from the bedside table. I rubbed the tough leather of my coat between the pads of my fingers, relishing the feel.

And then I started cutting.

I planned on taking off only the last few inches, then sewing the bottom so it wouldn't look ragged. After the first pass, I found myself cutting another long strip, then another. Before I knew it, I had cut half-a-dozen strips from the coat, my hands working without conscious effort. I held the coat up. It only went down to about midthigh now. It was too short to conceal my sword.

And for some reason, that's what did it.

I burst into tears, rocking back and forth amidst the ruins of my leather coat. Everything caught up with me: Thomas, Adrian, the Luna Cult, the cop I had attacked, everything. I couldn't take it. It was just too damn much.

I cried, letting out all my frustrations, hoping that when I was done, I would be able to face the night like I always had. I wasn't sure where that girl had gone, the one so willing to kill without a thought. If I was going to survive this, I needed to find her again. And I needed to do it fast.

22

I felt much better by the next night. The day was hard to get through, but I managed. The cry did me good. Without it, I wasn't so sure I would have made it through the day without going crazy. I itched for action.

As soon as night fell again, I was ready to go. I felt naked without my leather, and the shortened coat didn't help matters any. The T-shirt was loose enough; it didn't bother my wounds, though I wish I would have had Ethan come in to rebandage my back. While I managed to cover the gash, I hadn't done a very good job.

Ethan had at least set everything out for me down in the basement. I gently put on the shoulder holster. It rubbed up against the bandage, but the pain was minor compared with the pain I would feel if I got to Thomas too late.

I checked the Glock to make sure it was loaded, slammed it into the shoulder holster, and then threw on my belt, complete with sword and knives. I pocketed a half-dozen silver packets and prayed I wouldn't have to use them. A pair of spare magazines came next.

I headed upstairs to find Ethan waiting in the kitchen. "Be careful," was all he said as I headed out. He knew what was at stake. If this went south, there was a good chance I wasn't coming back.

The drive to the Luna Cult garage felt like it took forever. I could feel the seconds tick by. I just wanted to get started and get this over with. Once we had Thomas, I could worry about what to do next.

I waved toward the gloomy darkness, hoping someone was watching the cameras and would tell Jonathan I was coming. He was expecting me, sure, but I still liked being careful. I didn't want one of his guards to get a little overzealous, especially one of the new wolves. I'd hate to have to kill someone.

I reached the Den a few minutes later and pushed through the glass doors. I hardly blinked at the sudden light.

There was a disgusted grunt and my vision cleared in time for me to see Pablo turn and stalk away in a huff. Thinking back to the night I had come crawling in here, I was pretty sure he had been the one to discover me. I doubted anyone else would curse in Spanish. I was surprised he hadn't killed me when he'd had the chance.

Nathan appeared at the top of the stairs and motioned me up. I followed without question and he led me to the sitting room on the second floor. Two guards were standing on either side of the door, Jeremy Lincoln one of them. He did his best to give me a pleasant smile, but the tremble of his hands gave away his nervousness.

I brushed past the guards and entered the room behind Nathan. Jonathan was seated on the couch, staring into a glass of something ruby red. The faint scent of wine filled the room.

"I expected you last night," he said, rising. He carried the glass over to the bar. There was no one behind the counter.

"I had some things I needed to do," I said. "We weren't planning on doing anything last night anyway."

Nathan closed the door behind us, leaving just the three of us alone. He crossed the room and took up position behind the couch, arms behind his back. He glowered at the room in general.

"I almost went ahead without you," Jonathan said. "I was afraid you had gone off on your own." He crossed the room and stood between Nathan and I. "Of course, I don't know where you would have gone, so I was left with no choice but to wait."

"Did you tell Adrian?"

Nathan's shoulders bunched and his glower deepened. A low rumble came from his chest, but he kept his mouth shut.

"No," Jonathan said. "But it might be a good idea if we did."

"Why?"

"We don't have very many weres at our disposal here. I only trust the three of us to do this, honestly. The others are far too young, far too wild. They might not be able to control themselves, and a lack of control will get them killed."

"Then we do it without them."

Jonathan sat down on the couch. He faced me, brow furrowed with worry. "And how will we manage it with just three of us? You nearly died."

"If it wasn't for one of them getting lucky, I probably would have had them."

"And yet you still lost. We don't know how many of the Tainted your brother has at his command. Are you sure just the three of us can take them?"

I shrugged. "We have to try."

Jonathan sighed. He wiped his face with his hands, once again giving me the chills. It just didn't look natural with the glamour. I could almost see his hands passing through it.

"Please," he said, motioning to the chair across from him. "Sit. You're making me nervous."

My nerves were so frazzled, I was nearly bouncing from the walls, but I moved to take a seat. It felt good to get off my legs, though. I was definitely not fully recovered from my last encounter with Thomas.

"What's our plan?" Jonathan asked as soon as I was seated. "I've tried to come up with a way to do this and everything I come up with ends up with us dead. I don't see how we can pull this off."

"We go in, take down his Tainted, and pacify Thomas. Seems easy enough to me."

Jonathan gave me a doubtful look. "And how do you plan on doing that?"

I flipped my coat open a little, exposing the Glock in its holster. "Silver will stop them just as fast as it would any other vamp or wolf. As long as you and Nathan can watch my back, this should be easy enough."

"And what do you plan on doing with Thomas once we have him?"

I bit my lip. "I hadn't thought that far ahead."

"Well, you better figure it out," Jonathan said. "Silver will only last so long."

"I know."

"A cell." Nathan spoke without looking at me.

The thought of sticking Thomas in a cell made me want to hit something. It seemed almost cruel. Of course, we were going to kill those loyal to him and paralyze him with silver. Was throwing him in a cell while we figured out how to help him really any worse?

"Okay," I said. "We put him in a cell here."

Jonathan didn't seem to like the idea but nodded. "We can keep him until we figure out what to do with him. I don't like it, but it's all we have."

"Then it's settled," I said, starting to rise.

Jonathan raised a hand and motioned for me to stay seated. "I still think we need to tell Adrian."

"Why?"

"Because we have no idea how many Tainted we are dealing with here. It could be half a dozen, or it could be five times that. We just don't know."

"Could be," I admitted.

"Which is why we need to tell Adrian."

"No."

"I don't think we can do this without him."

"No."

"Kat . . ."

"I said no." My anger boiled over. "Adrian will kill him without a second thought. You know that as well as I do. I *will* not allow that to happen. We do this without him or I do it alone."

"We don't have the people for this."

"Then find some."

A knock at the door brought all our heads around.

"Come," Jonathan said, his voice tight.

Jeremy stepped inside, his face flushed. He closed the door behind him.

"What is it?"

"I want to go."

We all stared at him. He might have been a werewolf, but he was still just a kid. Taking him out on something like this was about as smart as taking a bunch of unarmed Purebloods. We all saw how that turned out the last time.

"No," I said.

"I agree," Jonathan said. "You are too young, too raw."

Jeremy's back stiffened. "I want to help. I overheard your argument and I agree with the Denmaster. You need more men. I might not fight as well as the rest of you, but I can be of some use."

"How?" I asked. "How in the hell do you think you can help us? You can hardly help yourself."

Jeremy breathed in and out slowly, as if controlling his inner beast. There was no flare of fire in his eye, no sudden sprouting of fur. I had to admit, he'd gained some control since the night he tried to stalk me.

"I can help," he said, glaring at us defiantly. "Even if I'm not involved in the fighting, I want to do something. I could watch for others, make sure no one tries to sneak up on us." He looked squarely at Jonathan. "You said it yourself, you need more people. Here I am."

"Jeremy—" Jonathan began, but Nathan cut him off.

"It might not be a bad idea."

Jonathan and I both turned incredulous looks on him. Nathan stared straight ahead, not meeting anyone's eye.

"It's a terrible idea," I said.

"Without Adrian and his weres, we will not survive." It sounded as if admitting it pained him. "Even though he is young, Mr. Lincoln could be useful. If we are going to do this, we should do it right. Turning away a willing participant will only make things harder than they have to be."

I stared at him, surprised. I had always thought of Nathan as more of a grunt. He did the heavy lifting, killed who needed to be killed, but didn't think too much.

Yet here he was, making perfect sense. There was a brain in there, and as much as I didn't want to admit it, he was right. Jeremy might not be a trained fighter, but he was a werewolf. He had his uses.

"Fine," I said. "Can we just move on and get this thing started? I'm tired of standing around talking about it."

Jonathan looked at me like I had betrayed him. He was the Denmaster, protector of the Cult. This had to go against nearly everything he has fought for. He was putting his own men in danger when he knew there was an easier way.

I shrugged and gave him a crooked smile. "He wants to come. I'm not going to tell him no again. He's got to get his feet wet eventually."

couldn't control his excitement. I had to admit, the kid had balls. I just hoped someone wouldn't rip them off and feed them to him if everything fell apart.

"Can we stop arguing and start worrying about how we are going to survive this?" Jonathan said. "We have no weapons here, other than what you brought with you. I for one do not wish to use them even if you were to offer. How do we go about this without getting killed?"

"Very carefully," I said. It wasn't much of a joke, but the tension in the room eased a little.

"Look," I said, "I've gone into some pretty bad situations where I didn't know all the facts beforehand. It's risky, sure, but we should be able to do this. We have the element of surprise."

All eyes were on me and I felt like a moron. I didn't like lecturing a bunch of werewolves. They knew what was at stake. Every time one of them went outside, it was a risk. Was this really any different?

"I think I know where Thomas is." I hated admitting I wasn't totally sure. "And if he is there, we won't have to worry about accidently killing any Purebloods. There might be werewolves, but they will probably stay clear since Thomas is what he is. This should be easy enough."

Jonathan nodded as I spoke. His gaze traveled past me as if he were lost in thought. Nathan continued to glower, but he no longer had that aggressive stance of his.

"Once we get to the location, I will point out the house we are looking for. We shouldn't linger. Once we stop, we need to move fast, hit them hard. Don't kill anyone unless I say it's okay. I don't want Thomas getting killed by mistake." I looked at Nathan when I said the last.

"You make it sound so easy," Jonathan said.

"Plans like this always sound simple. They never work out that way."

Jonathan closed his eyes and nodded. "Okay," he sa[id] "You can come, but no one else. I will not sacrifice a[n]y more of my own for this."

A look of defiant pride came into Jeremy's eyes as h[e] stepped farther into the room. I imagine he had bee[n] waiting for the day he could be included in the inner circle. He wasn't just another Cultist. He was a werewolf, which meant the Purebloods here worshipped him. It was a wonder he wasn't already lording over them.

"So, where will we find them?" Jonathan asked. "You said the other night that Thomas has gone home, but that means little to me."

"When the time comes, I'll show you," I said.

Nathan frowned, his eyes flickering my way.

"As much as I might want to, I still don't trust you," I said. "If I tell the wrong person the wrong thing, it will invariably come back and bite me on the ass. If I keep this to myself until we get there, then no one can betray me to Adrian. Once was enough."

That got to them. Gregory Hillis had been one of Jonathan's wolves. He had betrayed the Cult to Adrian and Count Tremaine, nearly getting us all killed. Bringing it up now was a bitchy thing to do, but hey, I never said I fought fair.

"All right," Jonathan said, resigned. "We'll follow you in my car. Don't go too fast. I don't want to stand out and risk having someone follow us."

"I don't like this," Nathan said. "We shouldn't be going in blind."

"There's no help for that," I said. "Even if I told you where we were going, you wouldn't really be prepared. You don't know the place. I'm just protecting my interests here. You'd do the same."

Nathan's jaw tensed, but he lapsed into silence. Jeremy stood a few feet away, rocking back and forth as if he

Jeremy paled a little bit, but it did nothing to lower his excitement level.

"Is there anything else?" Jonathan asked, standing.

"Nope, that's everything I know."

"Then let's get this over with."

I started to rise, but just then, my back chose to give out. I hissed in pain as I fell back in the chair. Jonathan rose as if I had been shot and came to my side. He reached out toward me and I cringed away.

"I'm fine," I said, pushing myself to my feet. Fresh blood oozed from beneath my bandage and trailed down my back. I was glad no one could see it. "Let's just do this."

Jonathan gave me a concerned look but didn't object. He turned and led the way out of the room, our little procession following after.

I had no idea how the wolves were going to survive this. I had been armed when I faced Thomas and his Tainted the last time and I had lost. Badly. And here they were, willing to waltz in with nothing but their claws and good intentions. I had a bad feeling they wouldn't all be coming out of this alive.

Anger broiled somewhere in my gut. I shouldn't be concerned about what happens to a few werewolves. They weren't what was important here. If I could get Thomas out of there alive, that was all that mattered.

I knew I was fooling myself. I did care. I was terrified something would happen to Jonathan, to Nathan, or even Jeremy. I wasn't so sure I wanted their deaths on my conscience.

We walked out of the Den without talking to anyone. The Cultists watched us go. I think they knew we were getting into something dangerous. They looked scared for all of us.

We kept silent as we headed for the Luna Cult garage

and went our separate ways once inside. I waited by the entrance, sitting atop my Honda, until Jonathan pulled up behind me in his car. He flashed his lights to tell me he was ready and we were on our way, heading for the house I still thought of as home.

23

The closer we came to our destination, the worse I felt. This wasn't physical pain. I had my share of that, of course. Every bump in the road sent slivers of pain lancing through my back and arm.

No, this was the kind of pain that comes when old memories, better left forgotten, get dredged back up and are not only forced to the fore of your mind, but are thrust into your face and waved about. This kind of pain was harder to ignore.

About a thousand different emotions vied for dominance within me. I fought them all, trying hard to just focus on the job so I could get to what really mattered: saving Thomas. But no matter how hard I tried, I just couldn't stop the emotions from flooding me.

And that scared me.

I was never one to show much in the way of emotion. Sure, anger was common, but that had a little to do with what I was. The vampire taint made my aggressiveness that much more pronounced. It was the same for werewolves. It was why I never could trust any of them.

And yet now, I was stuck feeling things I really didn't want to feel. I was scared we would fail. I was worried what would happen if we succeeded. Could I really keep doing what I did if Thomas was cured? I couldn't let him go out and risk himself again, not after this. Could I really stop all the killing and settle down and live a normal life?

I wasn't sure. And that was what scared me the most.

We approached the old neighborhood and I was able to forget my worries. It was nothing like I remembered. The houses here were still standing, but it was clear no one was really taking care of them. Rogue werewolves and perhaps a few vamps had moved in soon after my family and friends were killed at Count Valentino's word. Coming here would have been a death sentence before.

But now there was no one on the streets, despite the late hour. No wolves prowled the shadows; no eyes peered at me through parted curtains. It was as if everyone had up and moved away, deciding something far worse than a few rogue wolves had moved in and there was no sense in sticking around.

Those who hadn't moved were surely dead. I kind of expected it, really. If Thomas was out hunting again, then the wolves around his base of operation would surely have been the first to go.

I stopped in the middle of the street about a mile from the house where I'd grown up. I could see the curve in the road that was just this side of too sharp. More cars had crashed there than I could count. Even the barricade the city had placed at the side of the road couldn't stop people from slamming into the large tree that stood a few feet off the road. The spot had been a deathtrap.

I stared at the curve, afraid to go on. Once I took that turn, we would be heading straight for my old home. It would come into view, and there was nothing that could stop the flood of emotions I knew would come. I wasn't sure I could hold it together.

A car door opened behind me and I started forward again. Fuck them. I could do this. I didn't need Jonathan, or God forbid, Nathan, prodding me onward. If one of them came up to me and asked if I was okay, I would blow a fucking hole in his head.

I took the curve slowly, easing my way around it like I had done hundreds, if not thousands, of times before. I had to blink tears out of my eyes and was even more pissed for having to do so. This wasn't a time for weakness.

The old house came into view and the sight hit me like a brick. I swerved around a branch I almost didn't see and stopped a few houses down. The lights were off, but I didn't need them to tell me that someone was inside. The place felt occupied, even from here.

Jonathan pulled up behind me and shut off the engine. I dismounted from my bike, never taking my eyes off my old house.

Thomas was in there. I was sure of it.

"I don't like this," Nathan said, coming up beside me. "It smells wrong."

"It smells like death," Jonathan said, coming up on my other side.

I nodded. They were right. Even though my sense of smell wasn't as good as theirs, I could smell it too. It smelled wrong here. It was as if I could smell the old blood on the air.

And somehow, it made me feel better. If it had felt like home, I really would have lost it.

"Someone is living in the houses on either side," I said. "We would be best served to keep an eye on them on our approach. As long as no one spots us, we can get this over with quickly. We get inside, find Thomas, and get the fuck out of there. Kill everyone else."

Jeremy gulped behind me and I glanced back at him. "You can stay behind if you don't think you can handle it," I said. "I won't hold it against you."

"No," he said. "I'm coming."

I turned back to the house and gave it a long, hard look.

It was much as I remembered it despite its rundown state. The shutters had fallen off and a few of the windows were broken, but the door was closed and looked solid. The tree out front looked as strong as the day it was planted.

I tried to imagine where inside Thomas could be. Both our bedrooms had been on the second floor, though I wasn't so sure he would have claimed that room for his own now. Like me, he didn't need to sleep. And from where I stood, it was obvious the windows weren't blackened against the sun.

Of course, I wasn't sure he needed that. I didn't know if the Tainted could go out in sunlight or not. They were part vampire, but how much of a vampire were they really? I had never asked before.

Then again, it didn't matter either way. We were going to get this done tonight. If we were still there when the sun rose, we were probably already dead.

"I'm going straight for the basement," I said after a moment. "Nathan, guard the stairs leading to the second floor. Don't let anyone come down and get behind us. Jonathan, you come with me."

"And me?" Jeremy asked. His voice shook, betraying his terror. At least he hadn't pissed his pants yet.

"Watch the front door. Warn us if anyone tries to come through."

Now that the plan was fully in place and the time to fight had arrived, my gut was doing flips. This was it. Either we left with Thomas in tow or we wouldn't leave at all.

A nagging doubt eased into my mind. What made me so sure Thomas had come here? It had only been a hunch. He could very well have chosen a new location for his base. Hell, he might indeed have been taken in by some vamp Count who figured out how to control the mindless Tainted. I almost wished it was true. Then I wouldn't have to face him.

I pushed the doubt away. This had to be where Thomas was. It was the only thing that made sense. The place *felt* like him.

"Let's do this," I said, drawing my sword and gun and starting forward.

We moved fast. The yard was torn up as if a bunch of dogs had taken to burying their treasures in it. I zigzagged around the holes, not looking down in case I saw what was really buried there.

Nathan hit the front door first. He barreled in, taking the door right off its hinges. Instantly, a broken howl came from inside. It was quickly silenced.

I came in next, stepping over Nathan's torn clothing. He had shifted and the body of the Tainted lay beneath him. The beast was still twitching, though his head was barely hanging on to his neck. Nathan's claws had just about ripped it clean off.

Jeremy snarled as he shifted behind me. He spun to face the door, panting as if excited over the opportunity for violence.

I frowned at Nathan but didn't say anything. I had wanted to be able to close the door. Now we had to hope no one came charging in behind us, because I seriously doubted Jeremy would stop them, even as a wolf.

I quickly checked the other rooms before heading for the stairs leading to the basement. Nathan took up his position by the stairs, saliva dripping from his maw. Jonathan and I stopped at the closed basement door, listening.

No sounds came from below. Hell, the whole house was silent. I didn't like it. Everyone within a mile radius had to have heard the door crashing in.

I tested the doorknob and found it to be unlocked. I pulled open the door and trained my gun into the darkness below. Nothing moved.

With a quick nod to Jonathan, we started down the stairs, me in the lead. It was nearly pitch-black in the basement, but neither Jonathan nor I needed light to see by. His vision was better, but I could see well enough. Hell, I doubted the lights even worked these days.

I stepped down onto the basement floor, gun moving from side to side. My parents had sectioned off the large basement into three parts. The first part, the one we were in, was empty of life. There were a few old boxes, things I had been forced to leave behind, but nothing else. The other two sections were blocked off by closed doors.

Something was whimpering behind one of the doors. I eased forward, ready to fire the moment something moved. I didn't trust my senses here. I wasn't stupid. Nostalgia was hitting me hard, and it was a fight to keep myself from stopping to check the boxes to see what they held. I was surprised they were still even here.

There were so many memories in the house, things I wished I had been able to take with me. I doubted my old clothes were still upstairs in my bedroom. The rogue who had taken over probably had thrown them all away.

Then again, he could have kept my things and used them. It wasn't as if a rogue wolf had much time to take everything from his previous life with him, especially if he was forced to run and hide. If there were still a few boxes down here, it stood to reason there might be more of my old things elsewhere in the house.

I took a deep breath, pushing the thought away. I couldn't be thinking about that stuff now.

I paused at the door and listened. There was more than one creature inside whimpering in pain. I raised my hand and held up three fingers to Jonathan, who nodded.

I started dropping my fingers one by one. I tensed as the last finger fell; then I jerked open the door.

There were four of them lying on cots on the floor. They were all Tainted, stuck between shifting into a wolf, a vamp, and remaining human. Their eyes swiveled my way as I entered, but none of them made a move for me.

The smell of blood was heavy in the confined space. These creatures weren't in any condition to fight. One was missing both his legs at the knees. Another didn't have an arm. All were bleeding, all were dying.

I glanced around the room quickly to make sure there was no one hiding in the shadows. This room had been our ready room back when Thomas and I had hunted together. The tables were pushed back against the wall and old weapons were lying on top of them. The cots were new, however, so it was clear that Thomas had done a little re-decorating.

Just that knowledge alone told me there was something of Thomas left in there. A mindless beast wouldn't have thought to bring cots for the wounded. Someone who couldn't think wouldn't have brought their wounded back with them either.

I considered just closing the door and leaving the in-jured beasts lying there. They were no threat. If left un-tended like that, they would eventually die on their own.

I stepped back, ready to close the door and check the next room, when one of the Tainted screamed. It was a tor-tured half wail, half howl that resounded throughout the entire house.

I shot him out of reflex. I didn't want his howl to warn the others, which was stupid in itself, considering the gun-shot would alert anyone with ears. The beast fell limp as the bullet took him in the brain.

The door we had yet to check burst open and three more Tainted burst out. They were all naked, and all male, and they carried no weapons. They didn't need them. Their gaping maws and razor-sharp claws were weapons enough.

They charged and I shot the first one before he was much more than two steps from the doorway. Jonathan shifted beside me, his clothing tearing and falling away as his body contorted. Bones snapped and re-formed, his skin stretched. He screamed as his face elongated, turned into a wolfish snout.

It took only a few seconds for the shift to be complete. The Tainted had hesitated, eyes turning on him as he changed. The glamour fell from Jonathan's features and his mangled wolf-face looked all the more frightening.

He leaped into the midst of the two Tainted, taking one down. They rolled across the floor, jaws snapping at one another.

The other beast was distracted for an instant and I took advantage. I took two quick steps forward and took his head off with my sword. He didn't even have time to scream as his body crumpled to the ground.

Jonathan was holding his own against the other beast, so I took a moment to glance into the room the three had come from. There were more cots on the floor, as well as a broken television and couch that had been shredded. No one else was in the room.

"Fuck," I growled, turning back to the fight. Wherever Thomas was, he wasn't down there.

Jonathan had the crazed beast pinned to the floor, but he couldn't get his claws or teeth close enough to finish the job.

He didn't need to. I raised my gun and shot the thing between the eyes. Jonathan jerked back, nearly falling over himself in doing so. He gave me what I took as a shocked look, though it was hard to tell with his wolfish half face.

"Sorry," I said. I looked around the room, frowning. "He's not down here."

Of course, then the question became, where was he?

A moment later, I knew.

The scream of a tortured animal came from upstairs, followed by a heavy thump that just about shook the house. Snarls and growls came next and I rushed toward the stairs, ready to jump headfirst into the fight of my life.

24

I nearly tripped over Jeremy where he lay sprawled across the floor. His arm was hanging on by little more than skin and tendon. Claw marks crisscrossed his chest and face, his features turned to nothing more than chopped meat.

He wasn't moving.

I skidded to a stop and stared at him. The kid never should have been allowed to come. I didn't let him go free that night near The Bloody Stake just to have him die because of me. It was unacceptable.

Jonathan brushed past me, barely paying the bleeding Jeremy any mind. Bleeding was good. Bleeding meant he was still alive.

The Denmaster barreled into a pair of Tainted that had Nathan backed into a corner. The beasts had no weapons, but their teeth and claws were more than weapon enough. They had no fear, making them that much more dangerous. It was all Nathan could do to keep from being torn to shreds.

I forced myself to look away from Jeremy, from the battling werewolves, and my eyes fell on Thomas. He had a sword in hand and it took me a moment to realize it wasn't his old rusty sword.

This one was made of silver.

I cursed and raised my own blade. Thomas must have gone back and picked up my sword after our last fight. If he had grabbed the gun and knives, too, he could kill us all without breaking a sweat.

He snarled at me, not an ounce of recognition in his eyes. I wasn't even sure he recognized me from the night when he had nearly killed me. I was just another victim to him, a vamp that needed slaying.

"Thomas," I said, stepping over Jeremy, putting myself between the werewolf and my brother. "Leave him be."

Thomas sneered at me and charged. I brought my sword up to meet his downward swing. They rang loudly as they met, the force of the blow sending shock waves through my entire body. Thomas staggered back a step, but then charged right back in, swinging low this time.

I easily parried the swing and pushed him back, away from Jeremy. The front door had been shoved against the wall, leaving a clear path to the outdoors. I worked Thomas toward it, fighting off his blows and returning half-hearted swings of my own to keep him backpedaling. If I could keep him away from Jeremy, there was a chance the young wolf would survive.

Thomas suddenly came at me with a flurry of attacks. I was just barely able to block them, though I was forced back a step against his onslaught. I still had my gun in hand but refused to fire. If Jonathan and Nathan could dispatch their Tainted, then they could help me subdue Thomas. I would much rather not have to do it myself.

I deflected another swing and kicked out hard. My foot hit Thomas square in the stomach and he fell back. He gasped for air, but it didn't slow him for long.

I had only an instant to check the fight going on behind me. Jonathan was rolling around with one of the Tainted, fighting for his life. The beast snapped at him, tried to latch its fangs into his throat. Jonathan snapped at its face, nearly catching the Tainted's nose between his teeth.

Nathan was a few feet away, bleeding from multiple wounds and fighting for all he was worth. The creature was stalking him, lashing out with lightning-quick claws. Blood bubbled from Nathan's arm as the beast's claws slashed a deep groove in his bicep.

Thomas charged me and I barely turned back in time to parry his enraged swing. I swung myself around him, putting my back to the open doorway. I brought my gun up and fired. The bullet whizzed past Thomas's head and hit the beast threatening Nathan square in the back of the head. There was a muffled thump and it fell to the floor in a lifeless heap.

Nathan gave me a grateful nod before rushing to help Jonathan.

Thomas howled at the sight of his beast falling. He turned on me, face full of rage as he charged, attacking high and low. I backed toward the opening, wanting to lead him out into the yard where I had more room to maneuver.

Before I reached the doorway, Thomas came at me hard. I parried a vicious thrust that nearly took me in the gut, twisting out of the way so violently something in my back gave. I staggered back, slamming against the door frame, nearly slipping in Jeremy's blood. I cried out and Jonathan's head snapped around, momentarily distracted from the beast he was about to finish off. Nathan thankfully had it held down or it might have taken advantage.

Thomas came on. He swung at my knees and I was just barely able to drop my sword in time. The reverberations from our blades meeting had my entire arm and back twisting in pain. I could feel fresh blood dripping down my back. The wounds had broken open again and I hadn't truly fed to replenish the lost blood. I wouldn't last long like this.

I dodged a wild swing meant to take off my head. I dropped low and rolled, screaming as pain lanced through my body. I hit the floor hard and came up on my knees a few feet away, sword coming up just in time to block another of Thomas's blows.

He bared his fangs at me. I could see the hunger in his eyes. He wasn't going to just kill me.

He was going to eat me.

He hacked at me like he intended to chop me into small, bite-sized bits. I was weakening fast but managed to block every one of his swings. He swung again, downward as if to split my skull, and I blocked it with my sword. My elbow buckled and his sword brushed against my shoulder. The impact jarred me, but the blade didn't break through the leather.

Thomas howled in victory. My arm felt heavy. I wouldn't be able to stop his next blow.

Jonathan hit Thomas in the side as my brother brought his sword above his head. They slammed up against the wall so hard the entire house shook with the impact. They snarled and snapped at each other, with Thomas trying to bring up his sword and thrust it through Jonathan's chest as they struggled.

I tried to get to my feet, but my legs wouldn't cooperate. My vision swam and I cursed myself for being so stupid. I should have fed the night before instead of sulking in my room, worrying about what to do with Thomas.

Nathan flashed into view and he slammed into both Thomas and Jonathan, heedless of whom he hurt. He was bleeding pretty badly from numerous wounds, but instead of slowing him down, it seemed to enrage him further.

"Stop," I gasped, wincing as the pain in my back flared up. Even talking hurt.

The werewolves kept fighting, slashing at Thomas with their claws. Nathan managed to get a blow in past my brother's defenses, taking him on the shoulder. Blood spurted from the wound. Nathan howled, his face a mask of fury and hunger.

He was enraged, lost in the bloodlust. If I didn't do something, he would kill Thomas.

I growled and staggered to my feet. Everything went black for half a second and I found myself sitting again without remembering going down.

"Fuck," I said as I forced my way back up, slower this time. Now wasn't the time for weakness. If Nathan killed Thomas, I would never forgive myself.

"Get off him," I screamed, blood bubbling from my mouth. My fangs were fully extended. The sight of blood had brought my hunger, but at least the pain was keeping me from losing control. "Don't hurt him anymore."

Jonathan's eyes met mine and I saw he was just barely holding on to his own bloodlust. Seeing me must have triggered something in him, because his eyes regained some of their focus and he jerked away from Thomas as if he suddenly realized what he was doing.

Nathan, on the other hand, kept fighting. Thomas's sword was lying a few feet away, knocked away by one of Nathan's blows. Teeth snapped, claws swiped the air. They rolled around together, fighting with everything they had.

Jonathan howled, bringing Nathan's head up. The big wolf blinked, his head seeming to clear.

Unfortunately, Thomas wasn't affected the same way.

He thrashed under Nathan and managed to throw the bigger wolf. He sprang up, bleeding from seemingly everywhere, and attacked, hitting Nathan in the chest. He bared his fangs; then his head snaked forward.

Nathan jerked to the side just in time and Thomas's fangs went into his shoulder instead of his neck. Nathan screamed, his voice a mix of human and wolf.

I didn't know what to do. Nathan was thrashing under Thomas but was unable to get him off. Jonathan stood a few feet away, locked in place. He seemed conflicted: as if he wanted to help his wolf, but was afraid he would go too far. He looked at me with wolf eyes, pleading for me to do something.

I started to raise my gun but stopped. I couldn't do it. I couldn't shoot my own brother. Even if he killed us all, I just couldn't hurt him.

Jonathan growled and charged me. I was so stunned by his sudden movement, I nearly shot him instead. I jerked my aim away just in time and he knocked me back down. The pain in my back caused my muscles to seize, my fingers to spasm. I dropped my weapons, my hands tingling.

My lips peeled back in a snarl. Jonathan had turned on me at the worst possible time. He was going to kill me now while I was weak. Had he planned this the entire time?

Instead of finishing me off, Jonathan's claws scrabbled at my waist. He snatched a knife from the hidden sheath in my belt and spun away, leaving me lying on the floor.

Jonathan charged Thomas, who was still feeding on Nathan. The big wolf was still fighting hard but was fading fast. If it went on much longer, Thomas might bleed him dry. Even a werewolf would die of that.

Jonathan drove the knife awkwardly into Thomas's shoulder. Werewolf claws aren't meant to hold weapons, but they held enough of their human shape for it to be possible. He howled as he did it, and I wasn't sure if it was a howl of victory or one of anger. Either way, it got the job done.

Thomas jerked back with a scream, his fangs tearing from Nathan's shoulder. He shuddered, managing to keep himself from giving in to the silver for an instant, before finally collapsing on top of Nathan.

Nathan immediately pushed Thomas off him and staggered to his feet. He turned on me, eyes full of blood-red hatred. He snarled and took a threatening step toward me.

"Nathan," Jonathan said. He was shuddering on the

floor, bathed in a cold sweat. He was naked and human once more. "Shift."

Nathan spun on him and growled low in his throat. I grabbed my gun while he was distracted and brought it up so when he turned back to me, he would be looking straight down the barrel.

"I'd do as he says," I said through gritted teeth.

Nathan bared his teeth at me. There was fur stuck in them, as well as something thick and bloody. He spat it out and howled as he shifted.

It was almost as disturbing to watch as watching the wolves shift from human. His muscles bulged, bones shifted and popped. Even though it had to hurt like hell, he never cried out, never showed any sign that the change bothered him.

He kept his feet as his features settled. He stood before me, naked as the day he was born, and trembled in a combination of rage and pain. He was cut up pretty badly.

"She nearly got us killed," he said. His voice was still husky, tinged with a hint of animal.

"But she didn't," Jonathan said, standing. He hadn't had time to redo his glamour, so his head was only partially there. It had been so long since I had seen him like that, it was shocking.

"We should go," I said, looking away from the two naked men. They seemed comfortable without their clothing, and even though nudity didn't normally bother me, right then it seemed somehow obscene.

A howl came from somewhere outside. I couldn't tell if it was a werewolf or one of the Tainted.

"Soon," I added, not wanting to find out.

Jeremy managed to moan and all of us turned to look at him. He hadn't been able to shift back to human with the silver coursing through his body. He would be stuck that way until it ran its course.

"We've got to get him to Lei," Jonathan said. "And soon."

Nathan nodded and started toward Jeremy. He glared at me as he passed. I was in too much pain to return the favor.

He picked Jeremy up and a muffled scream came from deep within the boy's throat. His eyes bulged, but he couldn't otherwise move. He trembled in Nathan's arms for a few seconds, then blacked out.

"Help me," Jonathan said, going over to Thomas.

"What are we going to do?" I asked.

"We're going to put them both in the car. We'll take Jeremy to Doctor Lei and then bring Thomas back to the Den."

"And what about me?"

"You can meet us at the garage."

I didn't like it. I didn't want to leave Thomas's side, especially if Nathan was going to be around him. I didn't trust the big werewolf not to kill Thomas the moment he got the chance.

"Help me lift him," Jonathan said.

I hurried over and helped him lift Thomas. It wasn't easy. I bent over and grabbed Thomas by his legs. I tried to lift up, but my back wouldn't let me. I hissed in pain and dropped him.

"It's okay," Jonathan said. He lifted Thomas up and threw my incapacitated brother's arms over his shoulder. The knife was still in Thomas's back. Jonathan winced as if he was hurt somewhere I couldn't see, but at least he was able to hold Thomas up. "I've got it."

I felt useless standing there. Jonathan and Nathan took their charges out to the car and I followed them. Nathan put Jeremy in the back seat and then popped the trunk.

"No way," I said, hurrying after them. "You're not putting him in there."

"It's the safest way."

"You're not going to shove my brother in the fucking trunk."

Jonathan stared at me. I stared right back, but after

only a few seconds, I looked away. He was right. It was the safest way. If Thomas came out of his silver-induced paralysis before they were back, leaving him in the trunk was the best option.

"Fine," I growled, turning away. They could do it, but that didn't mean I had to watch them dump him in there like so much garbage.

When the trunk slammed closed, I looked back. Nathan was already behind the wheel. Jonathan had moved to the passenger side door. Neither had bothered getting dressed. It was kind of disturbing.

"Meet us at the garage," Jonathan said. "I don't want there to be any problems at the Den while we are away."

I nodded and walked away. I heard the car door slam but didn't look back. I went back into the house, gathered up my weapons, including the sword Thomas had used, and then did a search of the house, killing any Tainted that were still alive. Thankfully, only the wounded were left. A quick shot to the head ended their suffering.

It was mindless work. I didn't pity the poor souls. What I was doing was a mercy.

Somehow, it didn't quite feel that way.

After I was done, I put the house behind me. I would never go back. There were too many bad memories there now. I couldn't face that ever again.

I mounted my motorcycle, started the engine, and drove to the Luna Cult garage to wait for Jonathan's return.

25

The wait was killer.

I arrived at the Luna Cult garage and paced near the entrance. It was dark within the depths of the garage, making me that much more agitated. It wasn't much better outside.

The night was overcast, but at least it wasn't raining. I wasn't so sure I could take it if it was. The night had turned out bad enough, even with getting Thomas back.

Of course, I didn't really have him back yet. Jonathan and Nathan still had him, and I would need to figure out how to make Thomas understand I was there to help. He had yet to recognize me, but I figured it was only a matter of time.

I kicked at a fallen piece of concrete. It bounced off the wall, the sound echoing throughout the garage. I was the only one in there. I knew someone might be watching on the cameras, yet I still felt isolated, alone.

I should have gone with them. I never should have left Thomas with Nathan. I didn't care that Jonathan was with them. He couldn't watch the big wolf all the time. All it would take was one quick slice across the throat, and everything would have been for nothing.

"Come on," I growled, my pace increasing. They should have been back by now. Lei's wasn't that far away. What could possibly be taking them so long?

"Fuck it," I said. I would go find them. There were only so many ways to get here from Lei's. If they were still at the doc's place, I could deal with them then.

Just as I was about to turn, headlights came into view. I stood my ground, fists clenched, and waited. The car glided into the garage and pulled up beside me. The tinted driver's side window came down.

"Get in," Jonathan said.

I shook my head. I was too nervous to sit. My gaze traveled to the trunk. Was Thomas still in there? Was he still paralyzed? Was he dead?

Jonathan sighed but rolled up the window. He coasted down farther into the garage, going down two levels before shutting off the engine. I followed him at a near run, wanting nothing more than to check on my brother.

As I reached the trunk, it popped open. Jonathan got out of the car and came around to join me as I lifted the lid.

Thomas lay there, his body twisted in a painful-looking tangle. He must have been jostled pretty badly during the ride. Either that or when Jonathan put him in there, he'd been careless. Just the thought pissed me off.

I reached down and started working Thomas from the trunk. Jonathan leaned over to help. I was about to tell him to piss off but changed my mind. I was still hurt. As much as I hated to admit it, I would need his help to get Thomas to the Den.

We managed to wrangle him out of the tight space. Jonathan held him up as I closed the trunk. He started to drag him away when I noticed the knife still sticking out of my brother's back.

"Wait," I said. I marched to where Jonathan stood supporting Thomas and yanked out the knife. Fresh blood oozed from the wound and I grimaced at the sight. I was hungry, yet the sight my brother's blood only made me want to puke.

I lifted one of Thomas's arms and threw it over my shoulder. Jonathan adjusted his grip and did the same. Thomas's feet dragged uselessly behind us.

"I see you found some clothes," I said. I wasn't sure why I was talking. My mind was racing, my heart thumping in my chest. I just wanted to get Thomas somewhere safe so I could start working on him.

Jonathan laughed, though it was without humor. He was wearing a set of Lei's sweatpants and shirt. I had to admit, it looked better on him than it had on me.

The silence stretched on the farther we walked. For some reason, the sound of Thomas's feet dragging behind us was nearly enough to drive me completely batshit. I ground my teeth, just wishing the sound would stop. It was like dragging a corpse.

"It'll be all right," Jonathan said. "We'll figure this out."

As much as I wanted some sort of noise to mask the sound of his dragging feet, somehow talking didn't seem appropriate anymore. I wasn't so sure I could talk without breaking down and bawling.

And that only made me angrier. What did Jonathan care how I felt? We worked together because it was the best way to solve the problem of the murders. I wanted nothing to do with him after this. I just wanted to live my life, with Thomas and Ethan, and forget about this whole mess.

We reached the Den without a further word. Jonathan seemed to note my mood and let me brood in silence. He opened the doors, keeping as much of Thomas's weight on himself as he could, and we worked Thomas in through the doorway sideways.

Pablo was waiting for us as we entered. He glowered at me but didn't say anything as he took the burden from my shoulders. I was in too much pain to fight, so I let him. He took all of Thomas's weight as Jonathan let go.

"I'll be down in a minute," he said. "I need to change. Take him down to a cell." He took the stairs by twos.

My heart clenched at the thought of Thomas in a cell, but I let it go. No sense getting pissed about something I had no control over. There was nowhere else safe we could put him. Not unless I was willing to jam a silver knife in him and leave it, that is. And if I did that, I wouldn't be able to talk with him. There really was no other way.

Pablo led the way into the office. He carried Thomas all the way over to the desk, pressed the button that opened the secret door, and then headed down the stairs. I followed him, feeling like a weakling all the way. I wanted to help so bad, but I knew there was little I could do. I would only make it harder to get down the stairs if I tried to help.

He took Thomas to a middle cell. Pablo was quick to dump him on the cold concrete and back out of the cage. He slammed the door closed, locked it, and wiped his hands on his robe. He was sweating.

I stepped aside as he hurried out of the basement. I could feel both Davin's and the woman's eyes on me, though neither spoke. I ignored them and stared at Thomas where he lay.

He was twitching ever so slightly. I wasn't sure if it was just normal trembling from the silver or if he was actually trying to move. His eyes blazed as he watched me. I felt horrible. I knew what it was like to have silver tainting your blood, trying in vain to move, knowing you can't defend yourself. It was a nearly unbearable experience, one I never wanted to repeat.

A few minutes later, Jonathan came down, dressed in his own clothes. He had exchanged Lei's sweats for a pair of black slacks and a white button-down shirt. His glamour was back in place, making his head whole again.

"We'll have to wait," he said, stopping beside me. "Since he had the knife in him the entire ride, it will take longer than normal for him to break free of the silver's hold."

I bit my tongue to keep from saying something nasty. How hard would it have been to take the knife out of him before dumping him in the trunk?

"Why do you think it happened now?" Jonathan asked.

"What?"

"Why did he start acting this way all of a sudden?"

"You mean acting like a savage form of Thomas?"

"Yeah."

"I don't know. I wish I did."

Jonathan scratched at the side of his head. I noticed a few scrapes he had obtained during the battle. His shirt was long-sleeved, so I couldn't tell if he had been hurt badly or not. I hadn't thought to check before.

"The others acted like werewolves doing their master's bidding," Jonathan said. "They seemed organized, willing to fight together. I didn't believe it until I actually saw it in person."

"But why?" I kept coming to that. I really wanted to believe Thomas was getting better, but it was hard. Looking at him like that, paralyzed, eyes full of hate, it was hard to believe he was anything more than a monster.

Then again, weren't we all?

"Instinct," Jonathan said. "It has to be the reason. They are falling back on what their bodies had been trained to do."

"And what if it's more?" I shook my head. "What if he's in there, knowing I did this to him?"

Jonathan moved closer but didn't touch me. "He is long gone," he said. "As much as both of us would like him to still be in there, it just isn't feasible. His mind was lost the day he was tainted."

I had to contain my rage. I knew what Jonathan was saying was probably right. Deep down, I knew the chances of Thomas turning into the brother I once knew were slim.

But I didn't care. I had to believe we could fix this. Somehow, someway, we would bring him back.

We stood in silence, just watching Thomas. Davin coughed a few times and I vaguely wondered if they had given him his blood yet. He deserved that at least.

Thomas's arm twitched and I quickly knelt by his cage. He couldn't really move yet, but it was close.

"Thomas," I said as gently as I could. "It's me, Kat."

A low growl came from his chest, but that was the only sign that he heard me.

"Thomas." I kept saying his name, hoping it would trigger something. "Listen to me carefully. Can you do that?"

A foot jerked, the growl came again. My lip trembled as I tried to get out the next words. I hated seeing him like this. It tore me up inside like nothing else.

"We're going to help you," I said. "We're going to do whatever it takes to make sure you come out of this. You can have your life back, Thomas. I will make sure of that."

"He's a beast," the woman said from her cell. "Kill him now and do us all a favor."

I did my best to ignore her. What did she know?

"Thomas," I said. "Do you recognize me? Do you know where you are?"

Thomas's upper lip lifted, exposing his fangs. Saliva, mixed with blood, dripped from them. His clawed hands bunched into fists, but he couldn't otherwise move.

The woman laughed then. She pressed herself to the bars, facing us. "The Hand has a way of showing us what is to be tolerated. This abomination is His way of showing us that you all are nothing more than animals."

I couldn't stand the sound of her voice. It pierced straight into my head, brought out the raging beast I tried so hard to keep under control.

I leaped to my feet and charged her cell, blood spurting from my gums as my fangs dropped. I snarled at her as I snaked a hand through the bars and grabbed her by the throat.

"Kat, no." Jonathan started toward me. I turned to face him, baring my teeth. His eyes widened and he froze. Smart man.

I turned back to the woman, pressing my face as close to hers as I could manage. I could almost smell her blood. "That is my brother," I said. "Open your mouth again and I will rip out your tongue."

The woman smiled, her face turning a deep shade of red. I squeezed harder and her smile faltered. For a second, she looked scared for her life, but she quickly steeled herself, her face going blank.

I eased my grip and her color returned to a less alarming shade of red. She took deep, gasping breaths, though she tried to hide it. I started to turn away, but she grabbed me by the arm.

"Animals," she said through gasps. "You are damned." She smiled at me. "Your brother is no better than a dog now. Do you let him ride you like one?"

I snapped. I grabbed her arm and yanked her so hard against the bars, she screamed. She kept her grin in place, even as I latched my teeth into her wrist.

"Kat . . ." Jonathan pleaded, but I was oblivious to him. He was smart enough not to touch me. If he had so much as brushed a finger on my back, I would have torn him apart.

I sucked at her wrist, taking in the blood that would both replenish and heal me. It was all I could think of, was all that mattered.

The woman laughed, a maniacal sound. "Proof," she said. "A demon lives in you. Dance with him for as long as you can. Your time will come."

I screamed, ripping my fangs from her wrist. She opened her mouth to say something else, but I couldn't stand to hear another word from her lips. I grabbed her by the throat, relishing in the feel of her pulse pounding against my hand.

Everything fell silent for a heartbeat. Our eyes locked and I knew right then I would kill her if she said another word.

"His gra—"

. I squeezed.

My fingers burst through her skin. Her eyes widened, but that grin never left. I let go of her arm and yanked with all my might at her throat. Gristle and gore tore away. Blood splattered on the front of my clothes, over the cell bars, over the floor.

She fell to the ground, gurgling. I tossed the chunk of flesh through the bars at her. It landed on her chest, a bloody pulp of a mess. She opened her mouth and more blood poured out.

Then her eyes dimmed and she fell still.

I looked down at my hands, at the blood covering them, and instead of hunger, I felt disgusted. There was skin under my fingernails, blood all the way up my wrists, nearly to my elbows.

I turned and fled the basement. Jonathan didn't try to stop me. I brushed past him and nearly tripped on the stairs as I ran up them, trying my best to put what I had done behind me.

26

Jonathan found me in the sitting room, blood still on my hands. I was sitting on the floor, back pressed against the bar. I had run but hadn't gone far. Where was I to go? I couldn't leave Thomas there alone.

"Are you okay?" he asked, entering the room. He closed the door and walked over to stand next to me.

"No." I stared at the blood. It was already drying.

He stood there looking down at me. I refused to meet his gaze. What would I see there? Accusation? Pity? I didn't want his pity. I didn't want anything from him or anyone else right then.

"Let's get you cleaned up," he said, offering me a hand.

I stared at it without moving. His hands looked clean, though I could see small cuts that were already healing. He hadn't been hurt too badly during the fight, which was good. I don't think I could stand looking at someone else bleeding because of me.

"She was right," I said. I clasped my hands together. They felt sticky. "I'm nothing more than a monster."

"No, you're not."

I laughed. "Really? I just ripped a woman's throat out

because she pissed me off. What kind of normal person does that?"

Jonathan lowered his hand. "Some things you can't control," he said. "You can't help what you are. But that doesn't make you a bad person."

"Doesn't it?" I looked at him bitterly. "I kill people. Most deserve it, but there are those who don't. I make mistakes. I cause pain wherever I go."

I expected him to try to soothe me, to try to tell me some bullshit about how everyone makes mistakes. I wasn't stupid. I knew everyone made mistakes, but my mistakes caused people to lose their lives more often than not.

Jonathan reached out again, this time more insistent. "You're getting blood on my floor."

I blinked at him and then laughed. I couldn't help it. The absurdity of the statement was just too much.

He smiled as I reached out and took his hand. I let go as soon as I was on my feet. He led me across the room, through the hidden door, into the bedroom, and into the adjoining bathroom. He was already washing his hands by the time I stepped through the door.

I looked around while he scrubbed, trying to keep my mind off what I had done. The bathroom was pretty subdued compared with the bedroom. The walls were light blue, and the tub and sink looked like they could have come out of any other house or hotel. I had expected something else, something more glamorous.

Jonathan finished scrubbing his hands. He wiped them dry on a towel hanging from a hook beside the mirror over the sink. He left the water on for me.

"Thanks," I said, stepping in beside him. For some reason, the modest bathroom made me feel better. Maybe it was because it felt normal compared with everything else I was living. Maybe I was just getting over it. I'd killed before. What made this time any different?

"No problem," he said, stepping back to give me room.

I picked up the bar of soap and began scrubbing at my hands. I caught a glimpse of myself in the mirror and had to hide a grimace. I had blood on my face, caked in my hair. I was a mess.

"Here," Jonathan said as I kept scrubbing. "I want to check your stitches." He reached for my coat.

I tensed but let him take off the shortened coat. Now that he had mentioned it, my entire body started hurting again. With every movement of my arm, I could feel my shoulder holster rubbing against the bandage on my back.

I caught Jonathan's wince in the mirror. "That bad?" I asked. Now that the coat was off, I could scrub farther up my arms. Some blood had run up the sleeves, nearly all the way to my armpits.

"Come into the bedroom as soon as you are done," he said. "I'm going to clean that out."

I frowned at him, but he had already turned away. How bad could it really be?

I finished washing my hands and dried them on the same towel Jonathan had used. There was a faint scent of lilac on the towel and I wondered who did his laundry. I just didn't see him or Nathan using detergent that smelled so flowery.

Once my hands were dry, I returned to the mirror. I didn't check my back. I didn't want to see. Instead, I lifted my chin to check the stitches there. The wound was already healed closed, though it was still pretty red and angry looking. Another day or so and all I would have is a scar. It wouldn't be the first.

I took a deep breath, wincing as it tugged at my back. I didn't want to leave the room. I felt safe here, protected. Once I left the bathroom, I would be exposed again. It frightened me to no end.

I turned away from the mirror and left the bathroom. I knew I was just stalling. I had so much I needed to take care of, I couldn't stand around feeling sorry for myself. We had Thomas now. If I could just figure out how to cure him, all of this would be worth it.

I froze just inside the doorway, staring at Jonathan. He had his white shirt unbuttoned. As I watched, he slipped it from his shoulders and tossed it on the bed.

His back was covered in scars, but somehow, it added something to him, made him seem stronger, more real. His muscles rippled beneath his skin and I blushed. I couldn't take my eyes off of him. His arms were firm, powerful. I could almost imagine them holding me down . . .

"What are you doing?" I asked. I sounded pained, like I was on the verge of crying. I had to swallow hard to keep from choking.

He looked from me to the shirt, and I think he actually blushed. "I don't want to get blood on it," he said. "I've ruined enough clothing for one night."

I licked my lips and then realized how that must have looked. I turned away in an attempt to hide my face. I felt like an idiot.

"Sit on the bed," he said. "I'll get some supplies from the bathroom." He walked around me, going wider than he really needed to. I watched him disappear through the door. I couldn't help looking. He looked so damn good.

I looked away as soon as he was gone. I didn't need to be thinking about him like that, especially now. There was too much to do, too much shit I had to deal with without adding to it. I'd never even looked at someone that way before. Why was it happening now?

I slipped off my shoulder holster as I made my way to the bed, doing my best to focus on what was important. It didn't come away easily, sticking to the shirt. I couldn't quite feel it, but I was pretty sure I had bled through the bandage.

I sat on the bed and looked down at myself. The front of my shirt, as well as my jeans, was soaked in blood. It looked as though I had taken a bath in it. I hadn't even realized how much the woman had bled on me until then.

Jonathan returned from the bathroom a few moments later. I averted my eyes as he entered, not wanting a repeat of before. He had an armload of supplies, bandages and tubes of ointment, in his hands. I peeked up and noticed he still hadn't put on a shirt. His chest was bare, hairless, which struck me as odd on a werewolf. I would have thought he would be covered with it.

He sat down behind me, dumping his load onto the bed beside him. "I can't work on this with your shirt on," he said.

I glanced over my shoulder at him. "No way. You can deal with it like this."

"Your shirt is soaked back here." Jonathan looked worried. "I have a shirt you can wear home. It will be big on you, but it won't stick to you once I get this cleaned up."

I shook my head. "You aren't getting me out of my clothes."

He gave me a frank look. "I can't get to the gouges unless you take it off. I'm not trying to get you naked here." He said the last with such seriousness, it made me blush. What was I worried about? He was just trying to be helpful.

I sighed and started working my shirt up my body. It was wet with blood, so it didn't come off easily. And that's not to mention how much it fucking hurt. I groaned as the shirt peeled upward. The bandage came with it, slowly tearing from my skin.

As soon as it was off, I dropped the bloody rag to the floor. The air felt cold against my skin and I covered myself with my arms. I leaned forward, eyes closed. I was nearly shivering.

"This will probably sting." As soon as the words were out of his mouth, a bitingly cold liquid poured over my wound. I hissed in a breath and tensed, but I stayed where I was. I could feel the bubbles pouring from the gouge.

My throat constricted. Infections rarely set in with vampires or werewolves. Our bodies were just too damn resilient. So what did it mean that my back was bubbling like that? Had I made things worse?

Jonathan poured more of the liquid onto my back and I couldn't stop the grunt of pain. I licked my lips and did my best to ignore the flaring agony in my back. At least it took my mind off his body.

"What am I going to do?" I said. I needed to talk so I didn't scream.

"About?" Jonathan started dabbing at the wound with a moist cloth. It felt like he was using sandpaper dipped in salt.

"About Thomas," I said, nearly hissing the words. Good God, it hurt. "I don't know what to do. I can't take him home with me, but I can't leave him here either."

"We'll figure something out."

"But what about Adrian? Sooner or later he'll realize something is up."

"I'll deal with Adrian."

I started to say something more, but just then, Jonathan started poking his finger into the wound. "Fuck!" I yelled, jerking away from him. "What the fuck is wrong with you?"

"There's something in there," he said. "I need to get it out. I'm sorry."

I swallowed and closed my eyes. I couldn't even remember what we had been talking about.

Jonathan resumed poking into the wound. I could tell he was trying to be careful, but it was like he was stabbing me in the back with a scorching-hot poker. Couldn't he have found something smaller than his fingers to get whatever it was out?

I hated every moment that I sat there. It wasn't so much the pain, though that contributed to it. It was the fact I was letting a werewolf tend to my wounds. It was demeaning.

I should have just left as soon as we had Thomas locked up. I could have gone home, taken a bath, and let my body do all the healing on its own.

"Most of your stitching is busted," Jonathan said. "I can't fix it myself, but I think I can use some butterfly bandages to keep it closed until you can get back to Lei."

"I'll be fine," I said. "I'll heal. Just get this over with."

"But you don't want the scars to be too bad, do you?"

I shrugged one shoulder, the good shoulder. "No one is going to see them but me."

We fell silent and I drifted back to my own thoughts. I couldn't stop wondering if Thomas was going to be okay, if what we had done was the right thing. Would my intervention set back his recovery? If we had left him be, would he have eventually regained his sanity?

There was no sense in worrying about it now. He was downstairs and I would have to deal with the consequences, whatever they might be. At least he was off the streets. Adrian couldn't get to him now.

Jonathan finished dabbing at my wounds and started bandaging them up. I hated the feel of the tape on my back. It pulled my skin with every movement, making me feel restricted. As soon as I was home, they were coming off. Screw the scars. What were a few more anyway?

"Done," he said after a few more minutes. "Let's get you a shirt."

I sat on the edge of the bed and stared at the floor while he went to the closet. What was I going to do now? I was afraid to go home, afraid to face Ethan. Even though we had survived our encounter with Thomas, I still felt as though I had failed. It was dumb, I know, but I couldn't help it. Nothing was working out like I wanted it to.

What I needed was to get away. I could feel the pull of Delai. I wanted the comforts the small town offered. There, I could forget about my troubles, even if it was only for a little bit. Adrian wouldn't bother me there; Thomas wouldn't be there, half-crazed and ruined. I could just relax and let the world pass me by.

Fresh anger flared from my gut. Why in the hell was I thinking about that damn little town now? It seemed like every time things got tough, I was looking to run away these days. I couldn't do that, it wasn't me.

"What's wrong?" Jonathan asked. He was standing in front of me, shirt in hand. I hadn't even noticed him. He stared at me for a long second before sitting down beside me.

"I'm fine." It didn't sound convincing, even to me.

"Hey," he said. He reached out and gently lifted my chin so I was looking into his eyes. I jerked away from his touch but kept my gaze on his. "We'll figure this out." He wiped a finger under my eye and I was surprised to see a tear glimmering there.

I wanted to harden, to close up and tell him to leave me the fuck alone, but right then, I didn't have it in me. I just wanted to sit there and cry like a little baby. All the fight had gone out of me. It had been a long time since I'd been this screwed up.

At least I managed to turn off the tears. I wouldn't let him see me cry in earnest.

"I won't let Adrian hurt him," Jonathan said. "I'll keep Thomas here as long as you want me to. I'll protect him, keep him safe. We'll figure out how to help him. Maybe Lei will know what to do."

I nodded, unable to speak. Why was he being so damn nice to me? We weren't supposed to be getting along like this. I was supposed to hate him, to want to kill him. He was a werewolf.

How many times did I have to keep thinking that before I realized it just wasn't going to happen? Something about Jonathan comforted me. I wasn't quite sure what it was, but around him, I could relax more than I could in nearly anyone else's presence.

"I'm okay," I said. "Everything was just getting to me."

"You're human after all."

I looked up and he was smiling.

"Figuratively speaking."

I couldn't help but smile.

Our eyes locked and the entire world seemed to slip away. I could almost see through his glamour, see to the marred features of his face. I had done that to him, yet here he was, trying to make the murderer who had nearly cost him his life feel better. How could he have ever forgiven me?

He edged closer. I tensed, not knowing what to do. The shirt he had brought for me was balled up in his hands, and it reminded me I was sitting here topless. I hadn't put on a bra when I had gotten dressed since it would have rubbed against my wounds.

I let my arms fall away. I didn't care how much he saw. In fact, I almost welcomed it. My life had been filled with so much pain, so much death, it felt good to finally have something else, something deeper.

My lower lip trembled. I wasn't sure if it was from fear or something else. I was terrified, unsure what was going on. I didn't understand what was happening, and yet, deep down, something in me wanted it more than anything I had ever wanted in my life.

We were inches apart. I could feel his breath on my face and my own breathing quickened. I was shaking all over.

I started to reach out, to touch him. I caught myself at the last moment, my hand trembling as I held it inches from his bare chest. What was I doing? Thomas was downstairs, trapped. I couldn't be giving in like this.

The bedroom door suddenly opened, and both Jonathan and I jerked back. Nathan walked in, wearing a pair of Lei's sweats.

"Jeremy is—" He froze, foot hovering an inch off the floor. His face went hard, hateful.

Jonathan handed me the shirt and quickly stood. He

snatched up his white shirt and began to button it on. "Is he going to be okay?"

I yanked the shirt over my head. It was too big, but right then, it felt just right.

"He's still with Lei," Nathan said. His eyes flickered toward me and I saw pure hatred there before he turned back to his Denmaster. "She says he will live, but he might lose his arm. She won't know for sure until she sees how he heals."

I stood. The shirt went all the way down to my knees. Part of me wished it covered me from head to foot. I felt like a fool. I wasn't some girl who gave in to her emotions like that. I never should have let things get that far. I was somewhat thankful Nathan had arrived when he did. If he hadn't, I wasn't so sure how far things would have gone.

"Let's talk out there," Jonathan said, motioning toward the door to the sitting room.

Nathan huffed and turned away. Jonathan followed after him. He stopped at the doorway and looked back at me. There was a tenderness to his eyes that made me want to hit him. I didn't need this. Not now.

He left the room and I took a moment to compose myself before following after. We had work to do.

27

It turned out there wasn't much else to talk about. I couldn't face going back down into the basement to see Thomas, especially since the woman would most likely still be in her cell. Even if she wasn't, the blood would be there. I couldn't handle that right then.

Nathan spent most of the conversation glaring at everyone and everything. It was clear he thought more had gone on in the bedroom than what really had. I knew I should have said something, told him that nothing had happened, yet I was getting a perverse sense of pleasure seeing him squirm. It served him right, really. He didn't need to be concerned about my business anyway.

Eventually, it was decided there was little else we could do that night. Jonathan offered to let me spend the day in the Den, but I declined. I could almost feel Thomas below. It would drive me crazy knowing he was locked up somewhere beneath me.

I decided the best course of action would be for me to go home and try to relax. Maybe talking to Ethan would help me figure out how in the hell I was going to help Thomas get better. None of us had any ideas. It had taken

Thomas this long to get to where he was now. It could take years more before he improved further.

Jonathan walked me to the door, earning more foul looks from Nathan. Pablo, of course, had to join in, glaring from an alcove as we headed for the stairs. Maybe the two of them could get together and form an anti-Kat group where they could say all the nasty things they wanted about me. Whatever made them happy, right?

Jonathan assured me he wouldn't tell Adrian anything. He also promised to explain the woman's death away as an accident. Davin wouldn't let the truth slip, he was sure. Not if the vampire wanted his night under the stars.

I thanked him and hurried away before he decided to try to resume our little moment in the bedroom. I could tell the thought had crossed his mind. As much as I might have enjoyed seeing what it was like, it would be too much of a distraction. Besides, if I let him get that close again, I wasn't so sure I would be able to stop him from going further.

Still, the thought of what might have been made the walk back to the Den's garage lonely. Each step weighed on me. I knew I had done the right thing in capturing Thomas, in leaving the Den when I had. I just needed time to figure out what to do next.

I mounted my Honda and tore out of the garage as if I could outrun my thoughts. I needed to get away. The farther I went, the better it would be for everyone.

I found myself turning away from home and heading toward Delai. I could get away from everything there. I could almost hear the town calling to me. The place scared me a little, but at the same time, it made me feel good. What would one more night hurt?

The wind buffeted me as I sped along, intent on fleeing from my troubles. If Thomas hadn't been involved, I think I would have been okay. With him at the center of all of this, I was a mess inside. I could hardly tell which way was up.

I slowed, realizing running away wasn't going to help

anyone. Thomas needed me. Ethan would be waiting for me. I couldn't abandon either of them like that.

A strange sense of relief flowed over me as I did a U-turn, earning a few honks and curses, and headed toward home. It was as if I had escaped putting myself in even more danger without realizing it. Once all of this was over, I could consider paying Delai another visit. Maybe I could take Thomas. Maybe we'd both find a place to belong.

It was still pretty dark when I rode up my driveway. The living room light was on, and I pulled into the garage feeling guilty. I should have taken more time out of my night to spend with Ethan. He could use the company just as much as I could. And while I could just up and leave any time I wanted, Ethan couldn't. Just leaving the house gave him a massive panic attack.

I hurried inside and found Ethan waiting for me in the dining room. He was holding a cup of coffee up under his chin like he was trying to warm his face with the steam. The low sound of the television came from the other room.

"Are you . . . ?" He floundered for a moment before falling silent.

"I'm fine," I said. "We found Thomas."

Ethan's eyes widened and he set the cup down on the table. "Is he still alive?"

I nodded and my face must have fallen, because a look of concern crossed his visage. I tried to come up with something to say that would explain what condition Thomas was in, but nothing came to mind. Every time I tried to picture him, I kept seeing the woman in her cell, her blood pumping onto the cold concrete.

"Do you think you can fix him?" Ethan asked. "I mean, no one's ever found a cure as far as I know."

"I don't know."

He took a deep breath and started pacing. He ran his fingers through his hair, mussing his already wild locks.

I watched him and could see his growing agitation. He

wanted to say something, that much was clear. I waited him out, not wanting to interrupt his thought process. I trusted him to come up with a solution. He seemed to always know what to do, how best to help. It's what he did.

"I was thinking," he said after a few moments. "But I don't know if you want to hear it." He gave me a worried look.

"Go for it," I said. "I don't think you can say anything that will make my night any worse than it's already been."

He made a sound. I wasn't sure if it was a cough or a laugh. It was probably a little bit of both. "I'm not so sure about that."

"Don't worry about it," I said. "I'm too tired to let anything faze me tonight."

The concern crossed his face again. "Are you sure you're okay?" he asked. "You look beat."

I closed my eyes and fought against the urge to get angry. I wasn't even sure what I was angry about. Was it the constant questions asking how I was feeling? Was it thinking about Thomas? About the dead woman?

About Jonathan?

I felt myself start to blush and did my best to hide it. I so didn't need Ethan learning about what had nearly taken place in Jonathan's bedroom.

"I've been pummeled, torn, stitched, and had a close confrontation with a brother I thought lost forever," I said instead. "I'm more than beat."

He smiled nervously. "I can always talk to you about it later," he said. "I haven't worked on anything tonight and, well, I'm getting a little agitated myself."

My thoughts immediately went to his demon. I was positive that was what was making him anxious. I had no idea what kind of hold it had on him, but I could tell whatever it was, it was pretty strong.

"Say what you need to say," I said. "Then I'm going to go upstairs, take a long, hot bath, and spend the day trying to figure out what in the hell I'm going to do about this piss hole of a situation."

Ethan licked his lips and took a step away from me. "It's just that . . ." He trailed off and scrunched up his face like he was trying to figure out how to say something really bad. "You know about . . . well . . . Beligral." He nearly whispered the demon's name.

"Yeah," I said, suddenly wary. I really didn't want to have to worry about the demon on top of everything else.

"Well, you see, he's good at a lot of things," Ethan went on. He had stopped pacing and looked like he was ready to bolt the moment I showed a hint of anger. I didn't blame him.

"What's your point?"

"I was thinking that if you could bring Thomas here or something, maybe Beligral could, I don't know, help somehow?"

I closed my eyes and counted to ten. I couldn't believe he was dropping this on me now. As much as I liked Ethan, he could choose some piss-poor times to bring things up.

"But I can see you don't want to talk about that right now," he said. He backpedaled out of the dining room and headed for the stairs. His full cup of coffee was still sitting on the table. "I'll, uh, be downstairs for a little while. See you tomorrow night." He scurried out of sight before I could say anything.

I all but stomped up the stairs to my room, wondering why I put up with him sometimes. I was just glad he was so preoccupied with his demon shit, he hadn't commented on my overlarge shirt. I didn't want to have to explain that to him. I could hardly explain it to myself.

I was halfway down the hall before I realized I'd left my shortened coat at the Den. Hell, my gun and shoulder holster were still sitting beside Jonathan's bed.

I grumbled all the way into my bedroom. I slipped out of my clothes and started the bath. I couldn't believe I'd been so forgetful. The gun was loaded with silver bullets.

If Nathan found it first, what was to stop him from using it on me the next chance he got? The bullets would paralyze me just as fast as they would one of the wolves.

I was starting to get scatterbrained. I never left anything behind, and yet how many weapons have I lost in just the last few days? I just wanted everything to be over so things could get back to normal.

The bath was comforting, but it hurt. The bandages on my back slowly peeled away the longer I soaked, exposing the wounds to the hot water. I sort of wished I could melt away as easily. Sometimes it seemed like it would just be easier that way.

At least the stinging in my back kept my mind off of everything else. It wasn't until I slid out of the water and toweled dry that things started flooding back.

I was over the dead woman at least. It surprised me to realize I didn't feel bad any longer. She'd tried to kill me, would have killed others if given the chance. Why I'd ever felt guilty for killing her was beyond me. If she hadn't paralyzed me the night she attacked me, I would have killed her then. What were a few days in between?

I tried not to think about it. If I really looked at my actions back at the Den, I might start hating myself all over again. There were too many important things to worry about for me to start sulking again.

I wandered into the bedroom, picking up Jonathan's shirt as I crossed the room. I didn't even realize I was doing it until I was sitting on the bed, his long shirt draped over my shoulders, hanging to my knees. It felt good against my skin, almost like a favorite nightgown.

I sighed. What was my life coming to? I should have burnt the damn shirt the moment I had taken it off. I didn't need the reminder. I shouldn't have let Jonathan fix up my back. I could have used the bath to clean out the wound. I'd done as much before.

A cricket chirruped outside my window. The night was

fading and it would soon be morning. I was going to be stuck in my room for hours, alone with my own thoughts. I needed to be spending that time thinking about Thomas, not Jonathan.

But it was hard. Every time I thought about my brother, I thought about his rage-filled glare, the way he came at me, intent to kill. There was no doubt he would have torn my head from my shoulders if I had let him.

Everything I had, everything I believed in, was slowly falling apart.

The night eventually gave way to day and I couldn't make myself stop thinking. Nothing I came up with was helpful. I kept seeing the same visions, going over the same thoughts, without ever once coming to any sort of decision. I wasn't cut out for this.

About halfway through the day, I realized I was getting nowhere. It was like I had come up against a solid brick wall with no way around. I could beat at it all I wanted, but it wouldn't get me through to the other side. I knew the answers were there, just out of reach. I needed something to get to them.

And that was when it hit me.

I'd spent so long refusing to listen to anything that wasn't what I wanted to hear, I missed the bigger picture. No one had ever cured someone whose blood had been mixed. It was supposedly impossible. Even Lei wouldn't know what to do.

But Lei, like everyone else I knew, was only mortal. We were all limited by our knowledge, by what we have experienced. I needed someone who could go outside what we knew, look down other avenues for answers. The door to the other side of the wall was there. I just couldn't reach it by myself.

But I knew someone who could.

I waited impatiently for the sun to go down. As soon as night fell, I was out of my room, pounding on Ethan's door.

He opened it, eyes heavy. He stared at me a moment, then his eyes traveled down to my toes and back up again.

Uh," he said, his voice thick with sleep. He had definitely stayed up too late. He looked back down, his gaze settling around my knees.

I followed his gaze and felt a hint of aggravation. While Jonathan's shirt worked fine to lie around in alone, it wasn't long enough for me to walk around in without wearing pants. I might not be a prude, but that didn't mean I needed to be flashing so much leg around Ethan. It might distract him.

"Up here," I said, snapping my fingers. As much as I didn't care how much of me he saw, it did bother me he was staring so openly.

Ethan dragged his eyes to my face. He blinked a few more times as if he wasn't quite awake, then suddenly his eyes widened. "Oh," he said, taking a step back. "I didn't mean . . ." He glanced down again and nearly broke his own neck as he jerked his head back up. "Sorry."

"It's okay," I said. "I have something to ask of you."

"Sure," Ethan said. He tried to smooth down the wildness of his hair. He was still wearing the same clothes he had been wearing the night before. He smelled of stale sweat and pizza. He must have come upstairs and passed out right away.

"I've changed my mind," I said. Something clenched in my gut as I spoke. Did I really want to do this?

Ethan's brow crinkled. He rubbed at his face with both hands like he wasn't quite sure he was actually awake. He looked at me, slightly bewildered. "About?"

I stared into his eyes and wondered how Ethan was able to do this day after day. I knew his life was hard, knew every moment had to scare him to death. I mean, he was living with a vampire. No normal person could do that every day and stay sane.

I knew what I was about to ask of him was stupid,

would probably somehow make his life worse. I knew it would probably cause more harm than good, but what choice did I have? I couldn't stand to see my brother suffer any longer. If this had even the slightest chance of working, I was willing to take the chance that it would blow up in my face.

"Kat?" Ethan said. "What did you want?"

I took a deep breath and let it out slowly. There was no going back now.

"I want you to take me down into your lab," I said. It felt like the entire world suddenly stopped to wait for what I had to say next. I scarcely dared to breathe. "It's time I met your demon."

28

"Uh, what?"

"Your demon," I said. "I want to talk to him."

Ethan's mouth unhinged and slowly fell open. He gaped at me, completely at a loss for words.

"I'll wait for you downstairs. You have time to clean up, so there's no rush." I turned and walked away.

I went downstairs, sat at the table, then immediately stood up and went to the kitchen instead. I made sure to get a filter this time and made Ethan's coffee. I figured if he hadn't recovered by the time he came downstairs, a good jolt of caffeine should do it.

Once the coffee was perking, I went back to sit down, but before I was all the way in my seat, I realized I couldn't go downstairs to see his demon dressed as I was. I headed for the stairs, unconsciously pulling the edges of the shirt down. It might be long, but it wasn't long enough.

I passed Ethan in the hallway. His eyes were still wide, as if I had shocked him so bad his face got stuck that way. I could feel his eyes on my backside as I passed him and headed for the bedroom. There was a thump behind me and Ethan let out a startled "oof." I glanced back to see him stepping away from the door frame of the hall bathroom.

I shook my head as I stepped into the bedroom. I gave
Ethan a quick little wave and closed the door before he
could return it. A moment later, the shower started up and
I couldn't help but wonder if he was going to make it a
cold one.

I quickly got dressed in a loose-fitting shirt and jeans.
Something about visiting with Ethan's demon made me
want to dress in my leather, but I knew it would be a bad
idea. I'd much rather be able to move without pain than to
look good for a creature I wasn't so sure I really wanted to
meet.

I was downstairs again before Ethan's shower was done.
As soon as the water shut off, I poured him a cup of coffee
and took it to the table. I was pretty sure he took it straight
black but brought out the sugar bowl anyway. I'd never
seen him put anything into the coffee, but then again, I
never really paid close enough attention to know for sure.

Ethan came downstairs a few minutes later. His hair
was still damp, and the collar of his T-shirt was wet. He
looked as nervous as I felt.

"Thanks," he said as I handed him his mug. He took a
sip and started for the stairs without paying the sugar bowl
a glance.

I followed him down into the basement. He stopped at
the door to his lab and just stared at it. He took another
drink of his coffee, seemed to savor it, and then set the
mug down on the table beside the door.

"So this is it," he said.

"This isn't such a big deal," I said, though I wasn't con-
vinced of that myself.

He smiled. "If you say so."

He pulled a key from his pocket and inserted it into the
lock. The doorknob fell open, revealing a fingerprint
reader. I stared at it, surprised. I'd seen him go into the lab
before but never realized he had installed a reader there

too. I really needed to start paying better attention to what went on in my own house.

Ethan looked back at me, his hand hovering over the reader as if blocking off my view. "Are you sure?" he said. "This could be . . . unsettling."

"You were the one who said I should meet him."

Ethan shrugged. "Yeah, but I never thought you'd actually do it. It's like, you know, that whole I ask, you reject, we move on as we were kind of thing. I never expected you to take me up on it."

I rolled my eyes. "Open it."

He gave a nervous laugh and turned back to the door. I could tell he wasn't comfortable with letting me in, even if he *had* invited me. This had been his private sanctuary for years. How many times had he summoned that demon down there? How many times before I knew him? I was about to come face-to-face with a part of Ethan I'd never known existed until recently.

He pressed his thumb to the reader and the door clicked open. He led the way down into his lab.

The lab, unlike his bedroom, was clean and well maintained. Shelves lined one wall, holding various objects in jars and boxes. I couldn't tell what any of them were. The boxes were closed and the jars had been painted black. I probably didn't want to know what they contained.

A table much like what I used to hold my weapons upstairs stood across the room, and a workbench stood beside it. There were papers piled on one corner, and one of my recently used swords lay in the middle of the table. The walls behind the table held more partially finished weapons on hooks. I'd never seen one of my swords before it had been completed.

I looked around, expecting there to be a furnace or something, but as far as I could tell, there was no source of heat in the lab. He made my swords and knives down here, not to mention the silver bullets I used. There should have been some source of heat. It made me wonder how much of a hand Ethan really had in the creation of the weapons.

Finally, my eyes rested on the circle in the middle of the room. It looked to be made of silver, though I couldn't be sure unless I touched it. It took up a good portion of the room. There was nothing touching the circle, wasn't anything anywhere close to it other than a single recliner that sat within its confines. It looked well used.

"Nice place," I said, my skin crawling. This reminded me way too much of an evil scientist's lab in some old horror movie. The only thing missing were the wires and electrodes strewn all over the place.

"It suffices," Ethan said, moving across the room. He took a wide berth around the silver circle and sat down in a chair beside his workbench. He wheeled around to face me.

"So," I said, completely at a loss. "What now?"

"Now I tell you the rules," he said. He seemed suddenly serious.

"Okay."

"First, no weapons. I should have told you that before we came down. Beligral doesn't take well to threats of any kind. I should know." He looked down, his face reddening.

I looked down at myself. "Done." I hadn't even thought to grab my weapons before coming down. Now that Ethan brought it up, I felt like a fool. I never would have walked into a situation like this before without being armed. I knew far too little about demons to know whether they would have been effective or not anyway.

"Second, stay away from the circle. Do not touch it, do not cross it. Don't throw anything through it or reach for anything offered."

I nodded. "How do you get things from him then?"

"He leaves whatever I need behind. If I need him afterward, I just summon him again."

"All right," I said. "Anything else?"

"No deals," he said. "Absolutely none, zip, zilch, nada.

If he offers to fix Thomas and wants something from you, refuse. I don't care if it sounds simple, if it sounds like the perfect bargain, do *not* accept. I'll make the deals. He is my burden and I will shoulder it alone."

I frowned at that. "You are doing this because I want you to. Thomas and anything that comes along with him are my responsibility."

"No," Ethan said, firm. "I won't do it if you don't agree to this. I won't have you trapped like I am."

That stopped me. "Okay," I said. I hated agreeing to anything that might end up with Ethan in more trouble than he was already in. I simply had no choice.

"I mean it, Kat."

"I said okay."

He stared at me, then finally nodded. "All right, then. I think that about covers it. He'll try to get you to do something stupid. Just stay back, don't agree to anything, and this should be cake."

I wasn't so sure about that but nodded anyway. This was a lot more complicated than I'd expected.

Ethan rose from the chair. He opened one of the many drawers of his workbench and removed a large piece of sidewalk chalk. He walked around the circle, making a new chalk outline just outside the silver. He was murmuring something under his breath, but I didn't listen too closely. I didn't really want to hear what he was saying.

Once the circle was complete, he stepped back, dropping the chalk back into the drawer. "Can't be too careful," he said as he reached back in and removed five candles. At first I thought they were simple tan-colored candles, but as he started placing them around the circle, I noticed the thin red veins running through them.

I grimaced and tried really hard not to look at them. I wasn't sure if the candles were actually made of flesh or just crafted to look that way. I really didn't want to find out.

Ethan gave me a nervous smile as he continued working.

He produced a book of matches from his pocket and began
lighting the candles, whispering an incantation with each.
The candles seemed to burn brighter than they should and
gave off a peculiar scent that made my stomach churn.
They really did smell like burning flesh.

He finished with the last candle and backed away. "This
is it," he said. "If you want to back out now, I won't hold
it against you. This can be intense."

"I'm staying," I said. Ethan gave me a pleading look,
almost as if he wished I would back out. "I'm staying," I
repeated, and he nodded.

"All right," he said. He wiped his face with both hands,
leaving a smear of white chalk dust on his cheek. "Here
goes nothing."

I expected him to pull out a vial of blood or cut his palm
or something, but he only walked to the edge of the circle,
head down, and started chanting. The words made no sense
to me. They flowed one on top of the other, almost like a
song. He mumbled them, which made it even harder to understand what he was saying. I didn't know if that was for
my benefit or if that was the way it was supposed to be done.

At first, nothing seemed to happen. Ethan just stood
there, hands moving slowly in small circles at his waist,
head lowered, murmuring those words over and over.

I stared into the circle, waiting for something to happen.
After a few minutes, I began to wonder if my presence had
somehow mucked up the ritual.

The candles flared, drawing my eye. I could feel their
heat from clear across the room. The inside of the circle
seemed to grow a little darker as the light of the candles
grew that much brighter. The air felt thicker, as if there was
too much of it. Or not enough. I wasn't sure which.

A speck of darkness appeared near the floor within the
circle. It was about the size of a quarter and was so dark it
seemed as though that part of the floor had simply vanished. I only noticed it because I had been looking directly

at it when it appeared. Ethan's chanting increased, as did the heat from the candles. He was sweating profusely now. The back of his T-shirt was stuck to his skin and it was only getting hotter.

Slowly, the speck of darkness elongated vertically, almost like a zipper being opened. As it expanded, heat poured out. It was so hot my eyes started to burn, but I refused to look away. I didn't want to miss whatever was about to happen.

Light flashed in the middle of the circle, nearly blinding me. Five bars of pure white light shot from candle to candle, forming a perfect pentagram. The image hung for a moment and then winked out as the tear opened the rest of the way.

Something stepped out.

My mind couldn't make sense of what I was seeing at first. I saw skin, but it was red, blistered. Something black flapped behind the figure, almost like wings made of pure darkness. The image of the demon flashed as it stepped through the portal, and instead of the red-skinned monster I expected, a man dressed in a suit stepped forward.

He smiled at Ethan, displaying teeth that were clearly not human. Every yellow tooth ended in a point I knew was sharper than any knife.

Beligral's eyes turned toward me. They burned fiercely, red pits from the deepest hells. They bore straight through me, into what was left of my tattered soul. I was pinned there, unable to move, unable to think. It was so hot I could hardly breathe.

"Well, well, well," the demon said. He leaned forward on a cane I hadn't noticed before. I was almost positive he hadn't been holding it a moment ago. "What have we here?"

Ethan stepped back from the circle, hair matted to his head. He looked utterly exhausted. "Master," he said, drawing Beligral's gaze. I nearly screamed at the word, not liking the implications. "I bring to you Lady Death."

Beligral smiled, exposing those deadly teeth once more. He reeked of sulfur. The entire room did.

"Really?" he said. I shuddered at the sound of his voice. It sounded like two people speaking at once: One sound was normal, the voice he wanted us to hear; the other was like darkness incarnate. It was just barely there, almost beyond hearing. It grated and rolled from a face that I knew was a fake. It turned every word out of his mouth into a sort of blasphemy.

"Lady Death," he said. He moved across the circle and sat in the chair, propping one leg over the armrest. "I think this is going to be a very good night indeed."

Beligral laughed and right then, I truly knew what hell felt like.

I opened my mouth to speak but nearly choked on the oppressive heat. The room was far too hot, far too stuffy. His presence pressed down on me, weighed so heavily on me I could hardly move.

I fought against his gaze, tried to gain control of my body again. I couldn't speak, but I didn't need to. I just needed to get away.

I somehow managed to jerk my eyes away from him. As I did, the air suddenly seemed that much lighter, that much cooler. I sucked in large gasps of air, my entire body trembling.

I couldn't stay here. I couldn't stand to be pinned by his gaze again. Not if I wanted to keep my sanity.

Without saying a word, I turned and fled up the stairs, away from the demon whose very gaze seemed to burn my flesh, out of Ethan's lab, where the world suddenly seemed a lot more dangerous now that I knew what lay hidden just out of sight of mortal man.

As soon as I was clear of the room, I collapsed, trembling against the floor, terrified I had made the biggest mistake of my life.

29

"Pretty heavy, isn't it?"

I looked up, eyes wide, to see Ethan kneeling beside me. His hair was a mess and he looked terrible, but at least he was composed. It was more than I could say about myself.

"Is he gone?" I asked, standing. I refused to show any more weakness than I already had. I was really starting to get annoyed with how weak I'd been as of late. I should have been able to handle the demon.

Of course, I knew why I was so rattled. Thomas's discovery had really fucked me up. I needed to get my head on straight and start focusing like I was used to doing. I couldn't keep freaking out over every little thing.

"No," Ethan said.

"What? You left a fucking demon alone down there?" I couldn't help but scream it.

Ethan recoiled from me. "He can't get out," he said. "Only someone from the outside can break the circle. It's safe."

"It sure as hell didn't feel safe."

"It used to have that effect on me too," he admitted. "But you get used to it."

"I don't see how."

He shrugged. "Just like you got used to dealing with life as a vampire. Anyone can overcome anything if they really want to."

He was right. My anger ebbed, as did my fear. "You're being quite philosophical for someone who summons demons for a living."

Ethan smiled. "I have my moments."

I took a deep breath and let it out slowly. It did wonders for my composure. Now that I was standing in the basement, away from Beligral and his oppressive heat and stare, I felt stupid. He was trapped in his circle. I knew that. Ethan had been doing this since he was a kid. How dangerous could the demon really be?

"I want to go back down," I said, earning a surprised look from Ethan. "I have to know if he can help me or not."

"Are you sure?" He gave me a skeptical look. "I mean, you freaked back there. I don't want you to do something if you don't think you can handle it."

I glared at him. "I *can* handle it."

He grinned. "Okay, okay," he said. "I just want to be sure. I mean, I could ask him for you if you want. There's no need for you to go back down. He met you and that's good enough for me."

"No," I said. "I'm going to do this."

I didn't give him a chance to argue. I headed back down the stairs into the lab. It was still hot, but it was far more manageable now that I knew it was coming. I walked across the room and leaned against the table with my weapons just in case the circle wasn't as secure as Ethan thought it to be.

"Welcome back," Beligral said. "I'm surprised you returned."

I didn't answer. My eyes roamed the room, checking to make sure everything was normal. I still needed a few moments to fully compose myself anyway. Being in Beligral's presence was like standing in front of the sun. It was oppressive.

My eyes fell on the candles and I flinched in surprise. They were lit, but the flames weren't flickering. Instead, they were frozen in place, like they were a recording and someone had pressed pause.

Beligral laughed and I looked at him. He was sitting in the chair, cane lying across his lap. He would have looked like any other guy as long as you didn't look into his eyes or he didn't open his mouth. He could easily pass for human if he really wanted to.

Which was part of the ploy, I was sure. I'd seen glamours before, and I knew he was ramping up the glamour now. There was no way a demon could look like that. I could almost see the horns hidden behind the pleasant face.

"Do you know why I'm here?" I asked. It was a struggle to get out the words, but I managed. Each passing second seemed to get easier and easier. I would never be comfortable standing in the same room as a demon, but at least I was able to handle it now.

It did put the whole hanging around werewolves thing in perspective. That was nothing compared with this.

"You are here because you wish something of me," he said. "You wouldn't be here otherwise."

Ethan edged around me and stood by his workbench. He looked nervous again.

"Do you know what happens when vampire and werewolf blood mix?" I asked. It felt stupid to ask the question of a demon. He probably knew everything.

"Yes," Beligral answered, his mouth curving upward as if amused I had to ask.

"My brother has been tainted in this way. Can you cure him?"

The demon stretched and leaned back in his chair. "I don't know," he said. "This is something I personally have never tried before."

"It is possible?"

He shrugged. "Perhaps." He looked at his nails and started picking at them. "Do you know what the taint in your blood is? What makes your blood react so differently than that of a normal human?" His eyes flickered to Ethan at the last.

"No," I said. "And I don't care."

"Ah, but you might," he said. "You are a vampire, are you not? Wouldn't you like to know your origins?"

I tensed. I knew where I came from, who my parents were. I didn't need to know any more than that. "Can you help Thomas or not?"

"The blood is a funny thing," Beligral went on as if I hadn't spoken. "It can be manipulated to do quite extraordinary things. A hint of demon's blood, cursed to twist the body of those infected, can do quite a lot of unexpected things."

My throat locked up. Demon blood? Was he implying what I thought he was implying?

"I see you understand," he said, laughing. "Your blood, once pure, is now tainted. The taint, created in my world, spread because one of my kind thought it would make an interesting experiment." His red eyes burned into me. "His children are many, though they do not know his name."

I wanted to make him stop. All I wanted was an answer to my question about Thomas, and he was just making even more questions run through my head, questions I didn't want to think about.

"And there are more than you know," he said. "Your kind, the vampire, was not even the first. The werewolf, the other you know, is one of many. There are more, so many more." He paused and licked his lips as if savoring the words. "And I can show you. If you let me, I could show you all kinds of wonders, tell you of things you could only imagine."

"No," I managed. It was hard to breathe again, but this time it had nothing to do with the heat. "I just want to know if you can help Thomas or not. I don't care about the rest."

"Don't you?" he asked, his face showing mock surprise. "I would think it would be of great interest to you. If you know what you are, where you came from, then you might find a way to . . . shall we say, cure your malady?"

My knees went weak at that. I leaned heavily on the table, using it to support myself. "Cure?"

"Oh yes," he said. "I know a way." He smiled, displaying those too-sharp teeth. "If you wish it, I could make it so that you can see the sun again."

About a million thoughts zoomed through my brain. Could it be possible? Could the demon actually cure me of my vampirism? If so, then perhaps he really could save Thomas. Perhaps he could save anyone who wished to be free of the taint.

No. I couldn't believe him. If it was possible to cure the blood taint, someone would have discovered it by now. He was playing me, trying to get me to agree to something that would end up destroying me.

Still, the idea was lodged firmly in my brain. It would haunt me forever.

"Thomas," I said, forcing away the temptation to ask him to tell me more. As much as I wanted to be Pure-blooded again, I wanted Thomas cured more. "Can you help him?"

Beligral chuckled. It was like the rumbling of boulders. "Perhaps," he said, "if you are willing to pay my price."

"No," Ethan spoke up. "She will not make deals with you."

"Then I cannot help." Beligral crossed his arms and closed his eyes.

"What do you want?" I asked, surprising even myself.

"No, Kat," Ethan said. "You don't know what you're doing."

"Ah, but she does," the demon said, opening his eyes.

"She might not know it consciously, but she knows more than she realizes. It's in her blood."

"What do you want?" I repeated.

"It's quite simple, really. Bring this Thomas to me. I will see if there is anything left to save. All I ask in return is that you promise to visit me again. I tire of the same thing every night. I would like to see the fruits of my labors in action."

I knew it couldn't be that easy. Ethan had said not to make a deal with the demon, but really, he wasn't asking for much. It sounded simple enough, but I did have to wonder. What could possibly be in it for him?

Then again, did it really matter? This whole thing might be some sort of trap, but it was Thomas I was doing it for. I couldn't just turn away what might be the only chance I had of curing him. What more could the demon possibly do to me that hasn't already been done before?

"Fine," I said. "You help save Thomas and I will come and see you again."

Beligral smiled. "I will do my best," he said. "Do you agree to our terms?"

"Kat . . ."

"Yeah," I said, ignoring Ethan's pleading tone.

Beligral's smile widened. "Then it is done."

A searing pain behind my ear jolted me back against the table. It was gone almost as soon as it had happened.

"What the hell was that?" I gasped.

Ethan's eyes filled with tears. His mouth opened and closed a few times; then he turned away.

"No need to dismiss me," Beligral said. "I'll see you soon." He turned and flipped a hand upward. The air seemed to rip with the motion, exposing the blackness again. He glanced back at me once more, winked, and then stepped through. The hole closed as soon as he was gone. All five candles snuffed out at the same instant.

I groaned and slumped to the floor, all the energy flooding from my body. Had I really made a deal with a demon?

Ethan had yet to face me again. He walked around the circle, murmuring as he gathered his candles. He set them on the table and leaned against it. He was trembling.

I watched him clean up, wondering how he knew if the demon was really gone. If Beligral could hide his true nature, then couldn't he very well hide his presence? Hell, it was obvious he could dismiss himself from our world. Did that mean he could summon himself as well?

"I'll take you to the Den," I said, barely able to look up. "You can summon him where they have Thomas held."

Ethan spun around, eyes bulging from his head. "No," he said. "I can't do this anywhere else."

"I can't bring Thomas here," I said.

"You have to. I can't go   go out there." He looked up toward the ceiling as if he could see the night sky. "Everything I need is here."

I closed my eyes. My throat was dry, and my head and back hurt. I was sure I was bleeding again, but I just didn't care. "Fine," I said. "I'll find a way to get him here. Can you summon him again tonight?"

"Tonight?" Ethan bit his lower lip. "I could, but he doesn't like it."

"Tough," I said, standing. "I'll be back later, Thomas in tow. Be ready for me."

Ethan nodded. I started to turn away, but he stopped me. "You shouldn't have made a deal with him," he said in a small voice. "He has you now."

"He doesn't have a damn thing." I paused. I hadn't meant to snap at him like that. I softened my voice as I spoke. "I had to do it. For Thomas."

"You're marked," Ethan said. "You won't be able to escape him now."

I reached up and touched the spot behind my ear that had flared in pain. There was something there. The flesh was raised, bumpy.

I dropped my hand. I wanted to break down and cry, but I steeled myself instead. I was terrified. I'd probably made a mistake by making a deal with the demon, but what choice had I had?

"I'll deal with it," I said. "Just be ready when I return."

Ethan didn't say anything. He didn't have to.

I headed upstairs to get my gear. My hand drifted to the mark behind my ear. My hands were trembling, but at least Ethan hadn't seen it. What had I done?

I strapped on my weapons, checked to make sure the Glock was loaded and the knives were sharp. I smoothed back my hair, my hands still trembling, and headed for the door. There wasn't anything I could do about the mark now. I'd made my choice.

I left to get my brother.

30

A handful of terrified Cultists were standing just inside the door to the Den. They jumped as I came in, eyes wide, and for a moment, I thought they were afraid of me. When they instead crowded around me, I knew something bad had happened.

Thomas.

I bolted for the office. One of the Cultists tried to reach out and clutch at me, but I shook him off. Whatever had happened, it had to be bad if the Purebloods were looking to me for comfort.

The office was empty. The hidden doorway was hanging open, which couldn't be good. I could hear raised voices from down below, though I couldn't quite make out who was talking. At least there wasn't screaming. Yet.

I hit the stairs at a run. Even with my enhanced reflexes, I nearly tripped going down them. My legs just couldn't keep up with the speed my brain wanted. I needed to get down there before something happened.

But what made me so sure it already hadn't? Could Thomas have broken free? Could Nathan have killed him while Jonathan was distracted? Or was it something else? I had to know.

I leaped from the last stair and skidded to a stop when I saw the three men. Nathan and Jonathan both looked angry, though Jonathan seemed relieved I had arrived. They were both standing in front of Thomas's cage, my brother thrashing against the bars, but they weren't trying to keep him in.

They were trying to keep someone out.

"You kept this from me," Adrian said, turning to face me. Normally, his face was always blank, his voice controlled, yet now he was near bubbling with rage. His teeth were exposed, sharp and pointed. His eyes were a feral yellow. He was on the verge of shifting.

I had my gun out and had it trained on Adrian's forehead the moment I saw him. "Back the fuck away," I said. I glanced past him to make sure Thomas was okay. He was bleeding from his scalp, as well as his hands where he pounded them up against the wall. Otherwise, he looked unharmed.

"We were supposed to work together," Adrian said. "You betrayed me."

"We couldn't trust you." I made sure to include Jonathan and the Cult in my statement. I didn't want him thinking I did this on my own or forced their hand. I kind of hoped this would be the moment where Jonathan finally told me to kill the bastard.

Adrian took a deep, shuddering breath. He glanced over his shoulder at the two wolves at his back, then turned back to me as if they were no longer a threat. "Your bullet won't stop me," he said.

"It will if I hit you in just the right spot."

A smile curved his lips. "You could try."

I almost did it right then and there, but Jonathan stepped forward, hand outstretched.

"No," he said. "Not here. I will have no more bloodshed within my Den."

Nathan's fists clenched. It was obvious he wanted to kill Adrian as much as I did, if not more so.

From the far corner, a harsh, tortured laugh filled the room. Davin watched us, blood dribbling down his chin. He held an empty cup that had recently held blood. I ignored him.

"Adrian," I said. "I won't tell you again. Get away from him."

"Your brother?" he said, his face going to his more normal neutral. "He reminds me of you in many ways. There are so many similarities, even with him afflicted as such. I should have known."

I stepped forward, my aim never wavering. "Now."

He bowed his head slightly and stepped to the side. His eyes were still blazing, but he was in much more control of himself. It was like I was a calming influence on him. I didn't like that thought at all.

"Keep going." I stepped around him, making sure not to get too close. I didn't need him reaching out and grabbing my gun and using it on me. And I knew he could do it. You didn't live as long as Adrian had if you were slow.

He kept walking until we were standing opposite each other again. This time, I was standing in front of the cell with Adrian close to the stairs.

"Go," I said, "or I'll kill you." I was worried my bullet wouldn't affect him at all, even if I hit him in the head. He was resistant to silver, something I had seen with my own two eyes. What made me so sure he hadn't done something to make his skull hard enough to stop a bullet? Stranger things have happened.

Adrian glanced around the room, at the two wolves standing behind me. Some of his anger returned as he looked at them, but he did his best to hide it.

"I knew you couldn't be trusted," he said, looking squarely at Jonathan. "There are things I could say that would make you a target, things you thought buried." His eyes traveled to Nathan and he smirked. "And you . . ." He shrugged as if he didn't need to say more.

Finally, his eyes landed on me again. "Even after this betrayal, I still have a spot for you," he said. "Your willingness to stand up to me proves you are strong enough to stand by my side." His gaze flickered to the other wolves. "Think about it."

With that, he turned and walked away. I really wanted to pull the trigger and rid myself of Adrian once and for all, but Jonathan's whispered "No" kept me from doing it.

Adrian vanished up the stairs. I expected him to slam the door as he left, or maybe kill a few Cultists on his way out, but all remained silent upstairs.

"I'm sorry about that," Jonathan said.

I turned to face him, anger taking over. My gun was aimed at him now. "You let him down here?"

He shook his head, eyes on my gun. "He came in while I was checking on your brother. Nathan tried to stop him, but when Adrian wants to do something, he does it."

Nathan growled low in his throat. It was then I noticed the tear in his shirt. I was surprised the two hadn't killed one another.

I sighed and holstered my gun. My hands were trembling and I did my best to hide it. If I hadn't shown up when I did, Adrian might have torn through the two wolves to kill Thomas. Jonathan seemed so unwilling to fight sometimes, it wouldn't have surprised me if he had stepped aside and let Adrian do it.

"I'm taking him," I said, moving to the cell. "Tonight."

Jonathan's brow crinkled. "Tonight? Where are you going to take him? It isn't safe."

I looked into the cell, watched Thomas thrash against the bars, against the wall. He looked terrifying, but I pitied him. I should have been the one to suffer his fate. He was so much better at this than I was.

"Home," I said, glancing at Jonathan. "I have a plan."

He looked at me skeptically a moment, then joined me to look at Thomas. "How are you going to get him home like this? He hasn't stopped fighting since the moment he was able to move."

I pulled a knife from my belt and held it up. "Silver," I said. "It's the only way."

"Can you do it?"

I hesitated. Could I? Even with the knowledge that it was the only way to get Thomas to my house so Beligral could do his work, I wasn't so sure. Thomas was suffering enough as it was. Could I really cause him more pain?

Jonathan seemed to notice my indecision. "Go get a car ready," he said to Nathan. "Clear the way. I don't want anyone to see him leaving. Make sure Adrian is really gone."

Nathan nodded and left without a word.

As soon as he was gone, Jonathan faced me again, eyes worried. "I'm still not sure Gregory was the only one reporting to Adrian. I don't want him following you or finding out you took him."

"Thanks," I said. "But I can handle Adrian if he gets in my way. You should have let me shoot him."

Jonathan smiled. "Probably."

Thomas stopped beating himself against the walls. He was panting, staring at us, saliva dripping from his maw. His eyes were still wild. Blood ran from his forehead and dripped into his mouth.

"You need to invest in padded rooms if you plan on keeping any more like this," I said. I wasn't even sure if I was trying to tell a joke or if I was serious.

Jonathan gave me a faint smile, but it faded quickly. "How are we going to do this?" he asked. "It will be hard to get close to him."

"I know."

I looked at Thomas and searched for some hint of my brother behind his eyes. I wanted more than anything for him to just suddenly come out of it, to say my name and reach out for me. If he would do that, then all of the misery, all the pain, would be worth it.

But he just stood there, blood covering most of his body. His fur was caked with it. His chest was clear of hair, well-muscled, and I knew that every muscle in his body would react the moment I stepped within reach. He wouldn't hesitate to kill me if I gave him a chance.

I started forward, my knife clutched in my hand. I stopped and clenched my teeth. I knew it needed to be done, and yet I couldn't do it. I'd killed hundreds of vamps and wolves, but I couldn't harm my brother. It should have been easy. I was trying to help him.

Jonathan reached for the knife and took it from my hand. I let him, hating myself for my weakness. This was my problem and I should have to deal with it. I was taking the easy way out by letting him be the one to stab Thomas. Again.

I stepped back and lowered my eyes. Jonathan approached the cell. As expected, Thomas leaped forward, reaching out for the Denmaster. Jonathan moved lightning quick, jabbing his hand through the bars and embedding the knife in Thomas's side.

Thomas cried out, his clawed hand landing heavily on Jonathan's shoulder, but he didn't break the skin. He slid to the ground, the silver going to work.

"I'm sorry," I whispered, even though I hadn't been the one to do it. It had been my idea. It was my responsibility.

Jonathan opened the cell door and stepped back, allowing me room to enter. I went to my brother and removed the knife. After the last time, I refused to let it stay in him any longer than it had to. The silver would keep him down for a few hours. It was more than enough time to get him home and get this over with.

I wiped Thomas's blood onto my pants and then sheathed

the knife. I tried to lift him by myself, but my back nearly gave out. I cursed and before I could say anything more, Jonathan was there, helping me lift Thomas to his feet.

I hated the stitches, hated the pain. I was weaker than I'd been for a long time and I hated every moment of it.

But what could I do? If I wanted to get Thomas home, I had to accept Jonathan's help. I couldn't do it on my own, not if I wanted this done tonight.

We carried Thomas out of the Den, through the mostly abandoned campus. We saw no one until we entered the garage. Nathan was waiting, a car already running near the exit.

"Take the car," he said. "Nathan can drive you."

"No," I said. "I can do it myself."

"But what if—"

"I said no!"

Jonathan reluctantly agreed to let me go alone, although he did insist I take the car. It would be hard to get Thomas back home on my Honda, if not impossible. I wasn't about to tie him to me.

"I'll drop off your motorcycle later," Jonathan said as we slid Thomas into the back seat. "I have a truck I can use to transport it."

I didn't like the idea of Jonathan coming to my house again but didn't argue. I just wanted to get out of there and get back home. I needed to end the torture—for Thomas and me both.

"Be careful," Jonathan said as I slid into the driver's seat and slammed the door closed.

I just looked at him, giving nothing away. Inside, I was a mess of emotions. I was thankful I had Jonathan there to help me, to worry about me, but it kind of aggravated me as well. I didn't need his worry. I could handle things myself just fine.

I checked the car, relieved to find it to be an automatic.

I glanced into the rearview mirror and adjusted it so I could keep an eye on Thomas. I knew he would be incapacitated for quite a while, but I didn't want to take the chance of missing a jerk of an arm or the twitch of a leg that would warn me he was coming out of it.

I glanced at Jonathan and Nathan once more, gave them each a quick nod of thanks, and then put them behind me. I could still feel their eyes on me long after they were out of sight. Part of me wished Jonathan had come with me. I had a feeling I was going to need the support.

31

Ethan was waiting for me when I got home. I parked close to the garage and maneuvered Thomas from the back seat. Once I was through the front door, Ethan helped me get him down into the basement, though he stopped short of his lab.

"Maybe I should get things ready down there first?"

I nodded and he left to summon his demon. Thomas was propped up against the wall, eyes following me, but he had yet to show any signs of breaking free of his silver-induced paralysis. I removed my shoulder holster and belt, dropping them onto the table, and then slumped to the floor.

The pain in my back was still there, but it was finally starting to abate. I hated thinking that someone like me, someone who is supposed to be nearly indestructible, could suffer so much. I was just glad the healing process was finally kicking in full force. I still might not be fully functional for a few weeks, but I thought I could at least fight if I had to.

I opened my eyes and looked at Thomas. I didn't want to have to fight him. Nor did I want to have to poison him with more silver. This needed to work. I wasn't sure what I would do if it didn't.

Ethan returned a few minutes later. We worked Thomas

down into the lab. I might have been feeling a lot better, but I was still hovering on the weak side. Ethan was forced to bear much of his weight, making our progress slow.

Beligral was seated in his chair, waiting for us. He was smiling, displaying his full set of sharp teeth.

"Is this the creature you are so concerned about?" he asked, gesturing toward Thomas where we had gently lowered him to the floor.

I looked over at the demon. Oppressive heat, both real and imagined, slammed into me, and I had to take a deep breath before it overwhelmed me. How could Ethan stand this every single night?

"It is," Ethan said. He retreated next to his workbench, leaving me standing over Thomas.

Beligral rose and walked to the edge of his circle. He looked down at Thomas, face unreadable. He didn't smile, didn't frown. He just looked at my brother like he was just another slab of meat.

"This just won't do," he said. He turned his burning gaze on me. "Would you mind letting me out so I can get a good look at him. I can do nothing from here."

Ethan hissed in a breath, but I cut him off. "No," I said. "I don't think so."

Beligral smiled slyly and shrugged. "Then there is nothing I can do for him. If you wish me to examine him for a way to repair the damage done to his mind, you will have to allow me to touch him."

Just the thought of a demon touching Thomas made me sick. As much as he tried to look human, Beligral was far from it.

"Figure something out," I said.

He sighed and thought it over. Or at least he pretended to. I think he knew what he was going to do from the start.

"Then bring him into the circle with me. There is no harm in that. I can examine him and you can stay out there where you think it is safe."

Beligral's eyes fell on me and I took a step forward. I felt suddenly calm, as if this was something I did every day. I wanted to save Thomas, and to save him, I needed to bring him to the demon, it was that simple.

"Kat, no!" Ethan cried out as I reached down to pick up my brother. He ran forward and grabbed me by the arm.

I blinked, and the heat and fear came rushing back. Had Beligral done something to me? Was I that susceptible to his gaze?

I shuddered. I didn't know much about the sort of magic required to summon a demon, but I was pretty sure breaking the circle would release the demon to do whatever he pleased. I don't think Ethan would be able to send him back either. And in my carelessness, I'd nearly given Beligral exactly what he wanted.

The demon laughed. His two voices intertwined, flowed over me like a blanket covered in maggots. I had to look away, close my eyes, and focus on something else to make the feeling go away.

"It seems we are at an impasse," he said as his laughter died away. "I can do nothing trapped as I am. If you wish me to help your brother, you will need to figure out how to get him to me."

I remembered something Ethan had said earlier. "Dismiss him," I told Ethan. "Then I can drag Thomas into the circle and you can summon him again." I paused. "Is that safe?"

Beligral was smiling at me like he knew something I didn't. I kept my eyes averted, not wanting to consider how bad of an idea this really could be.

"I . . . I think so," Ethan said. "I've never had anyone inside a circle when I summon him. I guess there could be dangers."

"But, really," Beligral said, "what do you have to lose? He's already damned as it is. I'm the only chance you have."

I ground my teeth. I didn't want to have to make this sort of decision. What if it went wrong? What if the demon did something even more damning to Ethan? Could I live with myself then?

"Do it," I said, making the decision without really thinking about it. If I thought about it too hard, I would never be able to make the choice.

Ethan went about dismissing Beligral and resetting the circle. I knelt by Thomas and rested my hand on his arm. I felt the slightest flinch beneath my hand. It wasn't anything to worry about, but it did make me feel bad.

"It's ready," Ethan said, bringing my head up. New candles were arranged around the circle. "I'll redraw the safety circle once he is inside." He held the piece of chalk so I could see.

I winced as I rose, Thomas in my arms. Ethan rushed forward to help. "I've got it," I growled. Fresh blood oozed down my back, but I ignored it. Once this was over, I could heal all I wanted. Until then, I would bleed every day if that's what it took to bring Thomas back.

I stepped carefully over the silver circle, not wanting to screw anything up by touching it. The inside of the circle smelled hotter than the rest of the room, like an oven that had just been turned off. I set Thomas down on the chair, figuring it was the safest place for him to be.

I stood there, looking down at him, wishing there was some other way. Could I really leave him in there with a demon? If something went wrong, I couldn't get to him without setting Beligral free. Could I risk it?

"Kat," Ethan said, "you have to get out."

I didn't want to, but I stepped out of the circle and went to stand by the workbench. I hated every minute of this. What had I been thinking in bringing him here?

Ethan redrew the chalk outline and then started his chant again. I watched him numbly, barely hearing the different inflections of his voice. The air got hotter, the tear between realms opened, and Beligral stepped out. This time, I was too distracted watching my brother to notice if I could see Beligral's real face before the glamour came up.

Beligral gave both Ethan and I a casual glance before turning to Thomas. His back was to us, so I couldn't see what he was doing as he bent over my brother. He made a clucking sound with his tongue, ran his hands over Thomas's body from head to foot, and seemed to peer into his eyes, though I couldn't see his face from where I was standing to know exactly where he was looking.

It seemed to go on forever. I didn't feel any sort of power flowing from him, no spike in energies or heat that said he was doing anything mystical. As far as I could tell, the demon was simply going through the motions without really doing anything.

Finally, he straightened and turned to face me. He put his hands behind his back and stood straight up like he was about to give a long speech.

"He is too far gone," he said. "There is nothing but pure instinct left. He will function on that, but nothing more. He'll never recover."

"No," I said, refusing to believe him. After all I had gone through, it couldn't end like this. "Try again."

Beligral actually looked sympathetic when he spoke. "There is no need. His mind was destroyed when he was contaminated by both werewolf and vampire blood. There is nothing of him left to save."

"No," I repeated. "I've seen him. He's getting better."

"You might wish it, but it is not true."

"I saw it." I bit the inside of my mouth to keep from crying. Thomas couldn't be gone. I know what I saw.

"I'm sorry," Beligral said.

Hot tears burned my eyes and I refused to let them fall. "Then summon someone else who can," I said. "There has to be a demon or something that can fix him."

Beligral shook his head slowly. "There is not," he said. "As much as we would all like to see a miraculous recovery, it is not possible." He moved closer to the edge of the circle. "He is an animal now, barely human. He is of no use to you or this world."

My hands balled into fists. Every instinct in my body screamed at me to charge him, to beat the very life right out of the damnable demon. He was lying. He had to be.

But I knew attacking him would be a mistake. What reason would he have to lie to me? If I did something stupid and broke the circle, I would only make things worse. I knew this had been a long shot.

"You didn't try hard enough," I said, keeping myself pressed against the table. I would not make another mistake here.

The corners of Beligral's mouth twitched. "I did all I could." He glanced back at Thomas, then looked back at me. "But all is not lost. We can salvage something out of this situation."

"And what would that be?"

"Give him to me."

I blinked. Did he really just say what I thought he did?

As if seeing the question on my face, he repeated himself. "Give him to me. He is of no use to you."

"He is my brother."

"Your brother is gone. This is just a shell."

"No," I said, "you're wrong."

He broke into a grin. "Am I?" he said. "I know more about his situation than you could possibly know. I felt his mind, or should I say, felt where his mind should have been. There is nothing there. I can still use him, however. Give him to me and I will call us even. I will remove your mark and you will never have to see me again."

"No," I repeated. "I will *not* let you have him. Ever."

"I will free Ethan from his bonds."

Ethan gasped beside me, but I refused to be swayed. I couldn't let him take my brother from me. I would find a way to cure him.

"No," I said again.

"Do you really have a choice?"

My throat seized. He had Thomas in the circle with him. I had seen Beligral open the way to his own realm on his own before. Did that mean he could take something across? If so, what was to stop him from grabbing Thomas now and dragging him to whatever hell he had come from?

I couldn't let that happen.

"Dismiss him," I said. My hands were shaking, my knees were weak. I couldn't cross the circle and grab Thomas. Ethan was my only chance.

Ethan just stood there, staring dumbly at Beligral.

"Ethan," I said. He turned to face me. "Dismiss him. Now."

"No," Beligral said. "I don't believe he should. We aren't done here."

Ethan looked from me, to the demon, and back again.

"Ethan," I said, "I will break the circle and let the bastard free before I let him take Thomas."

"I . . . I . . ."

"Ethan!" I shouted, cutting off his stammer. "Do it!"

Beligral laughed, letting the full force of his nature out with it. The sound rumbled through me, shook me to my core. I staggered to the side, nearly fell. The air itself seemed to take on a thick consistency. I was suffocating.

This had been a mistake. Ethan seemed to be locked in place, afraid to obey one monster over the other. He was sweating profusely but didn't seem nearly as affected by the thickening air as I was.

I was going to lose everything—Ethan, Thomas, my life. Nothing would matter anymore. If Beligral decided to walk off with Thomas, make him some sort of demon slave, I would have nothing to fight for. I would never be able to live with myself.

"Please, Ethan . . ." I couldn't think of anything else to say. I was trapped, unable to do anything. I felt helpless.

Ethan looked at me, saw the pain in my eyes. He closed

his eyes and took a breath that looked to have pained him; then he turned to face his demon.

Beligral's laugh cut off. He was still smiling, as if he expected it to end this way the entire time. It was then I realized he had been playing us, seeing what we would do when he pressed us. This was all a game to him.

"Remember our deal," he said. "I don't want to have to remind you." He laughed again.

And then he was gone.

Thomas was still in the chair, seemingly untouched by the demon.

"I'm so sorry," Ethan said. "I never thought he would do that."

"He's a demon," I said. "What did you expect?" I wiped my hand across my eyes just in case and was thankful to find no tears. "Help me get him upstairs."

Ethan stammered a few words that made no sense and then rushed forward to help me get Thomas out of the chair. He helped me carry him up to the basement where the air wasn't so oppressive.

"Kat," Ethan started, but I shook him off.

"Forget it," I said. "It was a bad idea. It's over now. I'll never have to see that bastard again."

Ethan paled. "You made a deal," he said. "You won't be able to ignore that."

"Watch me."

He shook his head but said no more.

Thomas lay on the floor at my feet. The silver was still keeping him paralyzed, but he would come out of it in an hour or so. I really needed to figure out what to do with him before then. I didn't want to have to stab him.

I hated to admit it, but there really was only one thing I could do. I couldn't leave him here in the house. We had nowhere to put him. I doubted Ethan's summoning circle would hold him back like it did the demon.

I was about to tell Ethan my plans to return Thomas to the Luna Cult Den when a faint knock came from above.

My blood ran cold. Who the hell would be knocking at this hour?

"Stay here with Thomas," I said, grabbing my gun from the table. I checked to make sure it was still loaded and then headed for the stairs.

32

I hurried upstairs and tore open the front door without bothering to check who it was. I leveled my gun, my finger tensed on the trigger.

Jonathan's eyes widened and he raised his hands. "I brought back your bike," he said.

"Fuck." I dropped my aim and glanced out the door. My motorcycle was sitting in the driveway next to the car I had driven. There was no sign of any other vehicle.

"I walked it the rest of the way," he said. "The truck is parked down the road."

I slumped against the door frame, suddenly weary. This week was weighing on me more and more. I had no idea what I was going to do now. Everything was falling apart and I had no idea how I was going to put the pieces back together.

Instantly, I thought of the cop I had fed on. Did he fully recover? Was he still in the hospital? Did I really want to know?

"I take it your plan didn't work out," Jonathan said.

I didn't look up. "No, I'm going to take him back to the Den until I figure something else out. I'm at a loss as to what to do."

He reached out and lifted my chin with gentle fingers. My instincts told me to shoot him for touching me. Instead, I found myself leaning into his touch, almost savoring it. I wished he would drop his glamour. I needed to see his true face. Right then, I was tired of appearances. I wanted the truth.

"We'll figure something out," he said. His voice was gentle, soothing. "You don't have to do it alone."

"Yeah," I said, wishing I could believe him. I'd done nearly everything on my own since I learned how. I couldn't let anyone get too close to me. The more people I had to worry about, the harder my job became.

We just stood there, staring into each other's eyes. It was clear he wanted to say something. I waited him out. Whatever I did or said would probably ruin the mood.

The moon was drifting lazily across a sky that would soon start showing signs of the coming dawn. I still had more than enough time to get Thomas to the Den and return home. I didn't have to rush. Maybe I should finally give in and let someone else into my life.

Jonathan's thumb ran across my chin and a small shudder ran through me. Would it really be so bad to have someone else to worry about, to have someone else worry about me? It might make all of this shit worth it.

"I was thinking," Jonathan said. He cleared his throat and looked out into the night. Everything was still, quiet. "After this is over, maybe we could—" A crash from within the house cut him off.

I jerked away and gave Jonathan a terrified glance. I knew I still had a lot more time before the silver would wear off Thomas, but what else could have made the sound? Had Ethan dropped something? God, I hoped so.

I hurried toward the stairs and pounded down them, my heart hammering in my chest. I spun to the basement door and flew down the next flight just as fast. I skidded to a stop, eyes scanning the room, unable to believe what I was seeing.

Thomas was standing on one side of the room, panting. He was moving stiffly, as if the silver was still affecting him a little, but it wasn't enough to keep him down any longer.

Across the room, Ethan lay on the floor amidst scattered pieces of metal and tools that had once rested on a shelf. Thankfully, the shelf had fallen to the side and not on top of him or he might have been seriously hurt.

Thomas's head snapped my way and I froze. The gun was in my hand, but I couldn't force myself to shoot him. He stared at me, eyes burning as if he was a demon himself. Had Beligral done something to him?

Jonathan shot past me, clothes tearing from his body as he leaped at Thomas. I shouted at him to stop, but he didn't listen. He plowed into Thomas even as he shifted to wolf, bones and ligaments shifting to a new form. They went crashing against the table holding my weapons and hit the ground together, teeth snapping.

Ethan groaned and started to stand. He saw the wolf fighting Thomas a few feet away and his eyes widened and traveled to me. Blood was running down his chin from a busted lip, but he looked otherwise unharmed. As long as he stayed put, the most he might end up with were a few bruises.

Jonathan snarled and bit Thomas on the arm. My brother screamed an inhuman scream that sent shivers down my spine. It forcibly reminded me that Thomas wasn't what he once was.

Beligral had been right. My brother was nothing more than a shell, an animal running on pure instinct. Whatever I thought I had seen in him was just his training coming through. He had done it so much when he was a Pureblood, it had become the only thing he knew.

Thomas swung his other arm and connected solidly

with the side of Jonathan's head. The force of the blow forced Jonathan's teeth to tear free, ripping another scream from my brother.

"Stop it!" I shouted, wincing at Thomas's pain. I knew he needed to be stopped, but I couldn't bear to see him tortured any more than he already was. He had already been put through enough without making it worse.

My shout brought Jonathan's head whipping my way. He looked at me through wolf eyes, and I could see the understanding and pain in his eyes. He knew what this was doing to me, but he had no choice.

Thomas used the distraction to pull away from Jonathan's grip. He spun around the edge of the table, putting it between him and his adversary. He scanned all three of us, blood and froth bubbling from his mouth.

My heart broke then. That wasn't my brother. I couldn't think of him that way anymore.

And yet, I couldn't shoot him. The mind might not belong to him any longer, but it was still his body. I couldn't harm him, even if he was ripping out my throat. I just couldn't do it.

Jonathan leaped toward Thomas. My brother ducked down and took the impact on his shoulder. Jonathan's claws raked down his back, but he couldn't get a firm hold. He slipped free and slammed up against the wall.

I started to raise the gun. If I only shot him in the leg, or even the back, it would be enough. I didn't have to let this go on any longer. I could end this now. We could take him to the Den and put him where he would be safe. I didn't have to be so fucking weak.

But I was. My hand shook and I dropped my aim.

Jonathan was on his feet before Thomas could leap on him. He growled deep in his throat and I saw the bloodlust rise. I knew then he wouldn't just incapacitate Thomas. He was going to kill him.

Thomas rolled over the side of the table, landing on his

feet, just as Jonathan swung at him. He flexed his claws and growled in answer to Jonathan's challenge.

Jonathan leaped. His feet hit the table and he swiped at Thomas with his claws. The flattened side of his head pulsed with his anger, with his bloodlust.

Thomas dodged the blow by skittering backward. He howled and snarled, urging Jonathan to come at him again.

That was when I saw his hand twitch toward the sword lying on the table.

"Jonathan, no!" I raised the gun, intent on firing before the worst could happen. I was too slow.

Jonathan leaped from the table. Thomas instantly seized the sword, and with a practiced hand, slid it from its sheath. He swung the blade upward, ducking down just as I pulled the trigger. My bullet sailed harmlessly overhead.

Blood splattered the floor, the wall. Jonathan fell motionless to the concrete, his blood running from somewhere beneath him. I couldn't see how bad it was from my angle. Thomas raised the sword, blood dripping from the blade, poised to finish off the werewolf.

"Hey, poodle-mix," Ethan shouted from his corner. "Your momma ate kitty litter."

Thomas's head jerked up, though there was no way he understood what was being said.

My entire world felt poised on the edge of crumbling apart for good. My life had been bad before. This was worse, so much worse.

Thomas leaped over Jonathan and charged straight for Ethan. He moved lightning quick, so fast I couldn't get a bead on him. He brought his sword up and brought it down hard.

I screamed. My vision flashed red as he brought the blade arched downward. I was certain my hesitation had gotten Ethan killed.

Ethan's hands came out from behind his back. There was a loud clang as the sword met a spare muffler he had grabbed from the fallen shelf. Ethan screamed and dropped it, clutching his hands close to his body.

Thomas raised his sword again. It was now or never.

I raised my gun, tears blurring my vision. Thomas howled, a call of triumph.

A completely inhuman sound.

"Good-bye, Thomas."

My brother's head whipped around. There was a split second when something in Thomas's gaze changed. His eyes softened, a look of clarity came over him. "K—"

My bullet took him square between the eyes.

Thomas hitched once, blood pouring from the wound. All the air seemed to leave me as all life fled from his eyes. My brother fell to the floor, sword clattering loudly in the suddenly quiet basement.

33

I don't remember sitting down on the bottom step. The gun had fallen from my hand, clattered to the floor, much like Thomas's sword had fallen from his own. It laid there, an accusation all in itself.

Time passed. I'm not sure how long. I just sat there, staring at the body across the room. Nothing seemed to matter anymore. The blood was really on the walls, on the floor, yet I knew it was on my hands more than anything else.

"Kat?" Ethan approached slowly. I raised my head numbly toward him. He had a bloody towel in his hands. I didn't even remember him running past me to get it.

He looked at me and didn't say anything right away. There were tears on his face. It mixed with the blood covering him from nearly head to foot. How had he gotten so bloody?

It was then I remembered Jonathan. I turned my gaze to the limp form. More bloody towels lay next to him. He had been rolled over onto his back. Both his arms were draped across a towel resting on his stomach. His head was turned my way. He was alive.

"What are we going to do with him?" Ethan asked. "He's bleeding pretty badly and I don't know how to stop it."

I didn't know what to say. I swung my gaze back around to Thomas. He lay unmoving, his blood soaking the floor. I knew if I were to look into his eyes, there would be nothing there. He was dead.

And I had killed him.

"Kat?"

"I don't fucking care!" I shouted, rounding on Ethan. He winced and took a step back. He nearly slipped in blood.

Jonathan couldn't move, but I caught the tightness in his eyes. He looked hurt, but it wasn't in a physical sense.

And I didn't care.

"Get him out of here." I nearly spat the words.

"Should I take him somewhere?" Ethan asked, voice trembling. "I don't know what to do."

"Take him to a fucking doctor," I snarled. I put my head in my hands. I felt dead inside. Was there anything left to live for?

Ethan backed away and went to help Jonathan, who moaned as Ethan grabbed him under the arms. I didn't look at them. I didn't even move as Ethan worked the paralyzed werewolf past me and up the stairs.

Alone with the body, everything felt blacker. I had worked so hard to help Thomas, only to kill him instead. I'd been so distracted by everything else, I hadn't thought clearly. If Jonathan and the goddamn Cult hadn't always been lurking in the background, maybe I could have saved him.

I knew I was fooling myself. I wanted someone else to blame. Adrian hadn't been here. Jonathan hadn't pulled the trigger. I was taking my frustrations out on everyone but the one person who deserved it.

I rose to my feet and looked away from the body. I couldn't stand staring at it anymore. I would always see it every time I closed my eyes, would always hear the last sound he made. I didn't need to stare at him while my eyes were open.

I trembled and leaned my head against the wall. Had he tried to say my name? Had that last sound simply been another growl or snarl from a mindless beast? I'd never know, not after what I had done.

The door upstairs opened and closed. A few moments later, a car started up and the crunch of gravel quickly followed. I waited for the door to open again, figuring Ethan would come back so I could apologize to him.

He didn't return.

I numbly walked up the stairs. Ethan was gone. I should have known he would be forced to take Jonathan to a doctor somewhere. It probably was killing him to have to go out and leave me behind. He was afraid of the outdoors, and yet he managed to face his fear when someone's life was at stake.

And I hadn't.

I let Thomas break free. I could have used silver dust to paralyze him. I could have left a knife in his side, could have done any number of things and he would still be alive right now.

Disgust filled me. What had I done right recently? How many people had to die because of me, because of my weakness?

I found myself walking out the front door. My Honda was there waiting; I mounted up and started the engine. I tore out of the driveway and hit the road so fast I nearly spun out.

I didn't care. Someone could come along and hit me with a truck and I wouldn't give a fuck. Thomas was lying dead in my basement, as was my entire reason for living.

Tears coursed down my cheeks unabated. I couldn't hold them back any longer. They were the only thing that kept me from exploding.

The wind whipped at me, blew my hair around my face, concealing my misery. My back was bleeding again. I barely felt it. I was free, free to go and do whatever I wanted. What did I have holding me down?

I drove, heedless to where I was going. I just wanted to get away, remove myself from the spot where my world ended. I would drive and drive, and when I stopped, maybe then I could let the reality of what had happened hit me.

I knew I couldn't run from it, but I sure as hell was going to try.

A sign drifted by. I didn't have to look at it to know what it said.

Delai shone up ahead. There was no traffic here, just an empty road leading to oblivion. It was the only place I knew to go.

The day was quickly coming. I could feel the first hints of the sun's rays on my back. I felt weak, hardly able to keep my head up. I just wanted to lie down in the middle of the road and let the sun finish me off. I deserved nothing less.

But I kept driving. I passed DeeDee's, then turned down a road I had traveled only once before. I stopped in front of a house and sat there, staring at windows lit with a soft glow. Even now, in the wee hours of the morning, someone was awake.

I shut off the engine and headed for the front door. I didn't think, didn't consider what I was doing. I let my legs carry me, let them guide me to the one place I felt safe.

The door opened as I reached the front stoop. Levi stepped out, a smile on his face. He opened the door wide for me. He looked almost triumphant.

I walked past him, into the house, into my new sanctuary.

He closed the door behind me. The light by the sofa flickered.

A hand rested on my shoulder. I looked back and Levi's fingers tightened in assurance.

"Welcome home," he said.

I closed my eyes and let him lead me to my room.

Please turn the page for an exciting sneak peek
of E.S. Moore's
next Kat Redding novel

BLESSED BY A DEMON'S MARK

coming soon from Kensington Publishing!

1

A shudder ran through me as I huddled on the bed. My fingers squeezed into the mattress in a vain attempt to stop my hands from shaking. My throat was dry, constricted. Every breath burned. Every attempt to swallow ended with me just about choking on my tongue. Every fiber of my being screamed at me to feed, to leap across the room and tear the two men sitting across from me apart.

"You're doing fine, Kat," Levi said. His voice was a calming balm to my screaming mind. "Just relax. Breathe in slowly and let it out nice and easy. It will be over soon, I promise."

I bared my fangs at him. Blood dripped down my chin from where they'd ripped through my gums. I was breathing fast, hard, still too wired to relax. I felt like a junkie who'd been denied her fix. It was all I could do to keep from breaking something.

Or someone.

I closed my eyes and swallowed, shutting out anything and everything I could. I could do this. This was the last night of the full moon and if I made it through the torture, I could relax for another month before it would start all over again.

My breathing slowed now that I wasn't looking at anyone. I could still feel them there, watching me, but since I couldn't see the pulse in their necks, see the warmth radiating off them, I was able to get myself under some semblance of control.

"Good," Levi urged. "You're doing great. Don't you think she's doing great, Ronnie?"

I refused to open my eyes but could almost feel the slight dip of Ronnie's head as he gave his assent. It was the only kind of response I ever saw him give.

An image of Ronnie sprung to mind. He was staring blankly at me, waiting, neck exposed. I could feel his slow, easy breath, could almost taste his skin between my teeth. All I'd have to do was bite down and my mouth would fill with the sweet nectar of life. His blood would revitalize me, would make me strong, powerful.

A growl rumbled in my chest. My eyes opened and settled on Ronnie where he sat, looking just like I'd seen him in my head. I started to slip from the bed. One foot hit the floor. It would be so easy to propel myself off the bed and end the pain. I fought hard against myself, but it was a losing battle. My other foot touched the floor.

"Easy," Levi said. "You've controlled yourself spectacularly. Don't ruin it now by giving in to your baser instincts. Fight it. You don't have to give in to the hunger. You can do this."

A soothing warmth spread over me as he spoke. I relaxed and slid back onto the bed, easing my back against the headboard. I needed its firmness for support. I focused on breathing nice and easy, letting all violent thoughts flow from me like Levi had taught me to do in our previous sessions. I licked my lips clean of blood and settled my gaze onto Levi's own.

He was smiling at me. He sat with his legs crossed as if he knew I wouldn't attack; not this time anyway. He hadn't been so confident a month ago. I took that as a sign I was making progress.

Ronnie was in the chair beside him, seemingly oblivious to everything that was going on in the room. He was central to my training, though he probably didn't know it. I sometimes wondered if anyone was really in there. To look into his eyes was to see emptiness.

We started my training almost as soon as I'd moved in a few months back. Levi had promised he could teach me to control my inner hunger, that even during the full moon when the Madness took over, I'd be able to keep from feeding, from killing.

The first month had been an utter disaster. The moment the moon had risen, I was up and off the bed, trying to tear at him. He'd been forced to lock me in the room. Even then, it took me a good hour before I calmed down. After that, I was okay as long as no one bothered me, but the moment anyone came near me, all I wanted to do was feed.

But a mere three months later, I was able to sit here, albeit with much difficulty, with two men in the room, without killing either. Despite the hunger, despite the desire to tear them both to shreds, I felt good about what I'd accomplished thus far.

"Good." Levi's grin widened.

All of the tension eased out of my shoulders and I managed a smile of my own. I could still feel the Madness wanting to take hold, but I was able to keep it at bay. I hadn't had blood in five nights and was still able to hold on, which was a miracle in itself.

I took a deep breath and let it out slowly. A faint thump upstairs reminded me that Eilene and Sienna were in the house. They didn't know exactly what went on in my room during these full moon nights, though I suspected they had an idea. What else could we possibly be doing?

Knowing they were there sometimes helped. Other times, it made the hunger worse. Part of me wished Levi would make them leave the house so I wouldn't be tempted. Just because I was doing good now didn't mean I'd be so lucky the next time.

I glanced toward the wall, wishing there was a window in the room so I could look out at the sky. While there was a light dusting of snow and the cloud cover would hide the moon, it did little to abate the onset of the Full Moon Madness. Even the thick walls couldn't stop its effect on me. I'm not sure if seeing it would hinder my progress or help.

I felt myself calming even more as the seconds ticked by. Levi had done a good job teaching me how to control my inner beast. He'd done far more than I'd ever managed to do on my own. He kept a supply of blood bags in the fridge to drink from when the urge to feed was too great. It had been months since I'd fed on an actual living person.

The blood bags didn't completely erase the hunger, but they eased it enough so I wasn't constantly thinking about feeding. They tasted like shit, but it was a small price to pay for being free of the need to feed and kill for survival.

"I think we should up the stakes a bit," Levi said, sitting forward. The chair creaked with the movement and my anxiety level went through the roof.

My hands balled into the sheet again. I was terrified at what he might be planning to do. I mean, what else could he do to me that he hadn't already done? There was only so much I could take. I'd hate myself if I ended up killing him because he pushed me too far.

Levi studied me as if waiting for some sign that I was ready. He didn't look scared. In fact, he looked so calm you would have thought he was relaxing in his own room with a cup of tea and a good book instead of sitting in a room with a half-starved vampire.

I sat there, tense, afraid to move; but after a few seconds of his steadfast gaze, I found myself relaxing. My hands unclenched and I sat back, doing my best to appear calm and collected, though I felt anything but calm inside.

"Good," he said with a nod. "That's very good. You can control it whenever you want. Before long you'll fit right in. The desire for blood will no longer control you. No one would know you to be anything but human."

He reached into his pocket and removed a small penknife. He opened it and turned it so the light would catch the blade. It looked extremely sharp.

I tensed, unsure what he planned on doing with the knife. If he came anywhere near me with it, he wouldn't just lose the blade, but his arm as well. I was okay as long as everyone was just sitting there. If he were to intentionally antagonize me, I had serious doubts I could control myself.

"There is just one more test I need to run." He turned the knife over slowly in his hand. "If you can make it through this . . ." He left the rest unsaid.

Levi's grip on the knife firmed and he reached out, causing me to jerk back. But it wasn't me he reached for.

He went for Ronnie.

The other man didn't even flinch as Levi took his arm. Nothing on his face gave any indication he knew what was happening or cared one way or the other what was being done to him. He was like a living puppet, only moving when his master pulled his strings.

"No," I said, pushing back hard against the headboard. I didn't want to see him hurt Ronnie, even to test me. I had an idea I knew what was coming, and I wasn't so sure I could keep from losing it. "Please."

Levi's eyes locked on mine. "This is a necessary step to your recovery. I can't help you if you don't let me do this. You'll be fine."

Warmth flooded over me and I nodded. I sucked back the blood that was still dribbling from my gums, used it to temper the hunger raging inside of me.

My head felt cloudy, as if it was full of thick smoke. It made it hard to think clearly, made it hard to order my

thoughts. I knew if I were to really think about it, I would
never hurt Ronnie or Levi or the girls upstairs, but the
Madness had a way of fogging my mind. All it would
take is one moment of confusion and one of them would
be dead.

But here in Levi's presence, I did better. Something
about him allowed me to take control of my own brain,
forced me to see through the cloud and understand that the
moon didn't have complete control over me. Only I did.
Once I realized that, the rest would be easy.

Levi studied me a moment more before pressing the
knife into Ronnie's palm.

Blood immediately welled in the wound, filling his
hand. It spattered on the thin plastic sheeting Levi had
spread on the floor before we started.

My throat closed up as soon as the smell of blood hit
me. I couldn't look away from it even though I knew I
would have to soon or I wouldn't be able to stop myself
from flying off the bed. The urge was too powerful. There
was no way I was going to be able to control my hunger.

Levi tipped Ronnie's hand so the blood pooling in his
palm dripped onto the plastic. Each drop sounded like a
gong to my ears as it hit the floor.

I started panting. My every muscle tensed as if I was
going to spring, but yet I stayed put. I could almost taste
the blood, could almost feel it on my tongue. The scent
was overpowering, it filled my senses until it was the only
thing I knew.

And still, I held back. As much as I wanted to feed, I
knew I couldn't. I could hold on, I could wait it out. Levi
would eventually leave me alone in the room and I could
relax. I just needed to hold on for a few minutes more and
it would all be over.

I forced my gaze from Ronnie's bloody palm. His arm
was littered with tiny scars, as if this wasn't the first time
this had happened. It was easy to imagine him sitting there,

letting Levi cut him night after night, just so the bigger man could save someone just like me.

My hands dug into the mattress so hard it was a wonder my fingers didn't pop through. I forced myself to ease my grip even though I was half afraid to do so would be to ease the tentative grip I had on my control. Each finger unclenched slowly, the ligaments and joints popping as I straightened them. It hurt like hell.

"Get him the fuck out of here," I growled. I was shaking violently now. As much as I wanted to keep control of my hunger, it just wasn't happening. I was trying hard to breathe through my nose because I could taste the blood on my tongue every time I opened my mouth.

I felt myself moving forward and stopped just before I leaped from the bed. Ronnie was too close. I could be on him in half a second, could have my mouth on his hand, teeth tearing at the flesh, long before Levi could even think to pull him away. I could suck on the wound until the flow slowed and then finally stopped. It wouldn't kill him.

Not right away anyway. If I were to move my mouth a mere two to three inches up to his wrist, I could feed until completely sated.

I think the fear of not being able to stop was what kept me in place when Levi shook his head. If I moved, I would kill Ronnie, maybe Levi as well. Nothing could stop me. They were unarmed, aside from Levi's tiny knife. I could have them both dead before the girls upstairs heard the first scream.

A sudden wash of warmth flowed over me and I blinked, head suddenly clear. I was sitting on the very edge of the bed, almost all the way onto the floor. I hadn't even realized I'd been moving until that very moment.

I scooted back, dropping my head so I wouldn't have to look at the two men, at the blood still dripping onto the plastic. Even though I knew Levi was trying to help, part of me wanted to kill him for torturing me like this.

"I think we can call our little test a success," Levi said. The self-satisfaction was clear in his voice, as if *he* had been the one to have overcome the Madness and hunger. "You don't have complete control yet, but I'm sure you will soon enough."

I growled, letting him know how unlikely I thought that prospect to be.

Levi chuckled as he stood. "We'll leave you be. You've had a rough night and deserve a little respite from what I've put you through. I completely understand if you hate me." He winked. "And I'll be sure to lock the door for your peace of mind."

A simple door and lock wouldn't stop me if I really wanted to get out, but he was right, the idea of a locked door between me and the Purebloods did make me feel better.

"You did good," Levi said. "Tomorrow night we'll have dinner and toast your success."

My stomach clenched as Ronnie stood at a motion from Levi. His blood pumped just a little faster, making another small drop ooze from his palm. It was all I could do to keep from reaching out and grabbing his hand just so I could have a taste.

Levi opened the door and held it out for Ronnie, who walked past him without a word. Levi hesitated a moment, like he was going to say something else, but instead, he turned and walked out, closing the door behind him.

I waited until the lock clicked before leaping from the bed onto the plastic. My fingers tore into it as I pulled it up to my face. I lapped at the blood, sucked at the plastic to get every single drop.

I wanted more. The tiny amount of blood that had spilled from Ronnie's palm was far from enough to sate my hunger. A big part of me wanted to give in to the beast, to break through the door and find someone to feed upon. I could drain them, could keep the hunger at bay for a week more. I could end the pain.

I rose from the floor, blood on my chin, and started stalking around the room. I felt like a caged animal despite the fact I knew I could break free anytime I wanted. I was making strange growling sounds deep in my chest as I breathed in and out, like a beast that knew its food was sitting just out of reach.

I bit my lip, drawing blood. I refused to give in. I dug my fingers into my temples, closed my eyes, and tried to push away all thoughts of blood and food. I kept seeing the blood dripping from Ronnie's hand and was forced to open my eyes lest it took hold of my mind for good.

Another growl bubbled up from somewhere deep inside, but somehow my head cleared just a little bit. I might still be in near full-fledged bloodlust, but at least now I was able to think through it.

I sat heavily on the bed. The sun would be up soon, dampening the effects of the full moon, and from there, everything would be easy. I knew my control was shot because of the Madness. A few more hours and I'd be in full control of myself once more.

The urge to feed started to subside and I slumped down onto the bed. A tear fell from the corner of my eye. I wiped it angrily away.

Why was he doing this to me? Deep down I knew Levi was trying to help, but it was hard to see it through the hunger and fog in my head. It felt less like he was helping and more like he was torturing me for his own amusement.

And that's exactly what it was: torture. I'd seen vampire Counts do the same thing to their prisoners. They'd tempt them with blood kept just out of their reach until it drove them insane.

I found myself standing and heading toward the door. I didn't need Ronnie's blood or anyone else's as long as I got Levi's. He deserved to be punished for what he was doing to me. The bigger man would fill me up so much more than the smaller Ronnie or either of the girls upstairs.

The thought of Eilene and Sienna brought some sense back and I backed away from the door. My legs bumped against the edge of the bed and I sat down hard. I took a deep breath, let it out through my teeth, and found a smile spreading across my lips.

I'd done it. I'd controlled my hunger, controlled the Madness.

My fangs retracted, my head cleared a little more. I wiped away the last of the blood that had fallen from my gums and managed not to lick my hand clean.

I was doing better. I'd made it. I could defeat this thing, could do exactly what Levi said I could do.

I started to laugh, to exalt in my success, but that was when the pain hit.

It came from directly behind my left ear. It seared into my brain and I screamed. I clutched at my head like it might explode, and right then, it sure as hell felt like it was going to.

I fell back and immediately rolled off the bed. I hit the floor with a thump, and another jolt of pure agony caused me to scream again. My feet kicked out so hard I knocked over the chair Levi had been sitting in. It slammed against the wall with a crash, punching a small hole into the plaster.

My fangs were out again, but instead of hunger, all I could feel was the pain. It shot through me again, bowed my back off the floor. My eyeballs felt like they were about to pop from my skull from the building pressure.

The pain came again; this time it was so bad I couldn't even scream. My breath cut off and everything went black for an instant before my vision cleared. I gagged as my stomach heaved and the remnants of my last meal came shooting out of my mouth, drenching me in my own vomit.

I shuddered uncontrollably on the floor, gagging and spitting. The pain sliced through my head once more, but this time I barely felt it. A steady stream of drool fell from my lips onto the plastic, pooling beneath my face.

And then it was over.

Just like that, the pain stopped. I threw up again, but this time little more than bile came up.

I scooted back until my back bumped up against the bed. I brought both my legs up and curled into a little ball, terrified the pain would come again.

2

I was still shaky the following night. I got up and hurried to the shower upstairs, doing my best to avoid everyone. I didn't want to have to try to explain myself to Levi or one of the girls if I didn't have to.

Levi was talking to someone in the kitchen and I scrambled past, hoping it was his wife and adopted daughter. I made it all the way upstairs and into the bathroom without seeing anyone. I closed the door behind me with a sigh of relief.

The shower helped rid me of most of the shakes, and I was feeling mostly normal by the time I was dried off and dressed. Something about slipping into the warm clothes soothed my mind. Sienna had picked out both the black sweater and the blue jeans for me. It wasn't something I'd normally wear, but somehow it felt right. I think it was because Sienna had chosen them for me specifically that made the clothing feel perfect.

The steam was still heavy on the mirror as I began to brush out my hair. I was afraid to leave the bathroom, knowing I'd have to face the family when I did. I took my time to work out the tangles, inch by painful inch. Water droplets ran down the mirror, giving me a fractured look at myself in the trails they left behind.

From what I could see of my face, I looked haggard. The Madness hadn't been that bad for a long time, and what had come after had only made it worse. I wished I didn't know what the pain meant, but I knew. It was hard not to.

My fingers found the raised bumps behind my ear. Ethan's demon, Beligral, had marked me before I'd fled to Delai. I'd made a pact that I would return to see him. I'd almost forgotten about his mark and I supposed the agonizing pain had been his way to remind me.

My gut churned at the thought of the demon, of Ethan. And of home.

I sat on the toilet as the strength went out of my legs. I'd tried really hard to push thoughts of home out of my head. I'd killed my brother there, shot him just as he'd opened his mouth to speak. I didn't know if he was going to say my name or just snarl something inarticulate at me, but in the end, it really didn't matter what he might have said.

I killed him.

He will never speak again.

I stood in a rush and slammed the brush back into its drawer so hard I nearly tore it out of its tracks. I leaned on the sink and tried to control the anger that bubbled deep inside my chest.

I knew I was going to have to go home to confront Beligral. I was pretty sure if I didn't act soon, he would send more pain. The first time was bad enough, but what if he did it while I was talking to Levi or Eilene. I didn't even want to consider how Sienna would react.

It felt like I was being forced to choose between two homes. A big part of me just wanted to leave my past in the past and forget about everything I'd left behind. There was so much loss, so much pain in my old life, I really wasn't sure I wanted to go back to it.

Delai had become my home, a place I could live without fearing for my life every damn second of the night. Here, I didn't have to be Lady Death. I could simply be Kat Redding, vampire on the mend.

I smiled bitterly. When Levi told me he could help with my hunger, I'd thought he'd gone crazy. I figured at most he might be able to keep me from blindly killing someone, which was something I was already good at, but he'd gone so much further. While I'd never known a vampire who could completely control their hunger without going insane or becoming so emaciated they might as well have been dead, it wasn't out of the realm of possibility.

At least not now. I would never have been able to do this on my own. Something about Levi calmed me, helped me sort through the tangle of emotions that flooded my head every time I got hungry for blood. The blood bags he kept for me helped curb the need to feed on a living person. How much longer until I didn't need them at all?

"Kat?" Sienna's tentative voice drifted up the stairs. By the sound of it, I knew she'd heard me thrashing around last night.

I took one last look at myself in the mirror and tried to put on a face that didn't look so exhausted. It wasn't easy, but I managed.

"I'm coming," I called as I left the bathroom. I tried to sound cheerful, but it came out sounding strained.

Sienna was waiting at the bottom of the stairs, her blond hair pulled back out of her face. The concern was clear in her eyes as she watched me descend. While I was sure she'd heard me screaming the night before, I hoped she hadn't gone into the room to check on me while I was lying on the floor comatose.

"Dinner's ready." She gave me a weak smile that made her look even younger than her nineteen years. On a good day, she looked at most sixteen. She had one of those faces that would be eternally young, which was both a curse and a blessing. Any vamp who saw her would want to capture her young beauty for his own enjoyment.

I pushed the thought out of my mind and smiled at her. I rested my hand on her wrist, squeezing gently as I passed. My touch seemed to dispel any trepidation she might have had about my well-being. Her smile widened and she followed me out into the dining room.

Sienna's adopting mom, Eilene, was sitting at the table, hands resting in her lap. She'd been sick when I'd first moved in months ago and she hadn't improved since then. I wasn't sure what was wrong with her, but whatever it was, it left her weak and tired nearly all the time. Her features were wan and thin, her skin pulled tight over her cheekbones, while it sagged everywhere else. She couldn't weigh any more than eighty pounds.

She glanced up as we entered. She settled her tired eyes on me for only half a second before looking away.

"Levi will be in in a minute," she said, voice soft as if it hurt to speak.

Sienna took her place at the table, keeping her head low. She was always shy around her parents. I'd only ever seen her open up when neither of them were around, and that wasn't too often. One of them always seemed to be hovering around, though the young girl was worse when it was Levi who was in the room.

I studied Eilene for a few moments before sitting. The chair creaked as I sat down. It sounded loud in the hushed silence of the dining room.

Sienna glanced up at me and her mouth quirked in a small smile before she resumed looking at the top of the table. She brushed a stray strand of hair out of her face before dropping both her hands into her lap.

I felt bad for the girl. As much as I liked Levi, he did have a strong hand when it concerned his adopted daughter. She was never allowed to leave the house, had no friends I knew of. She spent most of her time in her room where I could only assume she read. There were no televisions in the house, no music ever drifted through the walls. It felt like we were living in a monastery sometimes.

Levi came in, drawing my attention away from the girl. His arms were laden with food. He always liked to feast after the full moon and tonight was no different.

"Dig in," he said, a wide smile on his face. He unloaded the plates on the table. "Tonight we will celebrate the accomplishments of our guest. She did wonderfully last night." He gave a little golf clap, though no one else at the table joined in.

He didn't seem to mind. Without missing a beat, Levi swept up his plate and began loading it with the food he must have spent hours cooking.

"Where's Ronnie?" I asked, picking up my own plate. The quiet man always ate dinner with us.

I picked at the food, choosing only small portions to be polite. I really wasn't hungry, but I didn't want to be rude either. Besides, I had to eat real food too. No sense starving myself over a rough night. I'd probably need my strength when I faced Beligral next.

A cold chill ran up my spine at the thought of the demon. I suppressed a shudder as I set my plate down in front of me.

"He's got things to do." Levi didn't look my way as he spoke, but it was clear he didn't want to discuss it.

I didn't press him, though I did wonder where Ronnie was. He didn't seem the type that could do much of anything on his own, and he almost never missed a meal.

Levi gave a brief nod at the table at large and we began to eat.

Sienna and Eilene didn't say a word throughout the meal. Levi chatted amiably, not really talking to anyone in particular. I barely listened to him and I doubted the other women did either. About halfway through the meal he started talking about how I handled the night before, though he left out the bit about what he'd done to Ronnie. I was pretty sure he didn't want them to know he was cutting up the poor man just to see if I would eat him.

The spot behind my ear began to throb, as if the memory of my bad night was going to bring back the pain. I was trying hard to forget about it, to just get through the meal so I could make a decision as to what to do about the demon. I didn't want anyone else to know about it if I could help it.

I found myself rubbing absently behind my ear and I jerked my hand away, but I was too late.

"Is everything okay?" Levi asked, giving me a concerned look.

I nodded and pretended nothing had happened.

"You don't look okay."

"I'm fine."

He frowned and crossed his thick, hairy arms in front of him. "I don't think so."

Sienna shifted uncomfortably in her seat. Eilene was watching the exchange with a faint frown. Neither woman would speak up knowing Levi wouldn't like them butting in to the conversation without his leave.

"It was a rough night," I said. "I have a headache."

"A headache?" He shook his head. "I doubt that. There's something else going on."

"Is there?"

He stared at me and I stared right back. I don't care how much he might have helped me, Levi didn't need to know every damn thought that went through my head.

Levi took a deep breath and a smile split his face. "Well, then," he said, voice booming in the room. "I guess that's that." He leaned forward and started eating again. He took a bite, glanced at me, and winked as if we were sharing a secret.

Sienna was staring at me and I could see the question in her eyes. I seriously doubted Levi would give up that easily, and it was obvious I was going to have to tell Sienna something. If I wanted the girl to trust me, I couldn't hold back on her.

It was strange having those sorts of feelings for the girl. I don't know why, but I'd grown attached to her over the past few months. Was it her innocence? The way she never flinched when I moved in. She treated me more like a person than most anyone I knew.

In a way, she reminded me of Ethan.

The rest of the meal passed without further incident. As soon as I was done, I excused myself and went back to my room. I didn't want to face any of the questions I knew were to come just yet. I hoped they'd be content to spend some family time together and let me sulk a while before bombarding me.

The plastic had been removed from my room, so someone had come down and seen the mess I'd left. Part of me hoped Eilene had done it. She was the only member of the family who wouldn't ask questions.

I started pacing the moment the door was closed. I kept looking at the closet, knowing my old clothes were in there. I hadn't worn them since the day I'd arrived. Eilene had washed them by hand before I'd shoved them as far back into the closet as I could get them.

I probably should have thrown them out. There were too many bad memories associated to those few articles of clothing.

But I hadn't. I needed the reminder of my old life so I didn't turn back into the person I had started to become before the day I'd ended my brother's life.

A part of me knew I'd come to Delai to die. It was the only place I knew where I could be left alone to fade away into nothing. I could die in peace here, could forget about everything I'd done, all the people I'd killed. It was supposed to be my final sanctuary.

But at some point, things changed. I'd gotten to know the family, had come to like them. They'd somehow *become* my family. While the peace might have been broken because of the demon mark, I still thought of Levi's house as home.

But thoughts of the demon made me think of Ethan. Tears sprang to my eyes and I sank down onto the bed. How could I have left him to fend for himself like this? The world was dangerous and he wasn't nearly as resilient as I was. I wasn't so sure he could survive in the harsh world without me.

Of course that wasn't true. Ethan was resourceful. He always found a way to conquer his fears. He'd even managed to leave the house despite his fear of the outdoors so he could save Jonathan.

I wondered if he'd managed to get the Luna Cult Denmaster somewhere safe all those months ago. The last I'd seen of both men, Ethan was helping the paralyzed wolf up the stairs after Jonathan's fight with my brother ended with him meeting the sharp end of one of my silver swords.

My hands clenched into fists and I just about punched the wall. I didn't know which way was up anymore. I thought I'd found a home here, a place away from the nightmares of my life, but I hadn't gone anywhere really. I was still the same person.

I was still a killer.

A knock at the door had me wiping away angry tears. "What?" I snapped, expecting it to be Levi. I so didn't want to be disturbed right then.

"I'll come back later." Sienna's small voice came from the other side of the door.

I groaned. I refused to turn her away of all people. "No, wait," I said, sighing. I rose and opened the door before she could walk away. "I'm sorry. I didn't mean to snap at you."

Sienna turned back to face me. She hadn't moved from in front of the door, as if she knew I'd answer for her. "I just wanted to make sure you were okay."

"I'm fine," I said, trying my damnedest to smile. It

didn't quite work, but at least I didn't grimace. "Where's your dad?"

"He's not here right now," Sienna said, and the relief was clear in her voice. "He went out after Ronnie or something."

"Do you know where he went?"

She shrugged. "He does that sometimes. Dad always tries to say he is doing something important, but I think Ronnie just gets it in his head to take a walk and forgets to stop. Usually he comes home before anyone knows he's gone. Last night must have been pretty bad for him not to have come back right away."

She didn't know the half of it.

"What was it you wanted?" I said, leaning against the door frame. Talking to Sienna always seemed to calm me a little. I really did like the young girl, even if she was far too timid for her own good. She would never survive outside Delai, I was sure.

Sienna licked her lips and looked shyly away. I found the insecure gesture endearing. "I was just wondering why you were so upset today. I could tell something was bothering you."

I paused to try to come up with an answer that wouldn't scare the girl. I mean, she knew I was a vampire, but I'd never gone full-on vamp around her. She might not know how bad I got, and I never wanted her to see it either.

Before I could come up with something to say, Eilene came down the stairs behind her.

"Sienna, go upstairs and clean your room."

The girl didn't hesitate. The moment her mom spoke, Sienna turned and hurried up the stairs. The sound of her footsteps receded and her bedroom door closed a few seconds later.

"You've got to leave." Eilene spoke before I could ask her why she'd sent the girl away. She leaned against the wall and closed her eyes like the effort to stand was too much for her.

I frowned. "Leave?" I said. "Why?"

"Because you have to." Eilene opened her eyes and looked up at me. She looked exhausted, like she'd been the one who stayed up all night fighting the urge to feed. "Something is forcing you away. I can feel it in the air, can see it when I look at you."

My hand went reflexively up and I touched the mark behind my ear. Other than the raised skin, I couldn't tell it was there. I wondered if she'd seen the mark and put two and two together somehow.

"I don't know," I said. "I don't want to go."

"That doesn't matter," she said with a sigh. "You need to leave."

"But Sienna—"

Eilene cut me off. "She'll get over it. I don't think you should tell her you're leaving. And you definitely don't want to tell Levi." She spoke her husband's name with such bitterness it took me aback.

I knew things were strained between the couple, but listening to her now, it appeared it was far worse than I'd thought. At first, I'd assumed she just didn't like how Levi was spending so much time with me, that she was jealous, but I quickly realized that wasn't the case. Levi had helped others before me. My time with him didn't seem to bother her in the slightest.

But there was definitely something else going on between them. The bitterness was there on a nightly basis. He pretended not to notice, but I sure as hell did.

"I'm not sure I want to go," I said. The thought of going home again made me sick.

"But you have to." Her gaze flickered to the side of my head, confirming my suspicion that she knew about the mark. "You have no choice."

She glanced up the stairs and forced herself erect. She crossed the room with small, shuffling steps, until she was standing a few inches from me. The fact that I was a vampire fazed her about as much as it had Sienna and Levi, which was to say, not at all.

"I sent Ronnie out," she said at a whisper. "It will take Levi a few hours to find him. You need to be gone before he knows you are even thinking of leaving or you'll stand no chance. He won't let you go if he senses your intent."

"What's going on?" I asked, starting to get uneasy.

"Just go," she said. "Please. Sienna will be crushed, but she'll understand."

"But why?" I wasn't sure if I was asking why I should go or why she was so insistent on pushing the issue. Did it really matter either way?

"Because if you don't go now, you'll never find the nerve to leave."

I didn't know what to say to that. Deep down, I knew she was right. I was already struggling with it. If Levi were to tell me to stay, I had a feeling I would.

Eilene stepped back. "Please," she said, "I don't want you to get hurt."

Before I could say anything to that, she turned and shuffled up the stairs as fast as her tired legs could take her. I watched her go, half expecting her to collapse from the strain, but she made it just fine.

I numbly turned and headed back into my room. I wanted to stay, I really did, but I knew Eilene was right. The demon mark would force me to leave one way or the other and now was as good of a time as any, especially since Levi was out of the house.

I stood at the edge of the bed, wondering if there was some way I could put this off. To leave now would feel like I was abandoning Sienna or turning my back on what Levi had tried to do.

But I couldn't stay, not as long as I had Beligral's mark.

With a heavy heart, I opened the closet door and began to pack for the journey home.